T0194606

MARY OUT O' THE EARTH

She Will Steal Your Heart Away

JOHN STCHUR

authorHOUSE®

AuthorHouse™
1663 Liberty Drive
Bloomington, IN 47403
www.authorhouse.com
Phone: 1 (800) 839-8640

Published by AuthorHouse 04/22/2019

ISBN: 978-1-7283-0403-8 (sc)
ISBN: 978-1-7283-0401-4 (hc)
ISBN: 978-1-7283-0402-1 (e)

Library of Congress Control Number: 2019902999

Print information available on the last page.

PROLOGUE

dis-ap-pear:
1. to cease to appear or to be perceived; pass from view either suddenly or gradually
2. to cease to be source: Webster's Third New International Dictionary

Disappear. There seems just a hint of magic in the word. It conjures up images of silk top hats, white gloves and perhaps an equally white rabbit or two. But as any grown-up knows, the magic is almost always fraudulent and the word itself a lame one, seldom able to fulfill the whole of its literal promise. Things – white rabbits, car keys, even people – "disappear" only in accordance with the first half of Webster's definition. And does anything, especially a person, ever fulfill the second half? Does anyone ever truly "cease to be?" Before answering, consider the case of David Lang, who in September of 1880 apparently did just that. And he did it, albeit unwillingly, while five pairs of eyes focused on him. On him, not on something draped over his person or on something he'd placed himself inside of or behind. On him. Which may or may not legitimize the magic but most certainly shades the hint of it black, because with the man was stolen his portion of the one commodity most vulnerable in all of us to the full power of the word disappear: his love.

According to Frank Edward's interesting but somewhat disturbing book Stranger than Science, the incident happened on a hot, dry afternoon, one of a seemingly endless succession of such days, in the area around Gallatin, Tennessee. With his wife and children watching, David Lang had just begun a short walk across the sun-browned, closely cropped pasture in front of their home when he spotted a horse and buggy coming up the lane toward the house. He waved, most likely recognizing the conveyance as that belonging to his close friend, Judge August Peck, and turned around and stepped into oblivion, because in the next few strides he disappeared within full view of all those present – winked out of existence just as cleanly and with all the abruptness of switching off a lamp at midnight. Mrs. Lang screamed and along with her children ran instinctively toward the spot where he had disappeared in mid-stride. They were quickly joined by Judge Peck and his brother-in-law, who had also been focused on the man when he "ceased to be." But they found nothing, not a single clue at the spot or anywhere else in the treeless, empty field to indicate how a grown man could have vanished in full view of his wife, children and two men in a buggy.

The search continued. Scores of neighbors and townspeople were brought in to help, and finally a county surveyor, who probed the area where Lang had vanished in hopes of finding a sinkhole or underground cave he might have fallen into. He found nothing. The entire field was supported on solid rock.

David Lang was never found, and one can but imagine the emptiness he left behind –greater as the weeks then months rolled by than if they had proof positive of his death. The only "evidence," if one can call it that, to mark his passing came the following spring when it was discovered that at precisely the spot where he had vanished there now grew a perfect circle of stunted, yellow grass approximately fifteen feet in diameter.

Nor is Mr. Lang's the only case of mysterious disappearances. Whole armies have vanished without a trace – no bodies, no record of capture, no subsequent contact of any kind – as recently as 1939. Ships have sailed around bends in rivers, planes have flown across well-charted land containing *neither* rivers, lakes nor seas . . . all into the same clueless oblivion David Lang managed to reach on foot. It's all there, the stories, the documentation, even the newspaper clippings, in scattered and diverse places, among them such monoliths of officialdom as the Library of Congress and the National Archives. But David Lang's case is special, even among these. His is the only case where human eyes actually witnessed the vanishing act as it took place. All eyes were focused on him.

On him.

The only case? Well, not exactly. In 1913 May Donegal also disappeared, from a small farm just outside of Valor, Michigan, and under circumstances remarkably similar to those surrounding David Lang. She too was crossing an open field, a pasture, in front of her home on a hot summer's day near the end of a months-long dry spell. She too had suddenly turned around and stepped back the way she had come . . . and she too "winked" out of existence after a very few steps, as someone watched. The reason, then, there is not mention of the occurrence anywhere more prestigious than in some age-yellowed court records stored in the basement of Valor's City Hall? Possibly the fact that the witnesses numbered but one. More likely that the observer was her husband, James Donegal, who just happened to be the area's best-known drunk, barroom brawler and all-around rogue, whom most people believed perfectly capable of murdering his wife then disposing of the body in such a way that it would never be found (although rumor had it that James loved her dearly and was as saintly in her presence as he was the devil's own away from her). At any rate, Jim's claim that he had done nothing more criminal than simply call out to Mary that she'd forgotten her sheet music as she'd set off across the fields to visit her friend and fellow music lover Emily Stevens, was never given much credence; and although authorities were never able to prove anything, they thought they pretty much knew what had really become of Mary.

Too bad for Jim, dead since '67, that they didn't believe him. Mary could have told them that the rumors of deep, abiding love were true, just as true as his claims of innocence. She could, in fact, have told them now, if any of them were still alive to listen, because early this morning she came back, one-hundred and six years later, not a day older . . . and changed.

PART I

THE ENIGMA

"It is a riddle wrapped in a mystery inside an enigma."
–Winston Churchill, 1939

"The awful thing is that beauty is mysterious as
well as terrible. God and devil are fighting there,
and the battlefield is the heart of man."
–Dostoevski, 1880

I

They sat across from each other, each, like most fathers and sons, an unbreakable yard-stick by which the other measured himself as a man. And neither of them believed in miracles.

"How you sittin' going into finals?" David asked between sips of black coffee. Inside he felt mild annoyance that Mark had picked the one spot to sit and eat his breakfast that directly blocked his view of the field across the road. Staring out the dining room window at the gone-to-seed field had become something of an early morning ritual, a form of self-hypnosis, after which he could usually get through most of a working day sufficiently numbed to avoid thinking about anything but the job at hand.

"They're not for another week yet," his son answered.

More sips. More raisin-brand consumed at the other end of the table.

"Yeah, I know, but are you going into them solid? Last year you had all those missing lab reports in biology, and it –"

"I'm solid, Dad. Up to date. Okay?" He got up from his chair, talking around his last mouthful. "You forget, fewer distractions this year, a changed attitude. This year I *want* to be kept busy." He said it without even a hint of irony or spite in his voice. Not that he needed it; the words themselves were enough. "As busy as, well a one-armed paperhanger, that's me!" Then he went over to the stairs, taking them slowly, deliberately, one step at a time, even though he was only eighteen – probably with the intention of going back to bed for a few house until his favorite Saturday morning nature shows came on, David thought. He left his unrinsed bowl and spoon on the table but David didn't call him back. Instead he stared out the window.

And that is when *she* appeared. Out in the field. Looking so much

1

like Pamela from a distance that for the span of several seconds David was absolutely sure he was only now awakening from an incredibly bad, incredibly vivid and complex dream; one in which his wife had died, he'd lived on for ten years without her, and his son had lost an arm. All of those things flashed in his mind the instant he saw her, the instant she . . . "came into being," especially the idea that maybe none of them had really happened because . . . that was Pamela out there, wasn't it? It was an emotionally devastating feeling, part panic, part suspicious joy, that did to this mind what riding the express elevator at the Detroit Renaissance Center, as it dropped you from the eightieth to the first floor in something under ten seconds, had once done to his insides.

Then reality reasserted itself – or he thought it did – in the form of Mark's size-eleven Reeboks resting on the floor. They were off to the left of the window but still within easy range of his peripheral vision without ever taking his eyes fully off the girl. And if the last ten years had been a dream and he was awake now . . . then Mark should still be eight and no eight year-old wore –

Not good enough, a more analytical portion of his brain piped in, because if you're not dreaming *now*, and you weren't dreaming *before* . . . then how do you explain the fact that a woman is standing in the middle of the south pasture when she wasn't there five seconds ago and you never looked away and she's a good sixty yards from the nearest cover?

David Rigert tuned out that voice. He'd never much liked that part of himself anyway, and as things had slid from bad to worse in the past year he'd found he couldn't afford to be too analytical about anything, because once you started thinking that way you got bitter, and there was enough bitterness in Mark for both of them. Instead you just did, and what needed doing right now was for him to get a closer look at this woman who reminded him so much of Pamela, ask her how she'd gotten there, and – oh, Jesus – see if she was all right, because she had just crumpled in a heap, not even catching herself, the way nobody who is still conscious goes down!

She didn't look so much like Pamela up close; but she was as beautiful as Pamela, and that realization weighted the wonder and confusion he was feeling, as he stared down at her collapsed form, with a guilt-ridden sadness. He had loved his wife very much and had always thought no woman could even come close to the way she had looked at her best. But *this* woman . . . The only half-absurd notion came to mind that this was a countenance, a persona, that had drifted elusively in and out of both his waking and sleeping dreams even before he'd met Pamela, each time his then-adolescent mind had played through the kinds of romantic/erotic fantasies he'd later concluded all young boys most likely have.

Her hair was more a true red than Pamela's strawberry-blond *(why did he keep making comparisons?)* and coiled on top of her head in a way that hadn't suggested at a distance its extreme length. Her complexion was more pale, too, though only slightly so, and every bit as smooth. And her figure . . . Small waisted and full breasted, but beyond that it was hard to tell because of her clothes

Her clothes. Again he was rocked by that sense of unreality he'd experience earlier when she had first "appeared." Because they were *old* clothes. Not just out-of-date or worn-out but *old*. Something from his grandmother or great-grandmother's era, he'd guess – and not just a copy or a costume but the real thing. These were what clothes stolen from a museum, where they had been miraculously preserved, would look like. Or maybe –

She moved. A shudder ran through her body, then a single convulsive twitch, the kind of spastic, involuntary twitch a run-over squirrel makes just before it dies, and it was that connection, made in his subconscious, that finally brought him to his senses. He'd been standing where she lay in the exact center of the field for a good ten seconds and she might be dying!

He dropped to his knees beside her, and the first thing that came to mind was that maybe she'd swallowed her tongue – lots of unconscious people did that – so he reached to tilt her head back. It was then he realized the thing that had kept him standing immobilized for so long was something more than wonder or awe. There was fear there, too, a mild yet steady undercurrent of it, because he hesitated for just a moment before actually placing his hands in a position to tilt her head back correctly thus opening her airway, hesitated in the same way he had as a child before touching the electric fence their neighbors had used to keep their heifers separated from the rest of the herd. And yet he'd always been compelled to touch that fence, just as now he would have been compelled to touch her flawless skin even if he were completely sure her breathing was unobstructed. And that was part of the fear, both then and now, knowing that he had to . . .

No shock. No sudden opening of her eyes and at the same time a possessing of his mind *(why did those things even occur to him?).* Just a sudden, sharp intake of air as soon as he touched her, then a half-sigh, half-moan as she shifted on her own from the partially twisted position she'd collapsed in to her back. She was coming around. Maybe if he spoke to her . . .

"Miss? Miss, are you all right?"

Nothing. Maybe he should touch her again, tap her shoulder.

He did and still no response, so he patted her cheek. "C'mon, girl-with-the-red-hair, you're scaring –"

Her eyes flew open. And for half a second they did possess him. It was the mental equivalent of the panic-strong arms of a drowning person thrown around their rescuer's neck in a grip just as likely to take them both down as to save either one of them. Then it was just-plain panic and the kind of helpless confusion anyone might feel who can't quite hang onto consciousness, before they closed again. If he had detected something else there, too, something behind the mask of confusion that was both knowing and feral, that was simply a product of the unnerving circumstances under which she had seemed to arrive, wasn't it? Still, he decided against any more tapping and patting as a means of rousing her (she'd moaned; maybe that meant she shouldn't be moved) and decided instead to simply sit and wait. And search his mind, not only for some plausible way to explain the illusion of her appearance from thin air, but also as to why, from the moment he'd looked into her eyes, the idea of falling in love again had suddenly become something more than the emotional gamble it had always been and had graduated instead to something frighteningly immediate and real.

"Shoes. High-button shoes, huh? That goes way back. And the dress . . . Some kind of muslin, isn't it? You know what it reminds me of? A schoolmarm's dress. Not a teacher but a schoolmarm. I think there's a picture or a painting somewhere, and it –

"Wait! I think I remember where! It's at my Aunt Ruth's!"

David paused, glancing down at her face as if he expected the fact that he'd remembered the painting's location might be a miraculous enough event to finally shock her into full consciousness. It wasn't, and he'd been sitting there next to her, still in the field, for fifteen minutes now. Five minutes ago he'd started talking to her, the way some doctors suggest might be good for someone in a coma.

"Anyway, the title of this picture is 'The Schoolmarm,' and the lady in it is wearing a dress a lot like yours: blousy sleeves, ankle-length, pleated but not full . . . and you know what? The date that picture was painted was 1910! I remember that!" He paused. "What are you doing in a dress like they wore in 1910?"

The rhythm of her breathing changed. He'd been watching the slow, steady-but-barely-perceptible rise and fall of her chest as he spoke, and it had stopped at the high point of an inhalation. It hovered there motionless for a good five seconds, then fell again, her breathing immediately resuming its normal pattern. His own took a little longer. "Okay," he said finally. "I think maybe we're getting somewhere, so let's try this: You're dressed like a *schoolmarm* from 1910, and you like to *paint*. Like to paint *dresses*. And you like to paint them for your *Aunt Ruth*. How's that? Notice how I got all the key words in without making it obvious? Pretty smooth, huh?" He paused. "Then why aren't you laughing or at least breathing different?"

The girl in the field slumbered on unaffected, and David began to think that maybe this wasn't such a good idea, that maybe he should be calling in someone with a little more medical expertise, even though she seemed to merely be sleeping now. But at the same time he was repelled by the idea – and forget the fact that he would have to either lie or have one hell of a time explaining how she got there, that revulsion was almost an instinctive thing, on par with his abhorrence of spiders and centipedes. No, it was more than that; it was almost as if a separate voice inside him were crying, *"NO! NOT YET! NO ONE ELSE!"*

"Okayyyy, Mary. I get the picture. No one else but –"

A sudden chill ran through his body, and despite the fact that at just past eight a.m. it was already in the low eighties, goose bumps danced up and down his forearms. "Mary? I called you Mary! And that *is* your name, isn't it? Somehow I know it is!" He rolled from a cross-legged sitting position to his knees, then turned on them so that he was facing her more directly and could study her inert face from a better angle. "You told me, didn't you? But if you tell me again once you're awake, I think I'll go crazy 'cause that can't be right, can it?" Nonetheless he leaned closer, close enough to catch the fullness of each breath against his cheek, and feeling much the same mixture of inevitability, fear and heady rush a compulsive shoplifter must feel each time they reach out their hand to steal, said in a shaky voice, "Mary, Mary, quite contrary, how does your red hair grow?" And that is when her eyes flew open for the second time and fixed on his with an alertness that suggested she had never really been unconscious at all.

I I

Thinking back on those first few minutes together, the" time travel" thing should have been obvious to him even then. He'd read enough H. G. Wells, Andre Norton and the like, after all, to be more than familiar with the concept; and hadn't it been prodding at his subconscious from the moment he'd seen her clothes? But then, if a pigeon off the top of the barn had suddenly swooped down and begun talking to him, would he worry about or even notice the fact that it was a passenger pigeon, extinct these last ninety years? He was still in a state of shock, he realized, at the very fact of her arrival. A numbed-logic, sensory overload kind of shock that had him accepting at face value events and conditions which might otherwise have precipitated too large and too sudden a crack in his construct of reality for him to remain sane. Still, the signs were obvious.

"Are you okay?" he'd asked after their eyes had remained locked for what seemed like whole minutes. His voice had possessed all the breathless control of an eighth-grader asking a girl out for the first time, and for some reason he thought she might scream. Not that there was the same degree of panic in those eyes as when she'd opened them the first time. Just confusion. And quite possibly mild suspicion.

She didn't answer. Or maybe he didn't give her enough time, especially if she were still groggy, before he followed up with: "Are you hurt?"

This time she found her voice. "No . . . I don't think so. Unless . . . *you* have . . . 'damaged' me." And suddenly the feral quality was back, at the very core of her eyes, as if it dwelled solely within her pupils. Only for a moment, though, before it disappeared again as quickly as it had come. *Masked over,* he thought. But the perfect beauty plus . . . "something else" there, when it was absent, made him doubt even that. Maybe it had never really been there at all.

"Was it you who struck me down?"

The question jarred him. And at the same time a word forced its way to the upper levels of his consciousness. *Intimate.* That was the "something else." Her eyes were not just beautiful, they were intimate. Eyes-for-him-only, the way Pam's eyes had let him know he was their whole world when she'd looked at him. Which was ridiculous of course, considering what she'd just said. "Do I look like the kind of person who would 'strike a woman down?"

She made a deliberate show of studying his face. "No. No, you don't. But I find it both confusing and alarming to awaken – and in the horizontal – with a strange man kneeling at my side. What . . . what has happened to me? And where is my husband?"

The scandalized tone and emphasis paid that single word, *horizontal*, might have brought a smile to his face if she hadn't seemed so upset, blushing a genuinely mortified blush the way he hadn't seen a woman do in years. Not since his own mother had died. "You fainted, I guess. You've been out for twenty minutes. But I really don't know how it happened – or where your husband is."

Again she studied his face, apparently trying to read how much truth there was in what he was saying, while at the same time her hands seemed to have discovered for the first time there was grass beneath their palms. They busied themselves frantically feeling along her sides like a blind person. Then both processes stopped, and she raised her head to look around. "I'm still in the field," she said as if that were some source of relief. "I think I remember now. You see, Jim and I live in that house over th–"

Her face went white and her eyes flicked back and forth repeatedly between the house and David's face. And each time they focused on the latter they looked a little more reproachful, more wounded. Finally, through grim-set lips, she said, "Please help me to my feet. I feel lightheaded, but I must stand."

He rose, offering her a hand and was surprised at the strength with which she grasped it and pulled herself up all in one fluid motion.

"The trees . . ! The house . . !" She gasped, sweeping the field and what lay beyond in a clockwise circle. Her eyes were wide now, nothing feral or intimate about them – the eyes of a deer caught in a fence as the hunter approaches.

"What about them?" he asked, trying to be nonchalant. But by then he thought he knew, and his heart was trip-hammering.

"They're – " She took a step backward away from him, and with eyes still panic-bright said, "Who are you?"

Right. Nonchalant. "I'm David Rigert. And I live in that house over there. Have lived in it for –"

"No!" She was backing further away now, shaking her head wildly. "Nooo, that's not true! And . . . I detest your boorish sense of humor! *I* live in that house, which you ruined with those dreadful blue shingles! Mrs. Mary Donegal, along with my husband Jim, who –"

What she was saying might have been enough. Plus the way she was saying it, the desperate, panic-stricken denial in her voice and eyes. But . . . *"Mary?"* She'd said "Mary!" And though he didn't quite go crazy or run away, that was enough to make her horrified, swooning reaction to the low-flying plane which had just now loomed into sight above the tall trees at the end of the field almost anticlimactic. And exacerbate the whole situation in his own mind from the disturbingly bizarre to something right out of the Twilight Zone.

She remembered being carried into the house only vaguely. It was as if this latest collapse had jarred the very essence of who she was loose. Her sense of self. And once loosened, it had been caught up in some inner maelstrom that had whirled it about and crashed it against the inside of her skull until it had broken, so that now there was this unsettling, confusing sense of . . . duality.

She was two people.

The one part was her old self, who was terrified. Here she was lying on a strange bed in a strange room – which she recognized at the same time as her own and Jim's room, only different – carried there by a man she did not know. Yet she prayed that this was her real self, the self that was dominant, because the *other* . . !

The other self was laughing at her, and it was the secret, part patronizing, part contemptuous laugh of a mean-spirited soul who

9

believes they are dealing with a moron or a fool. The "other" self was alien, not only to herself but to this world – and she did not even fully understand how she knew that, did not, with her turn-of-the-century schooling and culture, even fully grasp the concept. But it was there, the awareness was there. It was part of the maelstrom, manifesting itself as fragmented bits and pieces of memory, of mental pictures of creatures and landscapes like nothing on this world.

Alien.

She was not that other self, *could* not be that other self, who not only disdained all things good but even as the rest of her was still climbing to full consciousness had been busily analyzing the man named (David?) in much the same way her "real" self might have examined a cut of meat at the butcher's shop. And, dear God, with Jim dead how could she have any interest at all in another m–

Jim! Jim is dead! It hit her with all the certainty and jarring impact of a mule-kick to the stomach, and drove all the air from her just as effectively. But rather than an explosive "Huh!" like the sound her dear uncle had made the time Cooper Token had caught him in the bread-basket, it came out as a strangled sob, and she turned onto her side, curling up into a fetal position And the next thing she knew, the man named David was standing in the doorway staring down at her. "He's dead, isn't he? My Jim is dead."

The man had turned and gone once he'd seen she was all right. Into the kitchen by the sound of his footsteps – or what should have been the kitchen – and had returned a few moments later with a damp cloth, which he had placed on her forehead without even asking permission. It was at that point she'd asked him the all-important question.

"I don't know as I can answer that," he replied apologetically.

"Why?"

"Because there's a lot I don't know yet."

She smiled a sardonic smile, but not directly at him. Talk about the mole complaining to the groundhog that his house is dirty . . .

He was silent for a moment, and she used the time to mentally review what he looked like, standing there in the doorway, without actually turning her eyes in his direction. Tall, most likely six feet, with the raven-haired, blue eyes coloring of her pure-Irish father.

"I take it that means you don't know much either."

Now she did look at him. Sharply. "I know less and less all the time. And why is it you canno' tell me of Jim if you are allowed inside his – in *our* house?"

He looked down at his hands, as if the answer were perhaps written on their palms. They were large hands, at the ends of equally large and muscular arms – more muscular, she realized with a twinge of guilt, than Jim's, even, and shamelessly exposed to nearly the shoulder by the virtually sleeveless gray shirt he wore. And on its front, as if in further testament to his immodesty, were actual words, printed in bold green letters. They formed opposite halves of the same circle and said SPARTAN WRESTLING, which meant almost nothing to "most" of her, but somehow challenged that "other" self in some measuring, wary way.

"I think you're confused," he said, and the look in his eyes was at complete odds with the affected way that he dressed; it was pure empathy. "I think we're both confused. Me about where you came from . . . and you about whose house this is."

She said nothing, but felt her body stiffen.

"I'd like to ask you a few questions," he went on in a voice purposefully calm. "Are you up to that?"

She nodded. *Jim! Jim!* her mind screamed. *I did not love you perfectly, but –*

"Good." He drew a deep breath. "Okay" Another breath. "First I'd like to know what year you were born."

She felt her heart skip a beat and something heavy and premonitory settle in her chest. "1888," she answered. And the fact that a gentleman did not ask such questions of a lady barely gave her pause, if only he could help her to know –

But his eyes had flinched. She'd caught that despite his best efforts to hide it, and, dear God, what did that mean?

"And . . . what year . . ." he began again, then changed his tack and asked a different question entirely. "Who is President now?"

Enough. All of this was frightening her too much. Being careful of her skirts and of a small dizziness that still lingered behind her eyes, she sat up, swinging her feet over the edge of the bed and onto the floor so as to be at not quite so much of a physical disadvantage. "What can that possibly have to do with the moment?" she said bravely. "Or with how my Jim is? Is it to test my sanity? If so, I resent it and should perhaps be seeking proof of your own!"

He stepped back a step, and the shadow of a smile crossed his face. "Sorry. Maybe it is a test, but as much for me as for you. Just humor me."

The smile helped. Despite the awful, premonitory fear, it helped, and she decided to do just that, humor him, one last time. "Wilson, newly elected. There. Do I pass?"

But apparently she did not pass. She could see that much in his eyes. And just then, in a moment of total recall, she remembered looking up while they were still in the field and seeing the thing in the sky, that motorized . . . thing right out of a Jules Verne novel, and –

She was up on her feet, past the man named David and into the living room with an unfamiliar yet familiar catlike agility that only frightened her more. And then she stopped, frozen in horror. She could sense him come up behind her, a stranger, but she no longer cared. Because Jim was gone. All her friends and family, too. Gone or . . . very, very old. "Do you want to know something?" she said in a flat voice to the man whose blue-eyed stare she could feel on the back of her neck. And she said it without once breaking into a scream.

"What, Mary Donegal?"

She swayed but did not faint. What she was seeing held her up, made a stone pillar of both her body and her soul, like Lot's wife. Magic? Not God's magic. . . .

"When I was young I very much enjoyed the works of Washington Irving. Do you still know of him in this . . . 'age?'"

There was a long silence behind her before he finally answered. "The Legend of Sleepy Hollow, Rip . . .Van Winkle."

The extra care with which he pronounced the latter, almost as if the words themselves were tiny bombs which handled the least bit roughly might go off and wound them both, gave him away. She nodded in a kind of transfixed despair. "But as an adult they frightened me, especially the second. I often thought to myself that I would rather die than go through what that poor man endured . . ." Her voice broke then, and she had to grab at the air with a half-gasp before she could continue. "So please tell me, if you can, that I share . . . nothing with Rip Van Winkle!"

The silence behind her spun on and on; and in a terrible way it was louder, much louder, than the noise emanating from her front. But not so devastating, both to her senses and to her spirit, as what she saw rather than heard: a young man, not even twenty yet and missing an arm, staring up at her in open surprise from the overstuffed chair he occupied. And a "window" of sorts, suspended upon the wall in front of him, that till now he'd obviously been looking at. It looked out upon the impossible – a pride of lions walking across a dusty, grassy plain that was most certainly not beyond the walls of any dwelling here in southeast Michigan!

The first "decisive" move David made was to grab the controller and shut off the tele vision. It wasn't that he wanted to (the sound of *Animals Gone Wild* being infinitely preferable to the sound of a girl crying, which was what he expected to hear); it's just that he needed to know how bad off she was in there, in his bedroom, where she had made a swift and ashen- faced retreat, slamming the door behind her after viewing what to him was simply another nature show but to her must have been a vision as sanity-threatening as had one of the lions actually leapt out of the television and into the room. Bad enough that he should ignore her request to be left alone and knock on the door again? Bad enough that she might do something self-destructive?

He listened at the door. No crying. Instead there was a heavy silence that lay upon everything like a guilt-blanket. He felt responsible. Not only for the despair of the girl but for what his son, who was already having a tough enough time, must be feeling as well.

Mark stared first at the closed bedroom door, then back at him, and said, "Not your style, Dad! Definitely not your style!" Then he got up from his chair and stalked out of the house, quite obviously believing the girl had spent the night there, in what would always to him be his mom and dad's room. David heard the screen door off the kitchen squeak open then closed, and it was an accusatory sound, made even more so by the simple fact that this woman did manage to affect him like no other woman since Pamela.

So the second thing he did was go to the screen door himself and call for Mark to come back, but by then the boy was a good hundred yards away, headed cross fields towards the big woods northwest of the farm, and he pretended not to hear. Which brought him round to Decisive Action Number Three, returning to the living room and trying to make some sense of all this by talking through the closed bedroom door.

"Are you okay in there?" he asked hopefully after knocking lightly.

No answer. There was, in fact, no sound at all.

"Look, I know this is rough, but I think we should at least talk about it. You know, compare notes . . ? Maybe we can come up with something. Maybe –"

He stopped. The thought struck him that maybe she wasn't there at all; maybe she had simply "winked" out of existence the same way she had winked in. And that idea filled him with such a mix of relief, superstitious awe and personal loss that he broke into a sweat.

"Are you even there?" he asked in a voice sounding more alarmed than he would have preferred. "I mean, I'm just as mixed up as you are, and maybe I just dreamed you. Maybe I'm *still* dreaming – and sleepwalking – and should just open the door and get back in –"

"*Please*, sir . . !"

The dominant emotion was relief that she was still there. "Don't worry; I just needed to know you're all right. Look – uh – Mary, I would never hurt you, okay? In fact I want to help you – and myself – understand this. I mean, from my point of view it's like you came from nowhere. One minute I'm looking at an empty field and the next you're there – *poof* – from thin –"

Suddenly there was a tremendous, hissing snarl (at least that word came to mind, although he quickly convinced himself it must have been something, *anything* else instead) that sounded like a giant cat, and for the second time that day the hairs on the back of his neck stood on end. Along with it, or immediately after, was an enormous *THUMP* which seemed to shake the very walls. Then he was bursting into the room simultaneous to the thought that if Mary herself could enter this world from thin air, so might someone or something to harm her. But there was no one there, only Mary, with that feral light he'd seen twice before, which was a form of glimmering having nothing to do with photometry or luminary power, fading from her eyes. She was standing facing one of those walls, whole body stiffened in a way that (to him) suggested massive electric shock. And on that wall hung a Farmers' Almanac calendar. But it was what now appeared on either side of that calendar that shook him to his core: two deeply imbedded, splintered handprints punched into the plaster-and-wood-lath surface to the depth of an inch or more. The expression on her face once the "light" had died was something akin to what one might expect upon the continence of a sleepwalker, awakened to find themselves standing naked in the middle of Wrigley Field. While on her palms and on the tips of her fingers was the telltale crushed plaster dust which spoke volumes regarding the source of the damage.

"The date!" she gasped. "It says . . ." She held out her dust-covered palms in front of her, stared at them uncomprehendingly – and didn't they still seem to be just a little too rigid in a way that was almost claw-like? The fourth "decisive" move David made that day was to take a few steps backward, just in case she was still pissed off.

It was like that at first. The next several hours, especially, were filled with periods of near hysteria as proof that the impossible had actually occurred continued to mount against her soul in much the same way, with regard to hopelessness and despair, as each new shovelful of dirt must sound against the coffin lid to someone being buried alive. She fought, she clawed . . . first to resist it and then, David suspected, merely to hang onto her sanity. But it was all done inwardly and at no time did she again exhibit evidence of being the kind of person who might react with violence to any kind of shock or surprise, no matter how severe.

And each moment during those several hours was, if anything, severe, beginning with his own deliberately calm, almost phlegmatic recounting of what he had observed as she'd made her entrance into this world, during which she had finally clapped her hands over her ears and begged him to stop.

Five minutes later he brought her the "U" volume of the World Book Encyclopedia, opened midway through the article titled United States, History of the, and at least she did not close the door on him once he'd left the room to get it, although she got no further than the captioned-and-dated photo on the first page, which depicted troops massed on the bow of a ship bound for France during World War II. At that point she had cried out, "I am dead! I have died and this is my Purgatory!" And she had crossed herself.

A second glance at the television a few minutes later, while not sending her from the room again, had her just as pale as the first time; and when he used the remote to switch channels then turn it off, her eyes fixed on the gadget with all the wariness deserving of a coiled snake. The refrigerator in the kitchen, especially the freezer compartment, did the same, as did the hot water faucet, the microwave and the dropped-ceiling lighting.

Even the change in his pocket was a death notice in code.

But the thing that made him feel most helpless was the wounded way she would look at him, when she would look at him at all, as if to say, "Why are you doing this? This isn't real; it's something you're doing and won't you please stop?"

And even then he'd been under her spell, with the caved-in wall and everything else that should have served as warning fading to insignificance when she was near, while the simple fact of pleasing her loomed all-important. Until finally he said, "Look I did not bring you here. No magic and no machine can do that, not even in these times. And there's no way I want you to be going through what you're going through. Why would I want that? Why would I want to cause you pain?"

She didn't answer. She only shook her head.

"What would it take to convince you it's not me? That it's nothing I can do or undo. because we've got to work together on this. Whatever is happening to you is happening to me, too. If this is a dream, then we're both having the same bad dream!"

She only stared at him, and so he repeated himself. "What would it take?" And that is when she turned and fled from the house through the same screen door Mark had used two hours earlier.

He followed her of course, thinking even then that he had a choice. He followed, and if it hadn't been for her dress, which reached all the way to her ankles, he would never have been able to keep up with her; she ran like a deer. No, like some other kind of animal, more or less skimming the ground as opposed to leaps and bounds. But there was no time to get a handle on that now because they were fast approaching the southeast corner of the lot, which was also the point where Albrith

Road dead-ended into Forrester, and if she didn't pull up soon she would either hit the wire fence there or have to hurdle it in a dress that would not allow for such a thing. And then she did pull up, with him some ten feet behind her, and for the second time that morning he watched her whole body go rigid. Rigid back, rigid arms, held stiff and straight at her sides. Small, almost delicate fists – fists by appearance more suited for tying ribbons than slamming holes in walls – clenched with emotion. Carefully he moved up beside her, wanting to see just what it was she was seeing to have halted her so abruptly.

"So alone, so all alone!" she groaned, and his eyes followed her stare. There was a tree, an enormous beech more than fifty feet tall where the fences made their corner. Its bole was a good three feet in diameter and ran straight up and clean for a dozen feet before the first branch. Straight up and clean except for one spot approximately six feet off the ground. That spot was scarred, with a manmade scar in the shape of a heart.

It took only a little imagination to allow for the stretching, widening and general distortion close to a century of growth had affected on the letters themselves carved inside that heart, although he'd seen them a thousand times before and never once bothered. They read:

M. D.

+

J. D.

An awed thrill ran through his body. It was like witnessing a cripple or a paraplegic, made to walk again. "You're not alone," he said gently but with a certain shakiness in his voice. "And I promise you, you never will be as long as I'm around!"

She turned then, and looked at him sharply with eyes that managed to convey misery, reproach and a question he did not understand. Then there was only the misery, and he said, "Look, can I . . . help in any way? Sometimes it helps if . . ." He held out his arms, open wide in what must be a timeless and universal gesture. But she only stood there.

"Would that be so 'improper'?"

A single tear tracked its way down the side of her cheek to her jaw-line, where it lingered. When it refused to budge further she wiped it

17

away and said, "It would. You are neither my father nor my brother." Then she hesitated. "But . . . I can see your intentions are honorable, and I'm in your world now, with your ways . . . "But that is as far as whatever control she still had would take her, because at that point she broke down completely and was so wracked with convulsive sobs that taking her in his arms seemed no longer a question of propriety so much as one of protecting her from herself. And that is how, on the same morning he'd awakened with the decade-old emptiness which seemed a permanent fixture in his life especially strong, David Rigert found himself holding a carmine-haired houri from more than seventy years before he was even born in arms that just as soon would never have let her go, breathing the female musk of her scent. Murmuring soft assurances through lips pressed to the top of her head. Stroking her miraculous hair and achingly aware of the feel of her pressed up against him and of the way she seemed to press ever closer each time she moaned, "So alone! So all *alone!*"

III

At or about the same time his father stood holding a strange woman *(Not his mother, nothing LIKE his mother)* in his arms, feeling all the wonder and promise a person falling in love feels, Mark Rigert stood just inside Pfister Woods, looking back at the farm and contemplating life from a far different, far less hopeful perspective.

Bitter future, bitter past.

On the one hand he could look forward to a time, very soon now, when his father would no longer need him at all, a time when he just might put his dad's .38 to his head and end it all. On the other, he could close his eyes and relive that day, eight months ago, when God had allowed a metal monster to suck him partway into its mouth, chew on him a while, then rip his arm off at its roots.

That day, that bitter, deceitful day . . .

It hadn't begun as the kind that would make you think something terrible was about to happen, the kind of day on which someone's life, their real life, would end. In fact it had begun as a good day, a beautiful day. He remembered noticing as he stepped outside that there was a special crispness and healthy clarity to the air, to the October sunshine itself. And he remembered how he'd stood there on the porch steps, the smell of coffee wafting after him from the kitchen, how he'd stretched out both arms sideways and tightened the muscles till they quivered and sang.

Both arms . . .

His whole body used to sing to him back then, and it didn't sing anymore. Or if and when it did, it was such a pathetic, inept song, with the one note missing, that it would have been better if it could have been silenced completely, once and for all. Forever.

But it had been singing beautifully that morning, a song that was partly about the record 267 yards he'd gained rushing in last night's football game against Granger and partly about all the fabulous, glory producing, success-producing things it would do for him in the future. And the song had rung true; even the four college scouts who'd been in the stands would have nodded in agreement had they been able to hear its bold, sweet tones . . .

His father was waiting for him out by the chipper, a machine about half the size of a Volkswagen that was run off the power-drive of the tractor and that sucked in branches fed to it at one end and spit them out as wood chips and sawdust at the other. His father. All his life he'd wanted to be just like his father. All-state quarterback for two years in a row, captaining his team to a state championship his senior year; Mark knew all his father's stats. And in *wrestling* . . . The elder Rigert had been state champ at 180 three years running, 190 pound Big Ten champ at MSU the next three years, and had culminated his career by winning the NCAA title on the same day as his twenty-second birthday during his senior year. He'd always wanted to be just like his father, and during that crystal-clear moment he felt for the first time that maybe he was. If not quite as good a wrestler (*almost as good*), maybe a *better* ball player . . . And for sure, they were both school heroes. Hell, *town* heroes. In Valor, then and now, school sports were what the rest of the week waited for, and on weekends those who played them well were kings. As "King Mark" started towards his dad, the latter swung up onto the John Deere's seat and started the tractor. The sound, ornery, powerful, rumbling, had that same extra clarity, that same more-real-than-real edge to it that the air did. He remembered feeling a special kinship with the tractor at that moment, with its power and vitality . .

His father climbed back down from the seat, nodded at him with that little glint in his eye he always had the morning after Mark had played and played well. "Morning!" he shouted above the noise of the Deere. "Gonna bag up that maple for the Wentzle job. You think you can handle this?"

Mark nodded, surveying the sizable wagonload of brush and scrub trees they'd cleared from a developer's site last weekend with just a hint of distaste.

David Rigert reached up for the lever that would engage the tractor's power takeoff, which in turn would set the chipper's metal teeth and blades in motion, and hesitated. "You be careful! You get between it and somethin' it's got a hold of . . ." He didn't' finish. He already had, at least a score of times before. Instead he said, "Feed it the same way you'd hand feed a crazed gorilla that'd like nothing better than to reach through the bars and yank you in with it!"

Mark laughed, both at this new and ridiculous analogy (last week the machine had been a "foam-mouthed gator") and at the way his father said gorilla. GO-rilla. He would always remember that, because it was the last time he would ever laugh a real, genuine laugh. Then his father pulled the lever and walked off to do the hundred-and-one things necessary each morning to keep a family tree nursery/landscaping business running smoothly, and Mark was awash in the whooshing, ever-rising moan-sounds of the chipper with nothing in its maw, like the sound of jet turbines recorded then played back at half-speed.

He was unable to remember clearly beyond that point. Just the way he had felt stepping out onto the porch, his laughing at his father's remark, and the chipper's deadly song And his coat sleeve. He remembered his coat sleeve, or what was left of it after the accident. The way it fluttered and moved, carried on the in-draft of air from the chipper like a tattered, bloody rag. He'd known then that it couldn't be moving in quite that way if it had anything, anything at all, still *(Nooo! N-o-o-o-o! Fuckin' MACHINE! It took it ALL! It took the WHOLE THING!)* inside it.

It had happened right away; there wasn't even enough time for him to get bored and as a result, careless. He did remember that. It was the buckle-and strap arrangement of his jacket, located halfway up each sleeve so you could roll them up. That and a two-inch-thick length of sapling lying on the ground which his feet had slipped on like a rolling pin when he'd tried to brace himself and pull away. Something on the branch he was feeding into the chipper caught on the buckle of his left sleeve, and when his feet slipped he knew he was going in.

There had always been a split-second of something, dread maybe, that had accompanied the precise moment when the machine's metal teeth finally grabbed hold of a branch and yanked it viciously, hungrily forward – the power, the terrible, inexorable, irreversible power..! And now, with his feet no longer solidly beneath him, he knew the final, full-blown horror of which that dread thrill was only a whisper, only the *possibility* of something in the night and not the beast itself with its hot breath on your throat.

This *was* the beast, and for two, maybe three seconds of struggling to brace against and resist its pull, he knew – *knew* – it had him.

It was the measured, short-lived eternity between the moment at which your second chute, your reserve chute, fails to open and you splatter against the ground.

It was floating alone in a lifejacket in the middle of the Pacific as a gray-white fin four feet tall ceases in its circling and knifes through the water straight for you.

It was his hand, then his wrist, then his forearm, then his whole arm, and him screaming and fighting and asking God, ASKING GOD . . .

There was no pain; that would come later, drop on him like an anvil, and he would welcome it with open arms *(arm, ha-ha)*. Pain that would cloud the mind . . .

The people who investigated the accident, people who were supposed to know, all said he must quite literally have ripped his own arm off at its socket in his panic-crazed, adrenaline-laced struggles to resist its pulling the rest of him in too. They said the instinct for survival can be that strong. And maybe it can be if you want to live. But they were wrong in his case. It took his arm, he didn't give it! And by the time he heard the final gristle-popping, meat-tearing wrench, like the separating of a chicken leg from the thigh only magnified to infinity, he knew what was happening enough to no longer *want* to survive. *(It is the opening scenes of JAWS. The girl is out there in the water already, alone. She feels something brush by her, beneath her, something enormous. And deep in her heart she knows. She treads water, telling herself, No, this cannot be. She can see the shore not so very far away, and then the first strike comes, and she is jerked partway beneath the surface by something impossibly strong. "Uh!" And the audience knows that part of her, at least her feet, are already gone even before she does. It hits her again, and she exhales the kind of sound someone would make if they were hit in the gut with a sledge-hammer and more of her is gone. How much? Halfway up the calf, above the knee? And she knows. Maybe she reaches down and there's nothing there. It hits her again and again. Each time there is a violent tug from below, so overwhelmingly powerful that it is as if she is being yanked inside out. "UhhhUH!" And more of her is gone. She knows. She vomits. Maybe she is only half there now. Maybe everything that would have needed shorts, slacks, or the bot-tom half of her bikini to cover is gone now. And you'd better believe all she wants to do is die . . .)*

That's the way it was for Mark, too. That is the way it is when they take you a piece at a time: the violence, the resistance that is futile. The knowing . . .

But the thing he remembered absolutely clearly was the coat sleeve, his tattered, empty half-coat sleeve. Because once he was free, once it had finally torn off his whole arm, he had turned to run, and his father, who had heard his cries through the open barn door, had been right there. For just a moment they had stood staring at each other. Then he'd said, haltingly, "Dad? Dad, you gotta help me!" He didn't remember what his father had said back, if anything, but he remembered his eyes. They were filled with more horror, more pain and grief than Mark could stand, and they frightened him badly. And so he looked instead where they were looking, at his coat sleeve.

Somehow that machine had managed to take his whole arm but only half his sleeve. But he didn't know that yet, he didn't know how much of him was gone. And when he saw half his sleeve still there, he naturally assumed that half *(half? three-quarters? what difference did it make? No hand, no fingers, just a dead stick, a bread stick –)* his arm was there too, and his mind, in its shock and despair, seized upon that fact and blew it out of all proportion in an effort to shield him from reality. All this in the span of a second or two, then he saw the way the half-sleeve fluttered in the artificial breeze created by the chipper, the way its open end sprayed blood, fanned it everywhere, as if there were an inexhaustible supply, and he reached for it with his good hand, his only hand, and his fingers closed on emptiness.

He looked back at his father then. He wanted to tell him how cheated, how outraged he felt. He wanted to explain to him that it had taken his *whole* arm, and that this was simply too cruel, too unfair, and that he didn't think he could handle it. But when he opened his mouth to do so, a scream slipped out. He shut it again, abruptly, and stared at his father in disbelief. Then he was falling into blackness, or it was rushing up at him, with the speed of an express train.

The next thing he remembered was waking briefly in the back of the ambulance, the smell of human excrement so overwhelming in the confined space, made smaller by two men leaning over him, that it was a taste in his mouth. A part of his mind, separate from the rest, realized that it was him, that he'd shit his pants while caught in the chipper. He had to apologize for that, had to ex –

Noooo! My armmm! Dear Jesus –

There were voices. One of them said ". . . his father ever managed to compress the artery when there's nothing left of the humerus is a friggin miracle!" And the other said, "Shhh! He can hear you!" And he remembered *(Where? In the hospital or still in the ambulance?)* wanting his mother sooo *much*. Hurting for her with an ache a thousand times worse than the physical pain, wanting to be little again, back when she was still alive so she could hold him. It used to help so much . .

Maybe the nurse would hold him (so is was the hospital). Someone soft, loving, accepting . . .

Dear God, PLEASE, just this once! I want, I NEED my –

"Mother-r-r-r!"

(The Stag of the Forest looks at him – NO, at BAMBI! – with an aloof sadness. "She's gone," he says. "You'll never see your mother or your arm again.")

"Mom ?? Dad?? Please, don't let this be hap—"

"God?? Please??"

Then someone *was* holding him, someone he wanted to believe was his mother, and he asked her, "Why?" And he remembered listening, as he'd listened a thousand times since, for . . . nothing. For an answer that never came. And then, like now, he'd thought about dying.

I V

Both of them, father and son, sat in straight-back chairs turned backwards from the dining room table so they could stare out the window. Both of them, father and son, watched her simply stand there in the middle of the field. It was twelve-forty now, she'd been there since eleven, and ninety degrees was a cool and distant memory.

"She's crazy, Dad. You know she is." They were the first words Mark had spoken since coming back from wherever he'd been for the last three hours and David had attempted to explain who she was and how she'd gotten there. He knew the boy didn't believe him, wouldn't have believed him even if he'd offered a more conventional story.

"Then I'm crazy too," he said, "because I swear on your mother's grave –"

Mark jumped to his feet. "Don't say that! Don't ever say that!"

Their eyes locked, held for a long moment, and David flushed. "You're right. You're absolutely right. Poor choice of words." Then he nodded toward the window, which was the same window he'd been looking through that morning when she'd first appeared. "But that doesn't change the fact that I know what I saw. She just . . . appeared. Out of thin air."

Now Mark stared back out the window too, and as the edge left his anger they both watched Mary Donegal about-face suddenly and stride purposefully for six or seven strides away from them toward the south. Then she stopped, looked around, and back at the house, and her shoulders slumped. She'd been doing this or things similar, off and on, ever since she'd decided that if there is any chance at all of the whole "time phenomenon" reversing itself, it would most likely occur at the same spot, with her repeating the same actions. Next, David knew, she would retrace those strides, plus a few extra, by walking backwards . . . and somehow the whole pitiful charade seemed infinitely sad when contrasted with her beauty, her carriage, and that natural elegance which seemed more than anything else to mark her as part of a generation lost. It was like watching a racehorse forced to pull a plow.

"Yeah, out of thin air," Mark said sarcastically. "Like Tinkerbell. And that impressed you so much you asked her right off, could she *re*appear someplace more private, like your bedroom."

David flushed even darker. The anger was still there, in his son's eyes, just controlled a little bit better and mixed more equally with pain. It was that second ingredient that kept his voice calm.

"Look," he said, "I don't expect you to understand. It's all pretty far-fetched, and I'd probably have a hard time with it myself if the situation were reversed. But I do expect you to trust me. If I say it happened that way, it's because I believe it did. I don't lie. And I don't sneak around." Mark started to object, but he held up his hand.

"Now, there may come a time when I am interested in another woman. Maybe even that woman out there, which is what's really bugging you by the way. And when I am, when I'm sure that I am . . . I'll tell you. Give me that much, okay?"

"But right now the only thing I'm sure of is that that girl needs some help, some understanding – and maybe some protecting from the outside world too. From both of us. Because even if she only thinks she's from the past, she's got to be hurting. Not to mention the fact that hat or no hat, she's probably a prime candidate for sunstroke by now, and I think it's time to bring her in, whether she wants to come or not."

With that he stood up. But it was impossible to tell whether his little sermon had made things better or worse between them. To determine that he would have had to look Mark squarely in the eyes, and how could he do that when he'd just lied to him? Because he *was* sure of where his interests lay with regard to Mary Donegal; and even if the temperature had been a balmy seventy-two, he would have been just as anxious to get her out of that field, just in case his theory was correct.

She dreams . . . and in the dream she is once again transported across the light years, instantaneously. In the dream she is herself but absent a name. A female (she is profoundly aware of that much) in full prime, padding along a forest *(whose words are these? ALIEN words, alien–)* trail, reveling in the restrained power of her thighs, the killing force in her upper limbs . . .

Something moves on the trail ahead. Just a scuttle of motion, a blur, then a slithering in the plant-growth off to one side. But it is enough. She pounces on the spot where her instincts tell her their trajectories will intersect with dizzying speed, and she has it. It is a creature much like a large, tailless lizard, with soft, pink skin rather than scales, and as she separates its head from its body with an effortless wringing motion, she identifies what it is not by an assigned word or "name" but by racial memory of the wonderful way its flesh tastes and by the sound it makes as it dies. The body she folds as best she can and stuffs into a skin pouch at her side. The head she discards, after first sucking out what little sustenance it contains. Then she is on her way, pleased with herself, pleased with the knowledge that with her prize she can lie with any male she chooses tonight.

And then it happens. She stumbles upon a Collector (*?*) Plate, camouflaged beneath the packed dirt of the trail, and despite the fact that she springs straight up to a height twice that of her own head in a reflexive attempt to escape, the cloud of gas envelopes her. The last thing she remembers, before the scene changes, is falling, falling . . .

But the scene does change. And now she is not only *thinking* with alien words; she is in an alien world. Even her body is different, alien, though in other ways the same. She is standing in an open spot, a "field," beneath a sky that is startlingly blue rather than the various shades of gold and amber with which she is familiar. A "man" approaches her. He, too, is "different" yet strangely, generally familiar, and he says, "I'm – uh– not going to say anything lame like, 'I know what you must be feeling now, because I can't possibly know. But I do know two things: One, that at least you're still among people who care instead of back in the age of dinosaurs or forward to a time beyond people . . . and, two, that pretty soon now I'm going to have to carry you in – again – because you'll keel over from heat exhaustion and what good will that do?"

The man (*David?*) pauses, awaiting a reply. And in the dream she has to rely solely on the alien words, which she somehow understands, to do so, and that in itself is a strange thing, because they are nothing like what she would like to say with her mind. Out loud she says, "It . . . was kind of you to lend me your late wife's hat. But I really must insist you take it back now. You see, I've thought it all through, and I've concluded that with the hat there is even less chance I'll accomplish my purpose, so –"

But by then her mind is practically screaming at the man-David, ordering, demanding, cajoling him to take her with him, take her inside despite anything she might say aloud. Then she focuses entirely on the alien words *TIME OF DAY*; and when he almost immediately responds with, "Yeah. Sure. And what about the time of day? Have you thought that through? If you really want to duplicate this morning's conditions exactly, you do it in the morning," she knows that her mind-touch powers are not gone completely but only dulled by virtue of the fact that despite outward appearances, they are two separate species. She can still "touch" his mind, "suggest" things in such a way that it will seem as if the idea has originated within himself.

What follows after that is a whole series of familiar-yet-unfamiliar alien words, exchanged between them in such a way that it seems as if she is slowly convinced to return with the man-David to his *(house?)*, where she will clean herself, feed and rest. Then she is actually doing these things, ending with the last; she is resting, sleeping, dreaming on the man-David's bed.

Then she awakens, and the dream becomes a nightmare, because it continues. But once again the perspective is changed. What had been so alien – the field, the words, that "part" of herself that understood the words – is now wholly familiar; she is that part. She even has a name. While the "she" of the first half of her dream is as the mind of a beast set loose inside her head and only now beaten down, down, howling and protesting, into her subconscious.

Down, down . . . until finally it is sufficiently repressed that she, Mary Donegal, is left, at least for a little while, with nothing more specific to account for the sick dread she feels than its ghostly footprints on her soul.

At least for a little while. But it comes back again, the beast comes back. There is Mary, whose only displacement is time . . . and there is "Mary." And when, several hours later, David enters the room obviously excited, obviously filled with an idea, it is "Mary" who is waiting for him. "You know what might help? What we could do?" he says, but the question is rhetorical because he doesn't even half-pause before he goes on. "We could go see Mrs. Barrows; there's this old, old lady named Emma Barrows who's lived in the same house about a mile down the road all her life. She's in a nursing home now, but I know for a fact she was born in that house and that she's got to be well past a hundred by now . . .

Then he did pause, waiting for her to put two and two together. And when it seemed by her silence that she could not, he frowned. "Don't you see? She would have been born maybe less than a dozen years after 1913, and people talk you know. Maybe she might've heard about you, especially when she was young. She might even know if maybe you, uh . . ." He couldn't quite look at her directly as he finished the sentence. ". . . came back."

"No," Mary as played by "Mary" cut in. "Please, sir . . . no." And when he questioned why, she continued, "T'would turn everything to an uproar. We would have to explain our reason for such questions – at least a little bit. And can you imagine what a fuss there would be then? And who would then believe us? With no' benefit of having seen me arrive, who would believe us? They would think us insane!" But internally she simplified things. Because her powers of suggestion worked best when the words and/or concepts were briefly and succinctly expressed, she concentrated on the words *EXPOSURE, DANGEROUS* and *THINK INSANE,* and on a mental image of numerous other man-people standing nearby, listening as they quizzed the entity Emma Barrows. And was immensely relieved when moments later he came back with, "I guess you're right," even though a moment ago he'd been purely taken with the idea. "I guess right now all it could do is make people think we're crazy – and maybe scare old Mrs. Barrows half to death besides, because what if she'd seen pictures of you – way back when – and now here you are, looking pretty much the same a whole century later!"

Good. Good. But there was resistance there. With a mind as strong as this David's, even her most focused "suggestions" were subject to interpretation, minor variances. She would have to reinforce them constantly.

"*Would* she recognize you?' he then asked hopefully. "From a picture?" And "part" of her knew that the old woman might.

She shrugged. "I . . . knew her mother, though not well. We purchased our eggs from her almost weekly. I remember that much. Her name was Winifred, and I'm unsure I could look upon a daughter of hers, yet unborn, aged beyond imagining . . ." Then she projected an image of great loneliness, of weathered and tilted tombstones and of being left behind. She "pushed" it at him nonverbally, which was the most difficult way, and it worked. It worked so well that he blanched and had to turn away briefly to hide his face. It was, after all, half sincere, because there was Mary . . . and there was "Mary."

Earlier that day and hours before she'd been forced to think about Emma Barrows, Mary had dreamt. And now Mark dreamt too. Only his dreams were of the nocturnal variety rather than the midday heat-exhausted delirium of an enigma; and it wasn't the dreams themselves that disturbed him, it was their prelude. He dreamt of his mother. Always. And sometimes just before he drifted off to those dreams, he would call her name softly. Very softly, so his father wouldn't hear.

Tentatively.

"Mother . . ? Mom . . ? I –"

(*You what?*)

He'd been needing her a lot since the accident – even more since this morning when "Mary" had intruded on their lives. His mother was – had been – so good, so loving . . . He missed her gentleness, the way she made everything right simply because you knew that no matter what, she loved you. You were her son – *hers* – and she was all all-accepting.

She'd been beautiful, too. In her pictures she looked like an angel, a blond-haired angel. He remembered that because she used to grab a wisp of her hair while running her fingers through his own nearly black locks and say, "Hmmm. Are you sure you're mine?" But he knew that he was, and he would love her so much, feel so good when she would reach for him then, hug him fiercely and exclaim, "Of course you are!" The love would be like a deep physical ache inside him.

He'd been eight when she'd died, and she had been twenty-eight.

"Mom . . ?" Whispered softly. "Mom, I miss –"

("Shhh. Shhh. It's all right.")

She was there again, sitting on the edge of the bed, and her hand, cool when he was hot, warm when he was cold, stroked his forehead. She took his head in her lap, and he snuggled against her. And then, despite his size, he crawled entirely onto her lap. But he wasn't big anymore, he was little! He snuggled harder against her soft-but-not-fat abdomen, seeking to –

("Its okay, Mark. You CAN.")

He felt loved, protected and accepted. Joyous. She had never seemed so real as she did tonight. If she could only stay long enough, if he could only snuggle deeply enough, he could –

("Come back inside. I'll have you all over again; I don't mind. I'll give you all those years you missed. I'll have you when you're eight, if you want. I don't mind. You'll be – ")

Sick. It was sick for an eighteen-year-old to be thinking that way, wanting to be a baby again, back inside his mother's womb. Men didn't think that way, it wasn't right, and he felt guilty, subhuman in a way he didn't quite understand each time he played the fantasy through, which was often. Yet he couldn't help himself. Couldn't. And it was getting worse; she was so much more real than she'd ever been before . . .

Which was another reason why it was time to check out, maybe *the* reason. Because it was spilling over into the lives of the people he cared about, this self-pitying, less-than-a-man sickness of his, and it would soon become as much of a burden and embarrassment as were he to slowly, a little at a time, change into some kind of disfigured monster.

The process, the spilling over, had already begun with Jenny, the only girlfriend he's ever had, the only girlfriend he'd ever wanted. She just refused to acknowledge it so far. If he had any guts he would break things off with her. *Should* break things off . . . But each time he tried to tell her it was no good, that she deserved better than a cripple who wasn't even brave about it, especially now with Prom coming up, she'd stopped him cold with the same four words: "But I love you." And somehow those words, those simple words, said with that look, that glow of absolute certainty she always had in her eyes, would tie him in knots inside and render him incapable of further argument.

Jenny at fourteen. The both of them at fourteen. Her standing there in front of him in his bedroom, looking remarkably soft and innocent. The sound of the televised game and his dad moving about coming up through the register from below. There is an expression on her face, put there by him, by what he has asked – no, almost demanded – of her. It is an equal mix of fear, hurt and proud yet forced, bravery. Joan of Arc must have looked that way as they tied her to the stake. Her body, already most of the way to fulfilling its promise of becoming something truly extraordinary, is rigid. Her arms, too, are rigid; her fists clenched at her sides in miserable determination. All because he wanted to know, to SEE . . . All because he'd played The Game, the If-You-Love-Me-You'll-Let-Me-Do-This game . . .

"I'm afraid. And embarrassed," she says in a voice that tries hard not to sound pleading. "Do we have to?"

"We don't have to . . ." His words say one thing, their tone another.

She clenches her fists even tighter, and the pretty little nose he has "Eskimo kissed" since they were five by rubbing it with his own, scrunches up as she forces her eyes closed. There is a moment of silence, a quiet in-drawing of air, then she says it:

"For you . . . my life. Undress me."

And, of course, he hadn't.

For you my life.

Corny? Melodramatic? Screw the world if it thought so, because she had meant it – literally. He was sure that had God or the devil appeared before them and demanded his life, Jennifer Marie Kiley, she of the shining eyes and the gee-it's-a-great-world disposition, would, at fourteen years of age, have stepped in front of him and said, "Take me instead." And knowing that had, even then, made him feel so unworthy he'd wanted to cry.

He'd been trying to *be* worthy ever since. To be as – what would you call it? *Perfect* wasn't the word; perfect was far less reciprocal. As one-hundred percent as she was. And now, with his arm gone, with what it was doing to his manhood . . .

Especially with what it was doing to his manhood . . .

Tonight's little fantasy had been sick. Jenny didn't need the kind of self-pitying baby he was fast becoming, and his father didn't need him period. His father had Carol; and now he had this "Mary" too. And maybe if he wanted to be with his mother so much he should give everybody a break and really be with her. Except who would be around to remember her then? Who would let the world know that no one could take her place?

V

One of the worst days in Carol Schemansky's life was the day twenty-two years ago this spring when David Rigert had walked into Bob's Truck Stop, where both she and her mother worked, with Pamela Blake. And Pamela was wearing his ring.

David, who would never know that being close to him, being touched by him, was like being kissed all over and blushing with a lovely heat. David, hers and her mother's rock, who had stepped in after her father died and had kept on giving and giving – everything but his heart.

The bottom had dropped out of Carol's world that day. At eighteen she could look to the future with, at best, a dull apathy if it wasn't to be shared with David; and not even the poet Congreve's much-touted "fury of a woman scorned" was present in any degree to override the pain, because David had always been so good to her, good to them, and had never led her on. And the girl he had chosen was the one any fair-minded God would have matched him with, because Pam Blake was just as kind, just as good as he was; and if Carol Schemansky was the girl at Valor High School who in 1999 most resembled a slightly less tall version of Charlize Theron, then Pamela Blake was the only girl in town who was actually more beautiful than the famous actress. They were Lancelot and Guinevere, minus the tragedy (that would come later); they were destiny, and Carol knew that in her heart, which is why she didn't hang around Valor much past her graduation and might also explain why she was less than discerning when it came to men from that point on.

Three years later she married Nicholas Reeves, a second string offensive tackle for the Cleveland Browns, and very quickly became one of pro ball's many wives to fall victim to the Jekyll and Hyde personality changes affected on their husbands through the use and misuse of performance-enhancing drugs. Nevertheless, she stuck things through until the fall of '06, when an argument following a Halloween party hosted in their apartment ended with him beating her so badly (Nick always went for the body, never the face) that there was internal damage and her chances of ever conceiving a child were reduced to near zero. The divorce was finalized three months later.

For the next seven years Carol drifted, if not so much geographically then at least with regard to purpose and perspective. She divorced herself *from* herself at the same time she separated from Nick, and never once allowed herself more than the present moment. For fifteen comatose months she served drinks and waited tables in a bowling lounge in Sandusky, then spent a few years with Libby Owens in Toledo, and finally settled in for the duration as an assistant manager at Franklin Park Cinema in that same city.

It was around that time that her mother, who had stuck it out at "Bob's" and finally married the man himself, got cancer and died. It was 2014, Carol was thirty-five, and suddenly she was owner (Bob had died the year before) of a restaurant in Valor that represented, for her, the best of times, the "pre-Pamela" years when she thought David and she were destiny, and even now, the worst of times.

But she didn't see David again until a year later, when she finally got around to changing the name of the restaurant from "Bob's" to "Carol's Café." The day after the new sign went up, in he walked, looking genuinely dumbfounded. "Carol!" he'd exclaimed. "The sign said – " Then, with a grin that was the same wonderful grin he'd always had but with eyes tinged with a seemingly permanent sadness, he'd rushed over and taken her hand, "Geez, I didn't even know you were back in town! How are you? How's your mother?"

He hadn't known about her mother simply because he'd stopped checking on the woman once she'd remarried, something he'd done on a regular basis once Carol had moved away, right up until the day her mother had walked down the aisle. He only stayed long enough that first day to tell her how sorry he was, and for Carol to realize that she was still in love with him.

That had been in 2015, and for the next three years the link that kept their lives from drifting entirely in different directions again was Mark.

The only portion of David's soul not still mourning Pamela was that portion reserved for his son; and because Carol was genuinely interested in the boy, he would stop in from time to time and talk about him, and that seemed to bring him just a little bit of peace.

Then he'd started sitting with her at most of Mark's football games and wrestling meets, and started noticing little things about her, like the way she wore her hair. And finally, during the 2017 – 2018 season, he'd started taking her to the games, becoming increasingly attentive in an old-fashioned but somewhat reserved way, and Carol began to suspect that the tight hold he still kept on Pamela's ghost was now less an emotional reflex and more an act of conscious will, as if to do otherwise was some kind of betrayal.

Then Mark had lost his arm, and that was devastating for both of them, because by then Carol was beginning to love the boy not only because he was a part of David but because he was everything she would have wanted in a child had she been able to have one of her own. In her dreams, in fact, Mark *was* her child, *their* child, and it was a dream she didn't always try so hard to keep separate from reality. It was she who had finally held him that first night in the hospital when, in a delirium of medication, pain and despair, he'd cried out for his mother, and the nurses (some of whom had children of their own) had only stood and watched. And it was she who had fought hard to keep David from sliding all the way back into the same kind of grief-induced spiritual coma they'd both, for very different reasons, been immersed in for a quarter of their lives.

The best of times, the worst of times. Returning to Valor had started the cycle all over again. But the high point, a day not so long ago when David had looked into her eyes with a gaze that wasn't seeing Pamela at all and said, "I wouldn't have made it these last few months without you," had made it all seem worthwhile.

And then life's wheel had turned again, and she discovered that the day she'd first known he was Pamela's and the day Mark had lost his arm were merely warm-ups to keep her tear-ducts well-oiled for today – and the days to come. Because today she'd closed things down early at work and driven out to his farm to see if there was any particular reason he and Mark had missed their regular Sunday breakfast of Belgian waffles at the Café. And had almost turned in the drive before she'd spotted them and driven on instead. They were out on the West lawn she and Mark had helped him landscape so beautifully the summer before. He with his hand resting so possessively on this . . . "other" woman's shoulder, a red-haired beauty with a face, figure and sensual impact, even at a distance, that not even Pamela could have hoped to have matched.

V I

"Do you . . . think there could be another 'Earth,' then?" the student asked, clearly fascinated with the idea that among all the billions and billions of stars the odds were very much in favor of at least one of them being identical in every way to our sun, including its possessing a planet the same size, mass and elemental makeup as Earth, orbiting at exactly the same distance.

Professor William E. Haroldson, sixty-seven years old and a battle-weary veteran of Astronomy 101, pursed his lips, trying to appear learned and at the same time taken by surprise by the question, which in reality he welcomed. 101 was pretty basic stuff without these side excursions into the land of "What If?" and the popularity of his class was directly proportional to how easily he allowed himself to be misled. "A planet like Earth?" he repeated, after much feigned thought. "Quite probably."

"With conditions exactly like here? Intelligent life? Maybe even human beings?" The student's voice rose a few notes higher, either in skepticism or in awe, with each question, and the professor knew he had him. "At least bipedal," he said with a wink; and by the way the rest of the class giggled he knew he had them, too. Then he allowed his face to go serious. "Actually, I don't know. To say there is only one tiny mud-ball in all the teeming galaxies where intelligent life could evolve seems to me to be the height of presumption. But as to how closely such life might have followed the same evolutionary road as ourselves is another question altogether."

He paused for a moment, mouth partway open as if struck with sudden inspiration, which is exactly the impression he wanted to convey. It would never do for the class to know that he'd engineered this little side-trip from pure astronomy in a dozen classes before them, and that most of his lines were pre-planned. "Come to think of it, 'road' is a very apt word, here, to illustrate exactly what I mean. How many of you are familiar with Frost's poem, 'The Road Not Taken?'"

A smattering of hands went up, fewer, it seemed, with each passing year, and that was a shame.

"Well, anyway," he continued, "it ends with the verse:

> 'Two roads diverged in a wood, and I –
> I took the one less traveled by,
> And that has made all the difference.'"

He allowed time for the words to sink in. "I think one of several things the poet is trying to say here is that everything counts. Every occurrence, every decision, every attitude in the present has at least the potential for 'snowballing' us into one specific future among infinite possibilities. And keeping that in mind, the notion that life would evolve on Earth's 'twin sister' in exactly the same way flies even more surely in the face of the laws of probability than the idea that we occupy the only planet in the cosmos capable of evolving intelligent life. The number of opportunities for two parallel evolutionary paths to 'diverge' would be infinite."

Up till now he'd been pacing back and forth slowly, with his hands behind his back in a posture he believed best represented a preoccupied "genius-professor." Now he stopped in mid-stride and whirled on the class. "Suppose, for example, that it was, as many believe, Earth's collision with an enormous comet and the climatic changes it affected that wiped out the dinosaurs, and that no such comet struck Earth's twin. Or, moving things much closer to the present, what if a second comet passed by Earth's twin, causing cataclysmic weather changes much later along the evolutionary road – say when Homo sapiens was first developing? And what if for a brief time it dropped the average temperature in 'alternate-Africa' and 'alternate Asia' by forty degrees, wiping out that species, but Homo erectus – stronger, more savage, yet far less intelligent and destined, had not the comet changed things, to be wiped out by Sapiens – had survived, due to its greater numbers at that time?"

Just then the chimes in a nearby church tower sounded, signaling the approaching hour, and judging by all the rapt faces, he decided it was as good a time as any to break for the day. Always leave them wanting more, he thought to himself at the same time he said aloud, "Class dismissed," and he felt quite smug as he was packing his papers back into his case a few moments later. He would not have felt so smug if he had known about the bad dreams then, or how closely one of the examples he'd just used paralleled the truth.

VII

She had been there all of twenty-four hours, and already it seemed to David that life had never been so complicated. There was Mary herself, and the rush of confusing, conflicting emotions that tied his tongue and made it as difficult to think clearly whenever she was near as it would have been during the freefall portion of a skydive. Then there was Mark, who was not only deeply depressed but was dwelling more and more these days in a past where his mother had not yet died, so that Mary's presence was an affront that just might drive him over the edge. And then there was the more practical question, though no less complicated, of what do you do, so far as the rest of the world goes, with a girl from 1913? Especially one who slams holes in walls with her open palms and runs like a two-legged panther.

First things first. Mary. The confusion and emotional conflict were not all one-sided; she felt it too, and it was a separate turmoil from that brought about by the "time displacement" alone. On one level she was attracted to him, drawn to him, same as he was to her. It was there in her eyes, in the way she'd pressed up against him yesterday out by the tree with her initials carved on it . . . and if that wasn't enough, by what had happened last night.

He'd insisted she use the bed, and she hadn't really argued that much once he'd told her how he ended up out on the living room sofa most nights anyway due to its comfort (which was true, except that the "comfort" came wholly from its being less haunted with memories of Pam); and at around three in the morning he'd been awakened by the sounds of movement nearby. It was Mary; he'd been able to discern that much in the moonlight immediately. Still, her shadowed indistinct form seemed eerie and spectral in the way her floor-length dress masked

41

all foot movement so that for a few tense seconds she appeared to be floating across the room toward him. She must have sensed his eyes on her, because she said in a whisper-voice, "Please don't think me dissolute, but from childhood through marriage I've never slept alone." She laid a blanket she was carrying on the floor alongside the sofa and lay down on top of it. "And with you, David Rigert, I feel both my person and my virtue will be safe. Goodnight."

That had been it. Except that in the morning, after having lain awake for several hours before dozing off again, he'd awakened to find his right arm hanging off the couch, that hand held in her own with the back of it pressed to her cheek. She was asleep now, but at some point during the night she had made a conscious decision to do something that even today would be considered suggestive of a desired intimacy and most certainly would have been back in 1913! And this only twenty-four hours after she'd lost a husband to time.

It bothered him. Along with the caved-in wall it bothered him, although, looked at in another way, maybe it was a perfectly understandable response, coming from a girl raised to womanhood in an era determined to keep its females helpless and dependent. Maybe it only meant that she now recognized better than he the irreversible nature of whatever it was that had brought her here.

Still it bothered him. And part of the unease, he suspected, stemmed from the fact that in examining her loyalties he had to examine his own, which were no more complimentary to his lost partner than Mary's seemed to her "Jim," because the simple act of holding her hand had made him forget all about Pam for the time being. No, it had done more than that. Somehow it had been as intimate, as erotic in the tactile thrills that had coursed from her soft-warm skin directly to his loins and brain, as had she opened her dress and cupped his hand, instead, to her breast. It was almost as if there had been an actual current, non-electric but alive with sensual energy just the same, that had passed from her hand to his and caused his memory of what it had been like in the early years to hold Pamela's hand to be permanently dimmed. He had pulled his hand away, careful not to waken her, with the same reluctant force of will it must take for an alcoholic to pour out, half-finished, the first drink they have had in years.

Then there was Mark. Mark would never accept Mary. Mark was intent on stripping everything from his life but the double-loss of his mother and his arm. At present he was working on Jenny, the girl he'd been married to in his heart since they were both thirteen, shutting her out a little at a time. Sweet Jenny. They were best friends and had always taken such good care of each other – and if even she posed a threat to whatever dark, "pre-motherless" world he was retreating to . . .

That was it of course. Mark was so openly hostile because another woman in the house, in his father's bed, was too glaring and constant a reminder of the falseness of that imaginary world. Each time he saw Mary it made it that much more difficult to resurrect his mother, and proof of that was the way he'd reacted yesterday, after Mary had finally quit her noonday vigil in the sweltering field and been offered a bath and fresh clothes (he'd never quite been able to give away all of Pam's things). Mark had been stalking out of the room as they were entering it, and at mention of the clothes he'd whirled around, teeth clenched, eyes defiant, and said, "Not Mom's!" His eyes had purposely sought out Mary's and hurled a silent challenge, and their stares had remained locked for a surprisingly long period of time before the latter had said, "I understand completely. I'll simply wash out my own in the tub I bathe in and then wait in the lavatory till they dry." She'd turned to him then with a false bravery. "I assume you have the same miraculous hot-water plumbing there, too? In the lavatory?" And rather than confront Mark then and there on his rudeness thus embarrassing her more, he'd launched himself into an overly detailed explanation of the presence and function of their washer and dryer. Mark had slipped out halfway through it, gone out to his car and driven away. He hadn't come back till bedtime, and even then he'd made himself "unavailable for discussion." But then he was mostly unavailable these days, in one way or another. David had tried on numerous occasions to get him to see a psychiatrist or some other kind of professional, but the boy had absolutely refused. Once he'd even gone ahead and made an appointment, told Mark they were going, and the response had been, "I'll go . . . but I'll just sit there and not say a word, so you may as well save your money!"

Mark was bleeding emotionally and Mary was salt in his wounds.

And finally, there was the question of Mary's rather dubious

43

assimilability, of her ever being able to blend with a society where her survival skills were about as useless and obsolete as the ability to sit a horse in full armor. He closed his eyes and tried to imagine her at McDonald's or shopping for food at the local Kroger store, or trying to check into a room at a Holliday Inn. Even dressed right and with money, the mistakes, the confusion would be obvious. It wouldn't be long before someone, maybe even someone well-intentioned, would phone the police, figuring she was some kind of mental case who needed looking after. And it wouldn't be long after that before they would decide she was mentally incompetent and start proceedings, first to find out who or what institution was responsible for her *(her face on the six o'clock news: "Do you know this person?")*, then, when that failed, to have her put in a home. After all, what was she going to tell them? That she was Mary Donegal, born in 1888 and displaced from the year 1913 to the present during the act of taking a single step? Yeah. Sure. Even if they did check old records (and for some reason, every time he considered that possibility some sixth sense, something in his subconscious associated it with the single word *DANGER*) and actually found something, they would only conclude hers was a peculiar kind of dementia built around an obsession with the mysterious disappearance of a girl who had looked amazingly like her more than a century ago. No way was any rational person going to accept the real story of what had happened as anything but the ravings of a lunatic.

He would have to keep her in hiding. Here. No one but himself and Mark must know. At least until she became a little more acclimated to the modern world through books and television. Then they would take practice "field trips" over to Ann Arbor, maybe even Detroit, to get the metropolitan experience she would need, rather than risk going into Valor where he was known and where people would be bound to ask questions. The prospect of it all, the idea that he would in a way be her parent/teacher/confessor/friend upon her rebirth into this world thrilled him in a way that was strangely erotic. If in his adolescent fantasies he'd conjured up an image of his feminine ideal – which Mary resembled remarkably – part of the lure, the sensual excitement of that image came from the fact that it was his and his alone . . . and that the subject of his fantasies would be completely dependent on him.

Of course nothing in life was as simple or perfect as in one's fantasies. Mary was a real person with a mind of her own, and the kind of secret life he contemplated for her would ultimately be stifling. If he cared at all for her long-term happiness, he would have to do everything possible to move her towards a day when she possessed all the choices and options available to any other woman in the twenty-first century. She had to be prepared to enter the mainstream of society, and that is something you did not, could not do these days without a past, which meant numbers and papers: birth certificate, driver's license, social security card . . . a whole new identity. Up until a year ago the thought would have left him feeling hopeless; but last spring he'd finally gotten around to reading H. F. Saint's *Memoirs of an Invisible Man*, where the main character is forced to do just that. It was still around the house someplace, and it would at least serve as a jumping off point . . .

Twenty-four hours and life had never seemed so complicated. And just when he thought he had it all sorted out – not the answers but at least the nature of the questions – there was Carol, whom he loved in a more thoughtful, less hormonal way, almost pulling into the driveway before driving on by.

"Then it's agreed, you'll stay here for a while? At least until you think you're ready for the outside world?" Less than an hour of actual time had elapsed since he'd pretended not to notice Carol's car slowing for the turn into his driveway then speeding up again. They were still out on the west lawn, he and Mary, sitting in the shade at a picnic table there. Less than an hour, but time enough during the first half of it for Mary to become lost in her own dark thoughts after having spent the entire morning trying again unsuccessfully to "step back through" to her own time from the south field – and for him to think things through as clearly as they could be thought through.

The remainder of their time together out on the west lawn had been spent trying to explain to Mary the risks involved in contact with the world at large before she was ready, ending with the qualifier ". . . until *you* think you're ready." Because he didn't want her to feel trapped.

She shrugged. "Actually, I don't much care. If you say it's best, then . . . tis best."

David didn't like the toneless way she spoke or the way her eyes wouldn't focus on anything, simply stared straight ahead at some indeterminate point in space ."You've got to care, Mary," he said softly.

"Why? Something was tellin' me out in the field today that I'll never go back. That I have about as much chance o' goin' back as my uncle, who believes in the Wee people, has of one of them leadin' him to their pot 'o gold!"

He stared at her. And suddenly the guilt he'd been feeling since the moment he'd seen Carol's car seemed only a fraction as salient, as if he were separated from the incident by months rather than a single hour. *Irish.* It had been there almost from the moment she'd arrived, a minute hint of it, more in the lilt and cadence of her speech than in anything definite she'd said, and under more normal circumstances he would have picked up on it right away. But now the almost musical rhythm, the softening and rolling out of her contractions was so pronounced – and if ever there was a voice that was the voice of saints and angels, it was one spoken in an Irish brogue! That sudden realization had made him momentarily lose track of what she was saying.

(WHY CARE. CAN-NEVER-GO-BACK.)

"Why?" he said. "Because even if you can't go back you're still a woman with a lot of years ahead of you, and you don't want to live those years with people thinking you're insane, which is exactly what they will think if you don't take time to become acclimated to the 'now.'"

She frowned a petulant frown. "If I canno' go back, it does no' matter."

He considered that, the way she'd said it. "Why the brogue, Mary? Why now?"

Her frown deepened. "Because it does no' matter."

"What's that supposed to mean?"

"I was taught to hide it. Cover it up if I wanted to be taken seriously as a lady. But now I'll sing the song of foreigner and fool whether I keep a stiff tongue or not, so why bother?"

David glanced sideways at her from where they both sat at the picnic table's bench. It was obvious she was determined to keep her mood. "It doesn't have to be that bad."

"*Tis* that bad!"

46

If she had been standing, there was no question in David's mind that she would have stamped her foot, and on impulse or maybe because he was suddenly reminded she was really closer to Mark's age than his own, he said with mock seriousness, "Life's a bitch and then you die, huh?"

First she flinched – flinched as if the words had a physical weight and substance and had struck her in the face. Then she looked at him with such reproach that he was sure she'd missed the point completely. And finally she cast about furtively for someplace else to stare, someplace less cruel, her expression said, that wouldn't allow him to see her eyes filling with tears, and he felt the same kind of instant self-loathing and need to make things right he'd felt once when Mark was three and he'd accidentally caught the boy's fingers in a door (and once again, fourteen years later, just before the same boy passed out in front of a killer machine that *he* had assigned him work on). He was off the bench and kneeling in front of her, gripping both her hands before he was even aware of what he was doing. "God, I'm sorry!" he said. "It's just a saying! I was just trying to lighten the mood! Geez Mary, if I could snap my fingers and pop you back to 1913, don't you think I would? I – " Suddenly he let go of her hands and, managing to look both clownish and "inspired" at the same time, flung his arms out wide and said, "Hey. Why don't you just punch me? Go ahead, I deserve it! It'd make me feel a whole lot better . . !"

For the first time since the field the corners of her mouth twitched and there were the bare beginnings of a smile.

"See? I knew it! Tasteless twenty-first century humor does it every time! And once a smile breaks through . . ." He dropped his hands again to where hers lay resting in her lap, took them, and as he did, his own brushed her thighs – through the fabric of her skirts, but still he brushed them. And the promise there . . ! In some completely incongruous way it was like holding a lethal weapon in his hands, a .44 magnum maybe, only this danger, this latent power was wholly sexual in nature. "Anyway – uh – maybe you better not punch me," he breathed. "After what you did to the bedroom wall, you'd probably punch a hole right through me!"

It was the wrong thing to say. The smile faded. Her eyes went from merely sad to haunted, and she shook her head in mute denial.

"Hey, it's okay. Boards and plaster can be replaced."

She opened her mouth to speak and for a moment nothing came out. "No!" she finally said. "'Tis not okay! 'Tis part of it! I'm . . ." Her voice trailed off.

"You're what?"

"I'm . . . no' the same Mary I was."

It wasn't her eyes alone that lent an air of prophecy to the words. Something cold and unpleasant touched his heart; and though he would have liked to have laughed it off and made some clever play on words that set both their minds at ease, he found he could not. Instead, he found himself saying, "Whaddya mean? The wall? You were in shock. You'd just seen a date on a calendar that said more than a hundred years had gone by since you got up that morning. Didn't you ever hear of a mother picking up a car or something her kid was pinned under or somebody frail tearing a metal door right off its frame to get out of a burning building? It's called 'adrenalin rush,' and if you didn't have an excuse to have one, then . . ."

He didn't finish. The whole time she was shaking her head "no" emphatically, and now she interrupted him. "That's not it. This . . . 'Tis with me all the time. Besides –"

"Show me."

"No! I hate it! It's not me!" Each word was clipped and unbending.

"Besides," she went on, "the strength is only part o' my change. I'm changed *inside* as well. As if . . ." She frowned. "As if I'm only 'me' halfway deep: Mary Donegal's thoughts, Mary Donegal's memories . . . someone else's emotions and desires!" Her eyes stole to her lap where he still held both her hands, and she colored. Nevertheless, she continued. "The 'comfort' I take right now in your hand in mine is proof enough I'm no' the same_person I was. Tis beyond my understanding and a scandalous thing to boot to the half o' me I still know that I even say these things! And yet I . . ."

She would not look at him, until he said, "There's nothing wrong with not wanting to be alone. And you yourself are not any more 'changed' or abnormal than you should be, going through what you're going through. And I'm flattered I am some sort of comfort, that you trust me enough to – " He stopped, seized by a sudden train of thought he knew he would not like himself for pursuing. It was manipulative; and yet, because he told himself it would ease both their minds, he said, "You . . . do trust me, don't you?"

Now she met his eyes squarely. "I must. And even if I must not . . . I do."

He blinked, felt guiltier than ever, and filed away the implications of what she'd just said for future contemplation. "Then let me prove something to you. You say you're changed? And that part of the change, though not all of it, is that you're stronger now? Well, what if I can show you very easily – no muss, no fuss – that you're absolutely normal physically? Would that ease your mind some on the other things, too?

"No. I mean, perhaps it would, but I don't want –"

"Wait here," he said, knowing momentum was his greatest ally. "If you trust me." Then he was racing inside and up the stairs to Mark's second floor bedroom. In less than a minute he was back, carrying what at first glance looked like a metal box attached by means of a rope to a long steel pipe. His heart was pounding, not so much from exertion as from a form of nervous suspense. What she'd done to the wall was always there, a nagging uncertainty in the far corner of his mind, and he wanted to be sure.

"This," he said, "is an isokinetic machine. It goes way back to my college wrestling days and a time before they knew that exercise in a positive-only direction, what's called 'concentric contraction,' was of only limited use for building strength. The idea was that you stood on the box and pushed or pulled against the pipe as hard as you could, and something inside the box called a 'centrifugal clutch' matched your force and only fed the rope out at a set, slow speed. The red pointer between your feet tells you how much force you're applying. There's no actual numbers anymore; they were just glued on and fell off years ago. But each short, raised-metal line represents two pounds, each longer one twenty, and if you can't get it past the third long one the way I'm going to ask you to hold the bar, the deal with the wall was a fluke and you can quit worrying about how you've changed and start worrying about whether I have any taste when it comes to buying women's clothes."

He saw doubt, the slow but steady reassertion of misgivings, then refusal in the way her mouth was reshaping itself, and he knew he had to talk fast. "Now I want you to step up on the box, grab the bar palms up after I feed out enough rope to get it to waist height. That will be at the midpoint, where leverage is worst in what people who lift weights call a 'curl.' Then, keeping your elbows at your side, try to bend your arms further with everything you've got." He pantomimed a barbell curl. "Can you do that? C'mon, I know you can . . ."

Reluctantly, not saying a word, she stepped up onto the box and held the bar, poised, as he'd described.

"Now . . . curl the bar upwards! Go!"

She exerted force. The pointer swept past the first long line and kept moving. Past the second, slowing now, but not by much, and David's heart climbed a little higher in his chest, where its mad thumping was less insulated. If it hadn't been for the whirring, clicking noises the machine made as it grudgingly fed out line, it would have even been audible to Mary.

Closing in on the third long line . . .

He glanced up at Mary's face. She was watching the dial, too. "Look up!" he shouted. "C'mon! You can go harder that way!"

The needle finally peaked out at a little past the third long line.

"Okay! Stop!"

The noise died. And for just a moment he was aware of the gentle "shushing" of a summer breeze working its way through the leaves of the two maples that canopied most of the west lawn.

Of a cow lowing on the next farm .

Of distant traffic on U. S. 223 .

So normal, those sounds . . .

"Well . . ?" the girl from the unknown said, making it sound more like, "I hope you're happy now."

He forced himself to look at her and try to grin. "You – uh – can start worrying about those clothes now. You're normal."

She was visibly relieved, which was good, he thought.

"C'mon, let's go inside and see what they're wearing on some television shows; see which things you like."

She led, he followed – she with a lighter step, it seemed, he with one proportionately weighted down, wondering, wondering . . .

Why hadn't he told her the truth? Why had he told her each short line stood for two-pounds, each longer for twenty, when in truth they stood for ten and one-hundred pounds respectively? *Three-hundred pounds* she'd curled, not sixty! Three-hundred pounds, in that position, was more in keeping with what an adult male chimpanzee, supposedly five times as strong as a human being, might register!

Also wondering if even then she'd been giving it everything she had, because it sure hadn't looked like it. No, it hadn't looked like it at all!

Part II

Woman as Predator

"There is no animal more invincible than a woman,
none finer either, nor any wildcat so ruthless."

– Aristophanes (411 B. C.)

VIII

That night, Sunday night, was a night of unrest in the Rigert household. For Mark, that fact alone was nothing unusual. Mark fought all his major battles against depression, regression and self-pity after the lights went out and the house was quiet, save for the settling sounds, the creaks and groans his German grandmother insisted were the restless spirits of the living trees from whose wood boards the house was made. During the day he could keep the bad thoughts at bay with only minor skirmishes, provided he kept busy. Until yesterday. Now he had to both stay busy and stay away from *her*, and though he'd done both today, hanging out at the library till six then taking Jenny to a movie, things were building. Bad things. And it wasn't just because of the way his time with Jenny had gone, either – Jenny, who still refused to understand that wanting a life with a one-armed cripple was like building your house on sand.

Bad things . . .

For David the night was filled with questions. Plural. Not *the* question, which was with him every night and he'd learned not to grapple with because it had no real answer: why did Pamela have to die? These questions had answers; he was sure of it, if only he wrestled with them long and hard enough. Like, what should he do about Carol? Should he tell her the truth, as he believed it, about Mary? In all the world she would be the one person whose confidentiality he could trust completely and who would at least listen with an open mind. But at the same time she was also a person from whom he'd never been able to hide his true feelings, and because his feelings for Mary, whatever they were, would only hurt her, things were in limbo. It was a Catch 22 where any decision he made was a bad one and where all he could do at the moment was lie there feeling guilty and wishing he could call her with some explanation for what she'd seen on the west lawn today, but relieved at the same time that he hadn't.

And what were his feelings for Mary? What *was* Mary? His little test with the isokinetic machine had backfired and left him shaken. Three-hundred pounds? There were, he knew, two or three World's Strongest Man competitors who, incredibly, were capable of a three-hundred pound curl, but they all weighed over 350 themselves and would have had to strain mightily, which Mary hadn't. For anyone of Mary's size, male or female, to accomplish it was about as freaky as watching a six year-old step up to home plate in Comerica Park and belt one out of the stadium! Or should be . . . But that was the thing; with Mary it wasn't. With Mary the strength, the bizarre circumstances, even the snarls he'd thought he'd heard yesterday when she was alone in the bedroom kept slipping off the logic-center of his brain like someone had greased it with cooking oil. Slipping off and drowning in a pool of animal desire. Red lights and little alarm bells should be going off in his head. He should have been adding all the little freaky things together

(Two sharp teeth? Hates the sun?
Pale, pale skin? Better run!)

and coming up with a healthy case of the heebie-jeebies; and instead, even now, what was really on his mind was what she would look like, what she would feel like when they –
Christ.
What *was* Mary? The most hypnotic, most alluring, most female female he'd ever imagined existed, with a sensual draw that would have pulled Ulysses in the opposite direction from the Sirens' song. And what were his feelings for her? The fact that he lay here, pulse pounding, hoping she would come to him again tonight despite what that would say about her own insecurity pretty much said where he was at on the well-traveled road between lust and love . . .

Sunday night. For "Mary" it was a night of unrest too. She lay awake, thinking – or at least a part of her did. And if either David or Mark could have peeked inside her brain, the kinds of thoughts and images they would have been privy to there would have made their blood run cold. It would have been as if they had peeked inside the mind of a wolf, or perhaps a leopard. Alien. *Feral.*

First she thought about Mark. She thought about the fact that she was going to have to kill him. Mark was in her way; she sensed he would always be in her way. But she would have to be patient. She would have to do it not in the way she hungered for but through his own thoughts and weaknesses. She would have to kill his "sense of self" and hope that the rest of him followed suit.

And she thought about David, about how she had fooled him at his own game today. But it had been a hollow victory, necessary only because she had failed (*I'm not the same Mary I was.*) beforehand to control her 'other' self. She'd given too free a rein to the Mary he thought her to be and discovered too late how powerful that tame mind could be once it gained momentum.

Momentum. She panicked momentarily at the familiar-yet-unfamiliar ring to the word. Now she was even thinking in Mary's language – had been all evening, not even aware of when she'd made the change – and it made her wonder how much of herself *was* herself and how much was an inseparable meld of the two of them. For one wild, claustrophobic moment she knew what it must be like to drown, and would have turned on the "other" Mary and torn her to pieces had they not shared the same body. Then she calmed herself, realizing the change to Mary's language had been an instinctive thing, on a par with choosing one's footing through broken terrain without ever being aware on a conscious level of doing so. Instinctively she had recognized this "human" language as the better suited for the clear, step by step execution of her plan. Still, the fact that it was superior, at least for her present circumstances, served as warning that in the end her "other" self might prove to be the most formidable obstacle of all to the attainment of her goal, as well as her greatest ally.

Her goal. Her imperative. To spawn a hierarchy so powerful, so revered that it would be in a position to betray a whole planet! How perfect David was for the fulfillment of it, how perfect his seed!

Had she really fooled him today? She thought so. But then it was hard to tell, so hard to tell anything in a world where she could only send and not receive. His face had said he was fooled. His mouth had said so too, but she was too unskilled at discerning truth by those means alone to be sure. At least he could still "hear" her. At least she could still "touch" his mind on its most basic, primitive level, where primal desires meshed with the pure eroticism she broadcast at him in such a way that whenever she was near he was completely under her spell – as evidenced by the quickening of his pulse, which she could hear; the heat of his arousal, which she could feel, taste and smell. Through her powers of suggestion and partly through his own loneliness, his own natural desires, he was under her spell.

She thought about those things; but most of all she thought about her need, her "other" need, her hunger, which was not sexual in nature, had nothing at all to do with procreation but in many ways was just as instinctive a craving, just as necessary for the survival of her species and just as pleasurable to fulfill: she wanted, she lusted for, she had-to-have . . . a kill. She needed the feel of flesh tearing, life's blood pouring over and between her teeth. It was the thrill that kept her savage and pure, and it was the true focus that kept her from losing herself in the blend of hers and the "other" Mary's mind.

She needed to kill. Tonight. And again and again after that!

As she rose from the bed and crept from the room with a facile, shadowy silence that was uncanny, the "other" Mary broke through whatever mental bonds it was that held her momentarily and screamed. Screamed at what she was being carried away toward. But the scream only reverberated on the inside of their shared skull; it was never actualized as sound. And then even the impulse was crushed, before any momentum could build.

Outside the night breezes brought her scents from all manner of living things worth killing, while her sensitized mind brought her knowledge of even more. She could not, for example, "smell" old Mrs. Tomlins who lived alone and widowed in the farmhouse a half-mile west on Forrester Road, nor any of the four members of the Driggs family an equal distance to the east. Too far. Too far and too closed in. But not so far that she couldn't sense them there, as separate and distinct cognitive pressures on her mind. It was like being touched non-physically, and it was more pronounced as distance was reduced and intelligence grew, so that while she sensed the people a half-mile away, she could also sense a stray dog at half that distance, as well as a deer in the nearby woods, but mice, frogs and a flying bat much closer than those creatures, not at all.

Both David and Mark pressed heavily on her mind, and while their "touch" told her nothing with regard to what they were thinking, it told her a great deal about *how* they were thinking; and right now they were both still awake, restless and perturbed. It was not a good night to be seeking a kill, but she couldn't help herself.

First she had to be rid of her clothing; it was encumbering, would keep her from moving as swiftly and silently as her needs required, and would be hard to explain, all blood- stained, come next morning. Not here, though, not in the open. She moved off the back porch, across the gravel driveway which curved around the back of the house then out to Forrester again in a lazy, inverted "U," and toward the small barn fifty yards beyond that. She moved like a shadow.

Once inside, she discovered it was little more than an empty shell now, a husk. In her own time, in Mary's time, it had been much more than that. It had in fact been part granary, part milking parlor, part toolshed and part loft, with each of those functions kept separate from the other by inner walls and partitions. But now all its insides were gone, either rotted away or torn out for their lumber so that all that remained were the outer walls and the heavy-beamed super-structure; and the only thing inside was the John Deere tractor, the hulking, brooding machine that had collaborated with another machine in the taking of a young man's arm. The Deere and empty space. And all that empty space had a way of doing things with the night wind, as it passed through the outer wall's cracks and gaps, which were slightly less wide than in a picket fence but almost as frequent. Things that would have made even a phlegmatic wonder if something were creeping up on their blind side, but would have suited the kinds of things they imagined just fine.

Those sounds, the soughs, the moans and the hissings covered up the swish of Mary's skirts as she undressed, and that suited "Mary" just fine. Item by item she stripped, all the while casting about with one part of her mind for new scents, new "touches," while the rest

59

of her took care to lay each piece of clothing out in a way that would assure her not forgetting something if dressing again had to be done in haste. Finally, she stood naked, a lush, ripe hourglass of a woman so stunningly, erotically female that a compulsive Peeping Tom, having seen her, would most likely have been cured simply because this was that illusive, ultimate thrill he'd been after all his life, and he would know instinctively it would never be equaled again. That is if he had lived, which would have been doubtful. She would have sensed him, just as she'd sensed the others; and as he watched, a wholly inhuman growl would have rumbled from her throat. She would have looked right at him, wherever he was hiding. And he would have begun to suspect he was going to die even before she glided, catlike, in his direction . . .

There was no Peeping Tom of course. But there was a growl, and it did rumble from her throat in nonhuman enough fashion to qualify, at least to human ears, as a premature death knell, although in reality it was a growl of pleasure at the feel of the night air moving subtly over unfettered skin, a growl of pleasure and anticipation.

The deer. It would be the deer this first night because her human-logic side told her such an animal was not owned, was no one's pet and could die without creating a single ripple in the sea of man's concerns. She moved out of the barn via a back, north-facing door into the lesser darkness of the night.

The field directly behind the barn hadn't been cultivated in twenty years. It was rough, broken ground of no use for anything except pasture, and the last cow to graze there had been sold to a neighboring farm eight years ago. Consequently it was weed-choked as well as rough, and the first thing this "alternate-Mary" discovered, as she settled into a ground-eating lope that carried her in the direction of the woods, was that her feet, the feet she possessed now, were soft, much too soft for the hard use she intended to put them through. It made her angry. She was not herself; she was changed, just as the entity born Mary Donegal was changed. But till now it hadn't seemed a hindrance, and suddenly the bitter reality of it all – the fact of her being forced to occupy the cloned, altered body and "preserved" mind of an Earth-female dead (*and yet not dead)* for unimaginable years – filled her with a rage that was the rage of a tiger,declawed, muzzled and chained to a children's ride.

The fact that she was, on top of that, unshakably programmed to strive toward an imperative that was not her own was akin to surgically attaching chimes and bells onto that same tiger.

Her breasts, too, added fuel to the fire. If her feet had been changed to something small and delicate as well as made soft, the breasts she shared with the other Mary were swollen to a size as unsuited for running and swift attack as had two kill-pouches been strung across her chest. Kill pouches: the word/concept brought a wave of vertigo and displacement that, combined with her rage, made her want to cry out in a way that would ensure no kill tonight; and it was that possibility plus the knowledge that everything about her present endowments would make things easier with David that finally allowed her to calm herself. Next time she would prepare. Next time she would bind herself, wear skins on her feet, whatever it took.

The deer. The deer. If she could not run down the animal for her breasts and feet, then the animal would come to her. Even in the short time she had paused to regain her composure she sensed it had drifted closer. Not by much, but if it continued in the same direction all she would have to do is find a good hiding place and wait, as she was downwind. And so she waited.

A gully running east and west through which a small stream passed was her hiding place, and it was perfect. High waters following snow-melts and heavy rains had cut a groove in the field through the years that was three feet deep, more than six wide, and vertically banked. Now, though, only a small volume of water flowed there, an inch-deep stream occupying the middle eighteen inches or so at the gully's bottom. Small but lively, lively enough that its noise would mask any subtle movements of her own. The deer would not hear or smell her, while she would be able to track its every move and approach through mind-touch alone. Perfect. And the gully maintained its depth and steep-banked configuration east-to-west across the entire field so that she would have her cover no matter where the animal's meandering path encountered it.

She waited, crouched up close to the south bank, adjusting her position twice as the animal drifted more easterly than she had anticipated. At one point a large spider crossed from the bank onto her shoulder and she flicked it off with an uncanny rippling of her deltoid muscles – look ma, no hands – in the same manner cattle dislodge flies. Mosquitoes lit on her naked back and were dislodged in a similar manner. Most of them . . . And then the thing called "Mary" began to salivate, because her prey was at hand.

With all the power of her mind she willed herself to project thought-images of safety, of non-threatening normalcy, striving to do with the deer nonverbally what she had done to David that first day in the field, when she'd focused everything on the words, *TIME OF DAY.*

Closer. C-l-o-s-e-r . . . Less than five feet now, and it seemed to be working because surely it could see at least half of her form, jutting beyond the concealment of the bank, now, from that angle, but . . .

Ka-thud. Ka-thud-Ka-thud. In her mind the three mincing steps it moved closer were as heavy and distinct as a Clydesdale's, and now her body was pure adrenaline and knife-edged hunger for the kill; she couldn't help –

The doe – for that is what it was, a doe – stretched its neck forward inquisitively, and just as the blanket-image sense of safety abruptly fragmented, blown apart by "Mary's" rush of adrenaline, the beast-woman shot straight up and screamed and had the animal by the neck. It squealed – once – then was ripped from its legs-braced stance atop the bank as abruptly as a tin can hit by a shotgun blast. But with the latter, the trajectory, once hit, is a random one, unguided, while the unfortunate animal's was an effortless, blur-speed arc with a secret monster as its pivot. It was as if "Mary" were practicing judo throws on a straw dummy, incredibly vicious throws, where the anatomical part grasped was the victim's neck rather than an arm. The deer traversed its arc with all the ruinous speed and power of a sledge swung by John Henry, and its back struck the bare, hard clay lining the gully like it had been dropped from ten stories. It was almost certainly dead or at least paralyzed the moment it hit, but that wasn't enough, not nearly enough, for a creature as hungry for the kill as "Mary." The moment had come and gone too quickly, the victory too easily won, and now she tried to salvage just a little more pleasure from this, her first Earthly kill, by whipping and thrashing the limp body back and forth like a terrier with a rat. Then, after she was finished with the rough stuff, she decided a little "chiropractic manipulation" was probably in order, and with a gleeful, snarling chortle, the kind of noise a wolf might make if it could laugh, she braced a foot against the animal's shoulder, slid her grip onto its lifeless head and twisted. And pulled. And pulled and twisted. The sound effects, as vertebrae separated and popped, were truly amazing, and she worked it until there was literally nothing left to break. Then, and only then, was her "primary" hunger sated.

Now, if there was time, she would see what she could do about that "secondary" kind of hunger, the kind that had to do with only the belly.

She made the time,

Instinctively she knew that the place to break through the tough hide of the dead animal was at the soft underbelly. Not so instinctively she knew, after the experience with her feet, that the teeth she possessed now were not the instrument of choice. But no one told her her "woman's hands," especially her thumbs, were too frail or lacked the necessary strength to be used as instruments of butcher, and so she dug them into the soft flesh there, dug them in savagely until they pierced through. From that point on things got grisly. There was the wet whisper-sound of the outer fat layer being torn like some clinging, tallow-colored Jell-O. There was the spilling out of the intestines, all in one convoluted lump as if they were back-pressured, as she tore through the abdominal muscles themselves. And there were both her arms, embedded past the elbows, as she reached far up beneath the doe's ribs in a grotesque exaggerate parody of midwifery.

Grisly.

Macabre.

But the thing that would have rooted itself most firmly in a chance observer's mind, that dark cellar portion of the mind where little bits and pieces of insanity are kept under lock and key, was the way she looked when she finally rose from her kill, the contrast.

Beauty . . . and horror.

Even with the light from the nearly-full moon turning her pale, flawless skin a silver-blue, she was a vision so lovely, so imbued with an utter sensuality, that awed, stunned silence would have been the only first reaction possible any man observing her. His next reaction, however, would have been something slightly less reverent, as he noticed her forearms were painted with blood, that she was slowly raising something amorphous and dripping toward her mouth. And when she began to feed on that wet, quivery mass, which he might or might not have recognized as the still-warm liver, plucked from the animal at her feet, the rapture would metamorphose all the more rapidly toward full-blown horror. Then the blood would spill over from her voluptuous mouth, trickle down her chin, her throat, in rivulets turned purple by the same moonbeams which now seemed to cast such a ghastly pall on her skin. Down further, till it flowed in a stream between her upturned breasts. Down the soft concavity of her belly, which even now somehow gave promise of infinite fertility. Down, down . . . until finally it merged with a lush, hirsute triangle, red-gold in true light but the same bruised-purple as the blood itself in this, the light of witches and wolves . . . and the contrast, the hellish journey between beauty and horror, arousal and insanity would have been complete.

But no one did watch. And so she finished her meal without the pleasure of having to kill again, pausing only once to stare heavenward at a sky filled with stars, the farthest of which was still only a small fraction of the distance to her own. Then she lifted and carried the carcass to a place of tall weeds fifty yards from the gully as effortlessly as if it had been a bag of laundry, returned long enough to wash most of the blood from herself in the stream, and proceeded home.

No one watched. At least not from the outside.

I X

It was probably good that Mary hadn't come to him last night. It had allowed him to see things more clearly, know what was right with regard to Carol. If she had come to him he most likely wouldn't be where he was now.

He got out of his truck, crunched across the white crushed-stone parking lot and entered Carol's Café. The smells and noises that assailed his senses as soon as he stepped through the door – fresh-brewed coffee, frying bacon, the clatter of cups and saucers – evoked a strange, sad sense of nostalgia. Strange because they took him all the way back to a time when the sign outside said "Bob's" rather than "Carol's." Carol herself had been struggling to eke out a living there, working as a waitress alongside her mother, and he'd been almost a daily visitor, busily using whatever influence he had as something of a local sports hero to make sure all his friends stopped by, too – and didn't forget to tip. The sad part was a little tougher to get a handle on, and as his eyes caught Carol's from across the room he shrugged it off to guilt.

He sat down in his usual spot by the window with the lace curtains (the curtains lent a certain comfortable if dishonest air of domesticity to the considerable amount of time he spent with Carol there), and for a brief moment he fought a panicky notion that she would just ignore him, that she would send Janet over instead. Then she was sitting across from him, her eyes unreadable, and he felt the same kind of prickly-heat at his cheeks and up and down his sides as when he'd found a Playboy magazine on Mark's bed, been leafing through it, and Mark, who was fifteen at the time, had walked in.

"She's – uh – not my cousin from Pittsburgh. . ." he said with no preface whatsoever. "So I'll spare you that story."

She didn't say anything. The muscles along either side of her jaw knotted, and he thought only men did that when they were angry; but she didn't say anything.

"But she's not what you think either."

Then the mask fell away, and it struck him that people might also do that as a way to keep from crying. "What is she, then?" she said in a voice that sounded infinitely weary.

"What is she?" That, of course, was the killer-question. And because the answer was something even someone as accepting as Carol had to be "prepped" for, he approached it indirectly. "What would you say . . ." he asked, "if I told you she's an escapee from a mental institution who's just as sane as you or I? And that I'm hiding her?"

She studied his face for a long time, before she asked, "Is she?"

'No. But –"

She stood up as if to leave. "Don't do this to me, David. With me it's more than a game. If you don't want –"

"Wait! It's not a game! But I've got to tell it my own way, and I think you'll understand why once you've heard me out!" He said it much too loudly, and now a number of Carol's regulars were watching her protectively. "So let's take a walk outside and at least give it a shot."

She hesitated, then by way of an answer called over her shoulder, "Janet, you think you can handle things alone for a few minutes? I won't be long."

Outside, the sounds of a mini-caravan of eighteen-wheelers on U.S. 223, which was only the length of the parking lot away, made conversation at anything below a shout impossible, so they went around back where the building could block some of the noise. It was nice back there if you looked in any other direction than toward the back of the café itself, where the rear end of a wall-mounted air-conditioner, six well-used garbage cans and a peeling, green door were the only things to see. David faced straight away from the building, where the land dropped off in a gentle curve till it reached the Raisin River, with its cottonwood-and-willow borders, because everybody stared at rivers and it wouldn't seem quite so obvious he was avoiding her eyes.

"What I just said in there . . ." he began, "the

'mental-institution-sane-as-you-or-I' bit, isn't far off really. Except it's more like that's where she might *go*, along with me, if either one of us starts telling the world-at-large where she came from or how she got here."

Now he did glance at her face for just a moment, to see just how much skepticism was written there. Not too bad, so he went on. "Her for believing, absolutely, that she's from the year 1913 . . . and me for not only going along with her on that but for a bunch of other pretty weird things I'd have to swear to besides." He reached over blindly now and took her hand, hoping the physical contact would lend an added measure of credibility to his story. "Things I'm going to tell you about right now." He gave her hand a quick squeeze, the tactile equivalent of a wink he hoped. "I'll . . . entertain questions at the end."

He talked, she listened; and when he was done he'd told her everything he knew about Mary except that the time she'd cried she'd done it in his arms and where she had spent that first night. He tried hard to keep any and all emotion out of it, to make it as studied an effort in neutrality as any newscast; and yet the first thing Carol asked when he was done was, "Are you . . . 'falling' for her?" Not, "Have you lost your mind?" or some other protest of the facts themselves but, "Are you falling for her?"

He was stunned. "I don't know what to say."

"Just tell me. Or maybe you already have!"

"No! I haven't! I said she's pretty, and she is that – pretty . . . and needy. Two things I think most men have a hard time keeping separate in their mind. But . . . " He made the mistake of turning to face her again out of shock and surprise at the question, and then he wished he hadn't. "In love? No. Concerned, maybe even obligated? Yes."

It wasn't a total lie but it felt like one. And in that moment he wanted in the worst way for it to be the whole truth, so he concentrated hard on just holding her hand – and much to his dismay it felt like there was less of him, less of her, down where they were connected! An insane yet disturbing image of two astronauts drifting in space rose in his mind. They were drifting apart, yet still gripping each other's hands, and as the gap widened their arms began to elongate until finally they were separated by a thousand miles, still connected by these wire-thin limbs that couldn't possibly transmit the substance of who they were such incredible distances . . .

"If I asked you to send her away, if I was too jealous to handle it, would you?"

tseee-Whoosh Right back again. In a millisecond the elongated arms had retracted to normal size. Less than normal size. And the spacemen were eyeball to eye ball – strangers. There was silence, too much of it, before he said quietly, "If I asked you not to hide some guy, some innocent guy on the mob's hit-list, would you still do it?"

"It's not the same."

"Why not?"

"Because . . ." She faltered. "Because it's . . ."

"Far-fetched but not crazy? Because that could feasibly happen and mine couldn't? I think the basic problem here is that you don't believe me." He worked hard at putting some real hurt in his voice, but he couldn't, not with Carol. He couldn't be that manipulative, and it came out flat-sounding and toneless.

"That's not fair," she replied with the genuine emotion he'd been shooting for. "It's not fair to tell someone out of the blue that the moon is green and expect them to accept it on faith just because they care for you. And even if they did, that's not the 'basic problem.'" The last words were uttered with as much scorn as he'd ever heard Carol muster, and he braced himself for what was to follow.

"In order to understand the 'basic problem,' two other factors would have to be figured into your little shoe-on-the-other-foot equation," she went on, a little more composed. "Number one, my 'innocent-mob-target' would have to have the looks and sex appeal of Brad Pitt. And, two," –– her voice softened – "I'd have to be your reason for living, for dying . . . You know how the song goes."

Silence. If he'd been stunned earlier, now he was overwhelmed. All he could do was stare at her dumbly, stare into the loving, wonderful eyes made shiny and bright with a backup of tears held always in check for his sake and wish so much that he could say the right words. She deserved the right words . . .

"I . . . You know I care about you, too, don't you?" was what he said finally, instead.

She nodded bravely but he could see her flinch inside and he loathed himself.

"And as far as her looks . . ." He shrugged. "You help people who need help regardless of how they look. I apologize that she's –"

Just then the green door opened abruptly, Janet stuck her head out and with typical misinformed candor said, "Sorry to bother you two lovebirds, but every table's full in here . . ."

"I'll be there in a second," Carol said, a little louder than necessary, and the door swung shut just as abruptly.

There was a lull, shared between them, then Carol let go of his hand. She purposely allowed her eyes to move back and forth between his own and the abandoned extremity with the kind of sad reluctance on her face a child wears when returning a kitten to its rightful owner that they would just as soon keep. "It's breakfast rush," she said quietly. "I gotta go. But I'd like you to think about a few things."

Now she touched the tip of one raised index finger with the tip of the other in a typical "Carolesque" pose. She had always been as organized as he was unstructured, even to the point of numbering her thoughts, and for just a moment, as she said, "One . . . " he saw a different Carol, fifteen and riding on her father's combine, doing the same thing – and during that moment he felt that he could have spoken the right words. Then the feeling ebbed as she continued: "Everything has an explanation. No matter how magical or how far beyond the laws of nature something seems, there's a logical explanation."

The second finger went up and was duly acknowledged by its left-handed counterpart. "Two, why don't you have her stay with me? If she's truly from when you say and needs 'acclimating,' clothes, etcetera . . . the guidance of a modern woman would be better than the *mis*guidance of a modern man!" She didn't smile or wink, and there was nothing in her tone that gave him a clue she was anything but dead serious. Under any circumstances such implied criticism, so unlike her, would have surprised him; but now that response took a back seat to sudden total and unwilling recall of the snarls he'd heard coming from behind his closed bedroom door and the caved-in wall, and a clutch of fear-laced concern grew in the pit of his stomach. But before he could reply she said, "And, three . . ." She hesitated, got a funny look on her face. "If you were ever uncertain how I feel about you, you shouldn't be now, after what I said. So I've got nothing to lose when I tell you the only thing that kept me 'nice,' once Pamela got her ring, was the fact that she was so purely good. It was justice. Devastating, but. . . . justice." Again she paused. "This isn't justice, David. She's not better for you than me; I can tell that without even meeting her from the things you've said. She's either schizophrenic or part of some elaborate hoax. But I do intend to meet her, David. Soon. And this time I'll only be nice on the outside. On the inside I'll be looking for, well . . . justice."

She backed away from him then, toward the green door, still wearing that look that was part reproach, part restrained anger and part whistling in the dark. And when he opened his mouth to say something, she turned around, effectively cutting him off with her body language. She didn't want a response. She wanted and needed the last word, though he was only vaguely aware of how all of this fit within the framework of an argument. It was only after the door finally swung shut with her on the other side that he said to the empty air, "I . . . don't think you know what you're getting into!"

X

Life for David took on a whole new rhythm and structure with Mary around. Before her arrival it was divided neatly into two immutable halves, "work" and "after work," with the former comparable to the main theme in a symphony, complete with percussion, strings, woodwinds and brass, while the "after" portion was but a transitory strain involving a single violin. Before Mary, losing himself in the rigors of his landscaping business was the best he could look forward to.

Life was still a two-part deal even now; but the part that seemed mostly just a means to an end, a perfunctory kind of thing, was the "work" part now, while the other half was no longer its antithesis but "time with Mary". He tried to deny the almost adolescent level of excitement and anticipation he felt as he left his current job, the half-acre lot surrounding a Congregational church on the other side of Valor, a little earlier each day. Tried to convince himself it was simply the mind-boggling novelty of actually communicating with someone born more than a century ago, but it was more than that. History does not make your heart act like a monkey on a jungle gym. History, even the living, breathing variety, does not make you feel as if you are constantly falling, with an urgent kiss or the tactile ecstasy of running your fingers through red, abundant hair the thing you are falling toward rather than the ground itself – this despite the element of foreboding, so strong that very morning when Carol had hinted at a confrontation between herself and Mary.

But by the time he'd left the church grounds that first day of the new week around five he'd convinced himself there couldn't possibly be anything actually dangerous about a girl of Mary's beauty and charm. He'd also convinced himself he was under no moral obligation to Carol just for having been her friend all these years, and that having Mary around might actually be healthy for the relationship in that it would serve to clarify things one way or the other.

That evening they went shopping together for clothes. She had spent the day armed with an operator's knowledge of the television remote, a set of World Book Encyclopedias and a few dozen Time magazines and was awash in a somewhat bizarre mix of impressions, attitudes and ideas by the time he got home. She'd concluded, for example, that the unprecedented material wealth of today's populace (witness the game shows) had probably resulted in a slowing of the maturation process, because in the two "dramas" (soaps, he later ascertained) she had watched, all the men and women had acted as spoiled and selfish as children, although by their appearance and freedoms they must have been adults. She also wondered, upon seeing a Coca-Cola billboard on the way to their shopping later on, if it caused very many people to jump about and do the kinds of "extraordinary acrobatics" she had witnessed on television once they drank it.

There is something to be said for that kind of absolutely pure and unaffected naiveté'. It is one of the qualities that make babies and/ or the very young of any species so precious and stirs up feelings of protectiveness and love in a way that makes one want to cuddle and cradle its possessor. That feeling is almost erotic in its intensity, and when the subject is a beautiful young woman it *is* erotic . . . and so the fact that Mary wound up that evening viewing most of what David had to show her with thinly disguised wide-eyed wonder was enough in itself to have him falling even faster than before he'd gone to see Carol.

Her reaction to television, especially certain commercials, was merely a warm-up in the naiveté' department. On the way home from work he'd stopped at a family owned department store called "Kline's" and picked up an emerald-green *(green, he'd heard, always looked great on redheads)* jogging suit, figuring something that only came in small, medium and large would offer him his best chance of getting the size right, and also knowing that she would have to wear something other than the ankle-length dress she'd come in in order to accompany him shopping. It wasn't until he'd been waiting a good ten minutes outside his bedroom door while she tried it on, and her voice, a little perturbed, a little distrustful, called out, "There's not a single button on this jacket!" that he realized how basic and all-encompassing was her forgivable ignorance. Zippers were only just invented in 1913 . . !

From there it progressed to her entirely different views on what was modest and immodest dress. "You canno' mean for me to go out dressed in . . . in these woolies, can you?" was the next blushing remark to find its way through the closed bedroom door. It took half an hour of arguing, then finally passing a Walmart flyer depicting clothing through a crack in the door, before she would finally come out. And as it turned out, she was right. On her the jogging suit was as stimulating, in the way the clinging material revealed just how shapely she was, as a string bikini might have been on any other beauty; and if calling it immodest meant that the onlooker's prurient interests might be aroused, then it was immodest. On her a snowmobile suit just might have been immodest.

The rate at which he fell had now doubled.

The truck ride to Adrian Mall, which was the closest city large enough to have a mall, was also enlightening. While she was familiar with both the concept and the reality of automobiles, her idea of fast was twenty to twenty-five miles per hour, and the sixty he hit once they were on 223 had her involuntarily gripping the dash with both white-knuckled hands and her arms locked at the elbows. For some reason the position reminded him of a large dog sitting, paws braced, on its first car ride, although it was beyond him how anything about Mary could bring to mind the word *dog*. Anyway, she relaxed after a while, and was noticing things like the Coca-Cola sign by the time they were halfway there.

He wasn't sure when it was he first started teasing her by pronouncing the occasional word or phrase with a brogue of his own. After their stop in the lingerie department at the Macy's, he suspected ("Miss? My 'friend' is from Germany. She just got in, speaks no English, and all her luggage is lost. Could you help her select what she'll need for a two-week stay?"). All he knew was that it moved them a whole giant-step closer, because she was genuinely frightened and self-conscious at the mall, he could feel it in the way she clung to his arm; and then he was "Sure 'n" this and "canno' do" that and she was smiling, laughing just a little, and looking up at him with gratitude in her eyes as if he were her knight in shining armor.

That night she came to him again. He awoke sometime after three to find her standing there next to the couch. In the moonlight he could tell she was still wearing the jogging suit, which must have been uncomfortably warm on a hot summer night, and as she whispered, "You must think me an awful baby," the first, somewhat loosely-connected thought that crossed his mind was that he'd forgotten to buy her anything "modest" to sleep in. Then he offered her the couch; he would sleep on the floor.

"I wouldno' think of it," she replied. "The chair will do fine." He assumed she meant the nearby recliner. "It slides down and back, don't-you-know, almost like a bed."

She didn't take his hand that night, thus saving him from falling even faster. But she did say one last thing, as she levered the chair to the reclining position as if she'd been doing it all her life. She said, "You're a 'woman's man,' David Rigert: trustworthy and kind." Then she turned sideways, away from him, making it obvious no reply was expected or required, and he spent the rest of the night listening to her sleep and turning those words over and over in his mind: "A woman's man." Like everything else having to do with Mary, they were somehow more provocative than they should be.

On Tuesday he kissed her for the first time. He'd left the job even earlier than the day before, telling himself it was because Mark wasn't scheduled to work directly after school today the way he usually was and he didn't think it was wise to leave the two of them alone together considering his son's attitude. But that was just an excuse, because Mark's job as cook at the local Elias Brothers was one of unpredictable hours, and besides, school would be out soon and what would he do then? Then, halfway home, he realized it was Wednesdays that Mark came right home, not Tuesdays, and that part of him had known it almost from the moment he'd pulled away from the churchyard. But instead of turning around he stopped at a gift shop and bought her a comb and brush set for her hair.

She was wearing a cotton-print dress with, he decided later, every half and full-slip he'd bought for her underneath – for "modesty's sake" – and he didn't know which was more obvious, her delight that he was home early or how self-conscious she was at baring her legs. Or *his* delight with her bare, lovely legs.

"I'm lost when you're gone," she said by way of greeting. "You've no idea what tis like to know no one else in all the world." She said it liltingly, in a mock-scolding kind of way as she met him at the back door, and her shining eyes roved his face the way an eight-year-old might regard a giant hot-fudge sundae with whipped cream, which made the rigid way she stood, with her knees knocked together and her arms clamped stiffly to her sides, smoothing the knee-length dress down maybe an extra half-inch, seem all the more affected.

"Is this right? Do I look . . . 'modern'?" she went on, and now those eyes were desperately seeking approval. "The dresses are all so short, and I was afraid to try on the hosiery because they seemed so small and would surely tear if –"

"You look great." By this time they were only inches apart, and it could have happened then and there, she was so happy to see him. But he saw it only in retrospect and he went on: "And they don't tear; they stretch more than you would believe." He glanced at her stiff arms, still smoothing the dress. "But the dress won't, and you may as well get used to the fact that in this day bare legs are no more 'immodest' than the short-sleeve shirt I'm wearing, okay? We can't have you blushing all the time."

She backed up to let him through, into the kitchen; but as he passed she said, mostly under her breath, "Aye, and in my day the man who rolled his sleeves much past the elbow was called a 'peacock,' don't you know?"

It was an invitation of sorts – or, perhaps more accurately, a nudge. He sensed immediately that what she wanted was more of the same Irish banter they'd engaged in yesterday at the mall because, just like then, she was feeling self-conscious and it drew attention away from that. "Oh, you don't say? A peacock is it? Well fine! Now that I know you disapprove of all vanity I'll no' be showin' what I bought for you in this box!"

She put her hands on her hips, taking up her part without a hitch and, my God, she was beautiful! And smart, too! And – "Let me be the judge 'o what is vain." He held out the box to her, and after she'd opened it and the light in her eyes let him know how pleased she was, she said, "Vanity is a sin, to be sure. But good grooming is a part o' cleanliness, which is next to Godliness . . ."

He grinned. "So! You're a saint now, is it?"

Then without warning the game changed.

"No. You are. And I'm lucky, sooo lucky that of all the times and places I could ha' been 'whisked' to . . ." She dropped her eyes coyly to the brush and comb. "Let me put these to good use, for it is I, I admit, who is vain."

She left the room then. Left him standing there feeling as if he were on the edge of a beautiful precipice, while she went into the bedroom to comb and brush her hair. But he knew it wasn't over, knew this was just a lull in the middle of something inevitable, and after waiting two, maybe three minutes he was drawn across the kitchen, into the living room, then left, into the bedroom, like a windup toy set in motion.

She was seated at Pamela's vanity, and he didn't mind; brushing her lush, abundant hair, watching herself – watching him – in the mirror.

He came up behind her. The constant stroking had given it a depth and luster the pocket comb he'd lent her previously had failed to. He wanted to touch it, squeeze it, crush it against his face. She was absolutely silent, stopping even the brushing now, regarding him solemnly in the mirror. "L-let me do that for you," he said in a breathless half-voice.

Still silent, still watching in the mirror, she handed the brush up to him. He took it, ran it through her long, red-gold hair, following its path with his other hand in a smoothing motion, and it was, for that hand, what slipping naked into bed between satin sheets must be for the body as a whole.

She stood up, still facing the mirror so that he could reach the ends without having to bend. Then she tilted her head back with her eyes closed. Now her head, her hair, was so close he could have rested his chin on it. Instead, he pressed his whole face to it, breathed deeply of its flowers-and-musk aroma. "And is your hair red, Mary?" he murmured between heady inhalations.

"Aye . . . 'tis," she said back.

"Not orange but true-red, with just a hint o' the gold of sunsets in it?"

"If you say so, David Rigert."

"So you understand, then, why I want to kiss it? Kiss you?"

"Aye, I guess I do."

His heart was pounding so hard, suddenly, that there was a dull ache in his chest and he couldn't have stopped now if he'd wanted to. "And is it . . . all right?

"Right or wrong, 'tis what I want, too!" And they were in each other's arms, their mouths seeking each other's, finding each other's in a melting, mashing, making-love-with-their-lips kind of kiss that transported them hundreds of miles into space with the world spinning below on an axis formed by their union. They kissed again and again, until finally she pulled away and leaned her forehead against his chest. 'Slowly, slowly, sweet, David," she panted, as breathless as he. "The more we kiss, the more I want to be kissed, and that's no' what I was expecting a'tall! She took his hand, stepped away from him and led him toward the door. "And in the most dangerous room in the house, too! I need time, David. Sit on the couch and purely hold me for a while? Talk to me . . ?"

Yes. And yes. He would have done anything for her; he was in her power.

X I

Does a mass-murderer, a psychopath, ever scream inside, terrified of the monster that is him or herself? Mary did, but not frequently or for very long. Only, in fact, when the "shifting of gears" from woman to beast-woman was not done smoothly enough, because if she had been allowed more than a glimpse of her "other" self, more than an intimation of what she-as-beast had done or intended to do, she would have either ended her life or retreated into catatonia and ruined everybody's plans.

She was aware of her "other" self, when that entity took control, in about the same way an epileptic is aware of a grand mal seizure: he or she knows things have gone awry but has no memory of what exactly transpired, other than that they are sore and bruised. With Mary, the bruises were on her soul. And now, on top of everything else, she was falling in love.

Strange thing about time travel and love: all those years, skipped over in a trice, had a way of catching up with you. Every hour spent in the distant future seemed the equivalent of at least a year's absence from one's own time, in terms of dimmed memories and fading emotional ties, so that after three-and-a -half days in 2020, the one-hundred and seven years she was removed from her husband seemed as real, were as felt, as had she traversed them in the normal fashion. Consequently, the guilt she felt at her mounting unfaithfulness was losing its edge at the same time that her feelings for David grew, becoming more a "guilt of principle" than something heartfelt. Besides, Jim was dead now. Impossible that he could still be alive, especially with his drinking. He was dead; and even the grief she should have felt was muted, no more poignant or sharp than the memory of losing her brother to influenza when she was seven and he was but five years old. Or was that all part of her "other" self's power? That was certainly all veils and shadows, too, except for the very clear sense of evil she felt whenever she directed her thoughts in the "other's" direction. Her "other" self was dangerous, possibly even homicidal, and maybe all this "numbness" was part of her plan to –

(to what?)

Suddenly she was struck with a sense of dread so powerful it left her nauseous and dizzy, her thinking clouded so that she could no longer say for sure what is was she feared. She'd had it; for a half-moment she'd had the reason, and it had all made sense. But then it had become jumbled. Something to do with her feelings toward Jim and her past being numbed, while her feelings for David were "allowed" *(was that right?)* to grow. And yet when she tried to warn him she –

(She!)

– then it was all gone except for the lingering, completely inane notion, more a concept than actual words, of "stopped momentum," and all she wanted to think about was David, sweet David.

"Mary," her other self, had taken the reins again; and if that more savage and purely malevolent persona could soothe and evaporate the doubts, fears and suspicions of David, Mark and the outside world at large through her prodigious mental powers of suggestion, those same powers wielded on Mary were a hundred times as strong. There was, after all, a rather direct correlation between their strength and physical proximity to the subject; and who might "Mary" be closer to than someone with whom she shared the same mind? But no amount of sublimation, nothing her other self could "suggest," could have healed the bruises on Mary's soul.

Does a psychopath, a schizophrenic killer, ever scream inside? Not frequently or for very long. Because that would imply enough self-knowledge to either change their ways or force them to commit suicide. Most of the time they simply walk around hearing a distinct "ticking," which may or may not be a bomb, that they can never quite pin down and that keeps them forever ill at ease.

XII

As soon as the worst of the breakfast rush was over on Wednesday morning Carol told Janet there were some "family matters" that needed tending and that she would probably be gone for about two hours. Then she got into her car and headed west on 223, on her way to David's house. But not to see David.

She approached her destination with the same kind of tight-lipped, nervous-stomach trepidation she'd felt one other time half a lifetime ago when her mother-in-law-to-be, Mrs. Marybeth Reeves, had called her from Shaker Heights, Ohio and asked her to come up for the day because there were some things she wanted to discuss about Carol's engagement to her "Nicky." All the way there she'd been preparing herself for a variation on the "you're-not-good-enough-for-my-son" theme and was surprised instead to sit and listen to the woman pour out her soul regarding how she had failed their son and how Nicholas Reeves was now a "spoiled child in a man's body" who was prone to violence whenever he didn't get his own way. Any woman marrying him at this point in his life, she was told, was courting the worst kind of disaster. The memory of that meeting, both the tension she had felt preceding it and the way things had ultimately turned out, helped her to keep her resolve now, reminding her that sometimes "butting in" is exactly the right thing to do.

David's truck was gone when she got there, something she knew ahead of time because she'd watched it head east past the café this morning at just a little past six-thirty, the way it had every weekday morning for the last two weeks. All of which made the faint sounds of television coming from inside the house as she climbed from her car cause her heart to do little skip-steps with a flutter in between as she realized it meant she was still there and that she was about to meet the "other woman."

She knocked at the back door and waited.

No response.

She knocked harder, and when there was still no response it occurred to her that David might well have told her not to answer, believing in her "1913" story the way he did. So she tried the knob. It was unlocked.

And that is when any feeling of righteousness abandoned her. This felt wrong. Entering someone else's home, even David's, without permission was wrong. Yet she didn't turn back.

Mary was waiting for her. She was sitting in David's Boston rocker, watching the doorway between the kitchen and the living room with an expression that might have been anything from mild amusement to wariness but was certainly not surprise, and Carol wondered why she would expect someone to come in on their own.

"Sorry," she said. I knocked, but you must not have heard me. And David's never been one to stand on ceremony . . ." Something changed in this "Mary's" eyes, then was masked, at mention of David's name. "My name is Carol, Carol Schemansky, and I'm David's . . . 'friend.' He's told me about you, about your . . . fantastic arrival, so you don't have to worry."

"Mary" simply watched her – no, studied her – in an overtly bold way that seemed rude; and Carol studied her right back. And almost groaned aloud, because she was that beautiful, the kind of woman who makes every other woman feel frumpy and about as feminine as Winston Churchill as soon as she walks into a room.

"I was no' worried the moment I saw you," "Mary" said finally.

"Oh . . ? Why not?" Inside she reeled at the possibilities contained in that short reply.

"Because you look" – she shrugged – "harmless."

Carol set her teeth. "Harmless. Gee. Right in there between 'ordinary' and 'of little consequence.'"

"Mary" assumed a quizzical expression, which Carol was pretty sure was fake. "You would rather appear dangerous?"

Carol nodded coolly. "In a sense, yes. But why get hung up on semantics? I didn't come here to –"

"Why did you come, Carol Schemansky?"

Her eyes were cold, penetrating, not the same eyes they had been moments ago, and Carol was thrown off balance both by them and their owner's bluntness. She didn't like the feeling. "For David," she said in a quiet, low voice. "I could give you lots of other reasons – to offer my help, to offer my home . . . and just plain because I was curious – and they would all be true. But what it all boils down to is 'for David.' I love him and I don't want to see him hurt or taken advantage of."

The hardness left "Mary's" eyes and the expression she'd worn earlier when Carol first entered the room returned. Carol was sure, now, that it was amusement, and her throat tightened.

"Is that an accusation?" "Mary" asked calmly.

"It's a statement. It says, simply, that I find it hard to believe in time travel or people appearing from thin air. Therefore I can only assume you are either deliberately trying to mislead David or . . ." she faltered.

"Am crazy," "Mary" finished for her. "David said that's what everyone would believe."

Unfilled seconds crawled by, dispersing, finally, into the other world, where the television still played. But that all seemed as distant and insulated from them as if they were sealed inside a plastic bubble. The only immediate reality was "Mary's" face, that amused – no, mocking –expression.

"And what, Carol Schemansky?" "Mary" said at length, breaking the spell. "Is it a choice you'll be wanting from me now? Between the devil and the deep blue sea . . ?"

More silence passed. Carol said: "He's not a wealthy man, you know. Not even well-to-do."

The amusement gave way to a look of scorn. "Such compliments! Are you always so charitable to strangers? At least I know now which choice you would ha' made for me! Thank you for voting me merely a liar and a schemer and not insane!"

Not allowing herself to become flustered, Carol pursued her original purpose. "There is a way you could prove me wrong. You could stay with me instead of David. Surely the decorum of your day would deem that preferable to living with two men, neither of which is your husband."

"Mary" gave her hair a toss. The result was a thousand times more impressive than any shampoo commercial. "But not preferable to acceptin' help from someone who has just cast aspersions on my whole moral fiber! I think not, Carol Schemansky. I think, too, that we should end this discussion and that you should leave." With that she rose from the rocker in a way that suggested far less effort than is required of an ordinary person, almost as if she were weightless.

Strong. She's strong! a part of Carol's mind warned her, and for the first time she seriously considered the possibility that she might be arguing with someone who was insane. "I agree," she said, forcing some backbone into her voice. "But not because you have the authority to order me out; this isn't your house. I'll go because I've finished what I came here to say." She started to deliberately turn her back on the girl, then paused. "But I want you to know, whatever your plans are for David, I won't make them easy. I'll fight you every step of the way!"

Then she did turn around. So she didn't see "Mary's" fingers hook into claws. Or her shoulders haunch, apelike, so that her chin laid on her chest. Or her eyes go feral.

"Yes. 'Dangerous' is right. It does fit you after all," the voice at her back said. "But tell me . . . what of me? Am I 'dangerous' too? Or is that title reserved solely for the dangerously self-righteous?"

By the time Carol had turned back again, "Mary" had resumed a more normal posture. It wouldn't have mattered, though, because what she "saw," in the next several seconds had little to do with what was reflected onto her retina. It was a nightmare in stop-action sequence, a kaleidoscope of images viewed from a dozen different perspectives, all rushing headlong toward the same violent end. It was "Mary," transformed, compacted to something hideous and troll-like, coming at her with hands and feet like clubs. It was "Mary's" transfigured, brutish face, looming ever closer; hands that could and would rip her apart, *reaching.* It was herself viewed from one side as those same hands found what they were seeking, gouged and ripped her face so savagely that the cheek on the side visible was torn completely through and all her teeth exposed. And it was "Mary," naked and as beautiful as Carol somehow knew she would be, moving in long, languorous strokes astride David, possessing him body and soul, while she smiled at Carol through hooded eyes – and through it all, overwhelmingly strong, came a voiceless voice inside Carol's head, suggesting, demanding that she *LEAVE! LEAVE!*

She remembered little beyond that point. The next thing she was fully conscious of was sitting in her car, which was stopped in the middle of Forrester Road just around the first bend east of David's house. The motor was running, it was still in Drive, her foot was on the brake, and she was slumped against the steering wheel, crying.

Mark was next. If today was to be the day for confrontations, "Mary" decided, then she might as well get both of them out of the way. Her bout with the Carol-woman had offered up some pleasant surprises, the best being the fact that her powers of suggestion had strengthened considerably now that she was more familiar with the species "man." Unprepared for it, the flood of images she'd broadcast at the other female had so unnerved her that for a while she'd been unable to separate hallucination from reality. And what could she tell anyone, including David, about it? Who would believe her? In some ways it was the perfect weapon, because who would believe that she or anyone else could will a person to see things? Too bad it could be at least partially resisted once the subject caught on. Still, it boosted her confidence, made her almost eager for three o' clock to roll around, which was the time that the younger male would be arriving home.

Then there was the growing skill with which she was able to "operate" Mary, assuming dominance over their shared mind then relinquishing it again with hardly an eye's blink of observable reaction on the girl's part. That, too, made her feel more than ready to deal with Mark face to face and hopefully speed along the undermining process she'd begun at night.

By the time the hour had finally arrived she had read the first one-hundred pages of Langsam and Mitchell's *The World Since 1919*, a text book from Mark's junior year that he'd been forced to buy because it was so heavily damaged. David had borrowed it from his son's room last night, and now, as she listened to the latter's car turn in the drive, it occurred to her that keeping it visible in her lap went along with her purpose just fine. She did move to a chair in the kitchen, however, where it would be impossible for him to avoid at least a minimum of contact with her, unless he was blatantly rude.

He was blatantly rude. He came through the back kitchen door, saw her sitting there, scowled and walked right on by as if she didn't exist.

"Mark," she called out, "I think we should talk."

There was only silence behind her, where he stood. At least he'd stopped moving. Then, after a good five or six seconds, he surprised her with a sullen, "What about?"

"About us. About why you resent me so."

Again the long silence. She scooted her chair around so that she could look directly at him. He spotted the book and his scowl deepened. "Why?" he said finally. "It doesn't matter. It's not going to change anything."

"It matters. Maybe once we talked things out you'd –"

"You're sitting in her spot, sleeping in her bed . . !" he interrupted, and though he hadn't exactly shouted, the outrage, the hurt was there, heavy in his voice. The fact that she'd chosen that particular chair, which apparently had been hers, was another plus.

"She's gone Mark. But I know for a fact she would no' mind."

"Yeah. Sure. Everybody wants to be forgotten; it makes life so much more meaningful. And don't talk like you know her, either! Or anything about her! 'Cuz you don't!"

"Oh, but I do. I know a great deal."

For a moment she was sure she'd gone too far, too fast. Sure he was either going to become so angry he'd stop listening altogether or leave the room. Then, in a voice that was really more a growl, he said, "What's that supposed to mean? How?" and she thought that maybe she had him.

"Do . . . you believe that I came here through time?"

"No."

"Well, if you did, you might also believe that it has . . . 'changed' me in certain ways, made me more sensitive to certain things."

Mark's scowl faded, was supplanted by a crooked half-smile that tried hard for cynicism but failed to completely hide the fact that his interest was aroused. "Well, I don't believe you, but if I did . . . 'sensitive' how?"

She smiled back. Yes, she had him. "'Tis no' easy to explain. Let me use you as an example. I would know you were home, or nearby, even if

I was blindfolded in a closet and with my ears muffed up tight. I would 'feel' your presence, even know your mood, because your 'essence' would . . . " She smiled again, this time shrugging helplessly. "I would just feel it, that's all; and I guess there's nothing more to say, except that it's not limited to you or to David." She paused. "Or even to the living."

She stopped then. Better to let him fill in the rest. He'd accept it more readily if it came from his own mouth. She watched his face very quickly run a whole gamut of emotions, finally settling on a regretful wariness that told her he wanted more to believe her than prove her wrong. "You . . . 'hear' my mother?" he asked in a voice so low it was barely audible.

She nodded. "I do. And she misses you sooo much, Mark. You were her light, her dark-haired light. She tries to tell you that, how much she loves you, wants to be with you again – especially at night. Do you 'hear' her, Mark? Because you answer back sometimes. Maybe unaware you're so doin', but I . . . sense something from you . . ."

"No." He was shaking his head rapidly in denial and disbelief, but his eyes told a different story. "No."

"She laments all those years you missed together." Now she allowed her face to reflect just the right amount of perplexity. "She would . . . ha' you when you were eight?"

"No," he said again, this time in defeat.

"I tell you this only because I want you to understand I do know how you feel, how sacred your mother is to you, and I would never think to take her place. And, too, to caution you to go ahead and be close, be as close as her spirit will allow, to keep her strong and alive." She regarded him solemnly, sadly. "I know. My husband, Jim, surely gone forty, perhaps fifty years now, and with me no' there to keep his spirit alive, 'tis but a shadow of a shadow, so faint . . . Do everything you can, Mark, to be with her now, because she too will be fading!"

The horror of that thought filled his eyes with anguish, yet still he resisted her. "H-how. can I believe you have that power? To hear the dead!"

And then something happened that was sheer luck. Something with more validation power than all the rhetoric in the world. She sensed another human being close by. Not in the house but close – out on the road, she thought – and she said to Mark, "Listen. Do you hear anything, Mark? Someone passing by?"

He shook his head. The television was still on, and she knew it would have covered the sound. Good.

"Well, I do. With my mind. There are two, a boy and a girl. Go look, because, as you know, we canno' see from here."

Mark went into the living room, crossed it to the front windows. She concentrated on picking up anything she could from his emotions. "You . . . know who they are but do not really know them," she called from her chair in the kitchen.

He came back, white. "The Evans kids," he said in an awed voice. "On bikes. They live about a mile from here but go to parochial school, so I never – " he paused, turned even whiter – "really got to know them. That's why they're here, though. Parochial school gets out a week earlier than we do." He said it almost as if he were reciting a confession. And he slumped, his single arm hanging lifelessly at his side.

There was a silence, then: "Are you going to marry him?"

It caught her off guard. She'd expected more questions about his mother, about her powers, but apparently he was convinced on those subjects or had given up for the time being.

"It . . . could happen. He's a saint of a man . . ."

His shoulder slumped further, and she tried to project an image from her mind to his that she'd painstakingly constructed earlier, once she'd decided to have this second confrontation of the day. It was of herself and David, married, happy, maybe five years down the road. Mark was there, too, but off at a distance and obviously shut out. He was disheveled, unkempt and pathetic looking. And then David turns to look at him with both sadness and resentment in his eyes. Then on the heels of the first, another image – and she didn't know whether she could do this one – of his mother's face, which she'd seen in photographs, fading, fading . . . and mouthing the silent words, *Be with me.* And it must have registered in some way because his face, which was already even more twisted with pain than before the children had ridden by, flinched suddenly, as if someone had thrown ice water in it, and his eyes had flown wide. Then tears welled in his eyes, and she knew that for an eighteen-year-old boy that was the end. He would avoid all conflict now, avoid her, at all costs. And never tell his father any of this had taken place.

Everything had worked out perfectly – everything, that is, but one minor detail. As she rose from her chair and stepped toward him to lay a comforting hand on his shoulder, because she knew it would lend a certain validity to her entire performance, she felt a welling of genuine compassion. "There now, there . . ." her voice soothed, unbidden, and she stroked his cheek with gentle fingertips. "I would no' love the father without caring for the son, too." Her arms were about to go around him in an entirely motherly embrace before she realized it was Mary, and that those kinds of emotions – compassion, tenderness, charity – even convincingly feigned, required her to give even more free a rein to her more human half's psyche than during rituals with David of courting and romance, because she possessed them not at all! And though she quickly quashed her "other" self to semi-dormancy again, she quickly recognized this . . . "emotional lacking" as perhaps the greatest weakness revealed to her thus far.

XIII

The next several days were some of the happiest in David's life. He felt like he was seventeen again. All the joy, exuberance and wonder were there, just like when he and Pamela were falling in love; but this time, with Mary, he was old enough to savor it more completely, because he'd had so much more of the downside of life to compare it to. There was some truth to the adage, "Youth is wasted on the young."

Tuesday, after their first kiss, they did indeed just talk, although it was difficult at first for David to limit himself to just that because he also "purely" held her on the couch as per her request, and the feel of her snuggled up against him, the smell of her hair, were both intoxicating. Then Mark came home and despite the fact that he immediately made himself scarce, she seemed suddenly shy again and they moved apart. But the talk was stimulating, in that it revealed a mind that was sweet, sensitive and delightfully acute; and somehow, when she explained how her memories and sense of attachment to everything in 1913 were fading, as if she'd actually lived through all the intervening years, it had only relieved him in a moralistic, sense-of-propriety kind of way (after all, she'd left a husband back there). From the standpoint of order in the universe and the presence of a cosmic plan, it had seemed right.

At eleven she kissed him a lingering kiss goodnight and, in the words of John Cleland's *Fanny Hill* ". . . put, once more, all within in such an uproar."

She remained in her own bed that night.

On Wednesday he took a chance. On Wednesday Mark really did get home before he did, and he decided to leave it at that. So when he finally did arrive, he found himself doubly anxious. Not only was he concerned that some kind of problem might have developed between his son and

Mary, he was also afraid that the latter's feelings toward him might have cooled, almost as if the closeness they'd shared the night before were too good to be true.

He needn't have worried on either count. Mark, while still distant, seemed if anything less openly hostile than before, and Mary reported that he'd been a perfect gentleman although they hadn't really said much more to each other than hello. She told him that right after greeting him at the door with kiss number three, as sweet and intimate as the one last night, which pretty much took care of the rest of his concerns.

That evening he took her to Ann Arbor to a small seafood restaurant close to U of M's campus. They held hands beneath the table, stared into each other's eyes and did all the other things young lovers do. Each time she gave his hand a squeeze, each time he looked away then looked back again and was struck anew by her beauty, he wondered when the dream would end. Then his heart would take a giant leap as he realized it wasn't a dream.

There were moments, though, when how far off course they were from everyone else's charted reality was underscored in ways that left one or both of them uneasy. One such instance was when the waiter brought them the check and Mary happened to see the amount. When they had shopped for clothes on Monday she had still been overawed by their surroundings and by the throngs of people, and all her concentration had been focused on simply fitting in rather than on the price of things. Tonight, forty-eight hours later, she was more sure of herself, and when the check came and she read it, she gasped out loud. $48.29. He realized almost immediately that such a price tag for a meal would have been an unconscionable amount in 1913, but it wasn't until days later, in retrospect, that he was able to fully appreciate how shocking it must have been. It wasn't until 1914, one year after Mary had been snatched from the past, that Henry Ford set the world on its ear by paying his employees the unheard of wage of five dollars a day! In Mary's time, paying that much for a single meal would have been the equivalent, he figured, of paying, today, more than a thousand dollars!

Afterward they walked on campus hand in hand, visited a bookstore, where he bought her a paperback edition of Richard Matheson's *Somewhere in Time*, jokingly remarking that it was their situation in reverse, and talked. She was completely at ease again. In fact he marveled at how quickly she had adapted to life almost eleven decades in the future. She was only a little bit shy now, a little more reserved than a "modern" girl her age, and he liked that, especially the fact that it did not dampen her terrific sense of humor one bit. They were playing their Irish-banter game again and much of the humor came from that, and surprisingly, so did their next kiss. He was running out of witty things to say, in his fake Irish brogue, but he wanted to hear the sound of her throaty laughter just one more time because it was so dam sexy. "Do you know why the Irish use 239 beans in their soup and no' a bean more?" he asked, at the same time thinking inside, *"Whoa, she's not ready for this."*

She shook her head.

"Because a single bean more would be two-f-a-r-t-y!"

"Oh!" she said, looking as startled as had someone just pinched her bottom. "Oh dear!" Then she blushed, and somehow the only way to make things right again, the only thing in all the world he wanted to do was kiss her. And shocked or not, she kissed him back, kept on kissing him right there on the sidewalk on State Street in front of the Kelsey Museum of Archaeology, as though it were the last kiss she would ever be part of.

That evening she came to him again. On their way home from Ann Arbor he'd finally remembered to buy her something to sleep in, and late, long after Mark had finally gone to bed, she was there, suddenly, standing next to the couch wearing one of the nightgowns. It was almost as if she'd "appeared" there, the way she'd appeared in the field, but by now he was used to how silently she could move and all that really mattered anyway was that she was there. She sat down tentatively on the couch's edge. Even in the semi-darkness he could sense how nervous she was. "I . . . Perhaps 'tis too much to ask o' the man you are, what I'm about to ask." she said in a meek, quiet voice.

Silence. Then: "Go ahead. Ask."

"I . . . my heart that is, needs to be with you, yet I canno'. I'm no' ready, that is, to . . ."

He understood and he held out his arms. "I'll just 'purely' hold you," he said, only a little teasingly. "Nothing more."

Then, with a sigh that was barely audible, she lay down next to him and somehow they both fit just fine on the couch's narrow width. They fit each other too, her curves to his hollows, and the rightness of it transcended even the sensual thrill of having her that close, feeling the heat of her body through the single, thin layer of cotton nightgown. He felt complete, content in a way that he hadn't for ten years. The last thing she said to him that night was, "Please, I canno' still be here when Mark wakes up."

But of course she was. David always awakened at first light and yet on this Thursday morning they were both brought 'round by the sound of clinking cereal bowls and the opening and closing of the refrigerator door in the kitchen. He could feel Mary stiffen next to him, and then she was up and on her way back to "her" room with such furtive grace and speed that he thought for a minute there might just be a chance she'd make it unnoticed despite the fact that her route had to take her past the open doorway between the kitchen and living room. That hope was quickly dashed, though, when he got up a half-minute later, walked into the kitchen and Mark said immediately, "You know, you two belong together. You even looked like you do, sleeping there . . ." And then, looking David straight in the face with eyes that were, for the first time ever, unreadable even by his father, he went on, "I'm happy for you, Dad. I mean it." Then he left for school, and it wasn't until several minutes later that they noticed he'd left his bowl of cereal with the milk already poured, sitting on the kitchen table untouched. It was a bad start to a bad day that didn't get much better till late in the evening, and even then it was at best an "eight" as compared to Tuesday's and Wednesday's "tens."

Stopping at the Café on the way to work didn't help. Guilt and a sense of duty are never acceptable reasons to see someone who cares about you and knows you well, and he might just as well have worn a sign, printed in "Carol-vision," informing her of those motives. She handled it with class, though. Carol had always possessed a certain innate class, and she kept up the appearances of normalcy for his sake by still coming over to their table, sitting with him and never once bringing up the subject of Mary until they were outside and she was walking him toward his truck. He found himself wishing in an odd, almost nostalgic way, during those moments right before they stepped outside, that Mary had never happened, because he knew things would have worked for him and Carol, that they would have married eventually and that it would have been a good marriage; and, at the same time, he suddenly wondered if his feelings for Mary weren't more like a mind-bending addiction than true love. It was one of those flash-fire revelations, here and gone again, the kind he usually only experienced near the end of a dream right before waking, all vague and only half-remembered once he was fully awake, with the only impression remaining with any clarity being the conviction that it *(whatever "it" was)* rang of truth and was life-shaping. For David, the thing that made it all dissolve was what Carol said as she reached the truck's door:

"She's dangerous, you now."

Instantly he was on the defensive. "No. I don't know."

"Not just conniving or crazy but dangerous. While I was out there yesterday, she – "

"You were out there yesterday? Why didn't you tell me?" His voice was strident, as angry as he suddenly felt.

Her eyes widened. "I thought you knew."

"No, I didn't know. And I don't like finding out this way – after the fact!"

The hurt registered in her eyes but she kept quiet.

"Look," he went on in a slightly softer tone, "I know you have my best interests at heart. Lord knows why but you do. But doing what you did isn't it. All it does is make me feel . . ." he groped for the right words. ". . . the same as if you went through my drawers. Can you understand that?" But inside he was seething. How dare anyone try and get between himself and Mary? He climbed into his truck and closed the door. The window was down and Carol put her hands on the ledge.

"What I understand," she said urgently, "is that your 'Mary' is not what she seems to be. And even in the simplest form, that deception is going to hurt you and already *has* hurt me!"

She leaned in closer, trying to capture and hold his eyes with the gravity of her stare. "And it's not harmless, David. You know me and premonitions. I don't usually believe in such things; yet, when I was out there I got one so strong . . !" She leaned in even closer, as if she were telling him some intimate secret. "She's a monster, David. A human monster. Some kind of psycho, like that lady back in the nineties who walked into that school in Illinois and started shooting kids. She–"

He started the engine, the noise effectively blocking out what she said next. The accusations made him all the more angry, and now when he looked at Carol it was as if he were seeing a stranger. "I'm sorry," he said once the motor had settled to an idle. "But I can't buy that. I'm sorry if either she or I hurt you, too. It's the last thing in the world I wanted to do."

He put the truck in reverse and started to back from the spot. "I'll stop by again in a few days just to prove everything is okay. Is that all right?"

Again she didn't answer. She simply walked with him, hands still on the window as he backed around in an arc. It was disconcerting. Then he said, "Bye," shifted into first and carefully pulled away. Just before she finally lifted her hands and stepped back, she said one last time, "She's dangerous."

Work dragged that day. Mary had been subdued and a little cool that morning, having heard what Mark said about seeing them on the couch from where she waited in the bedroom, and that, combined with the nature of the day's work – removing a row of stumps from the north end of the church's property – made David supremely anxious to be done. Yet each frequent glance at his watch showed less than a quarter the time passed that he'd imagined. Finally he finished, and when he got home he found her not so much cool – she still greeted him at the door enthusiastically enough – as distracted and preoccupied, the way Mark used to be the night of a game. It was almost as if she were hyperactive. She would sit next to him, take his hand, squeeze it, then jump up and pace as she told him something new and miraculous she had learned that day about "these times." Then she would sit again, maybe give him a light kiss on the cheek, and jump up again to recount yet another newly acquired tidbit. And maybe the pre-game analogy wasn't exactly it either; in some ways it reminded him equally of a dog he'd once had, a cross between a Black lab and maybe an otter and a mischievous child, named Sheena. Whenever Sheena had done something wrong or intended to *do* something wrong she had behaved in the same animated way, only with her it was rush up and lick your face and burrow her nose into any available recess, then sprint off and run in frenetic circles until it was time to repeat the whole process. Of course with Mary the affection/distraction was all done with dignity and grace, and there was nothing at all even vaguely canine about it, just . . . animated. Still it left him with the feeling that something was up.

Then, just before bedtime, he thought he discovered what it was. They were saying goodnight and she'd allowed her hips to arch against him during their kiss in a way she never had before, and things were fast approaching critical mass when she pulled away abruptly and said, "Stop! I canno' be trusted for more! I must think things through 'n be sure 'tis love I'm feeling along with my fleshly desires! And for that I canno' be close to temptation! I'll be keeping my bed tonight, sweet David, only for that reason – and please tell me you at least think you love me too?"

He'd told her. Then he'd told her again. Something was up alright. His spirits, his heart rate . . . And all because of the last word he'd heard her say: "Too."

XIV

Something *was* up. It was "Mary's" bloodlust. It was eating at her, getting out of hand. If she didn't satisfy it soon it would force her into a blunder and set her nerves so on edge that she would no longer be able to maintain the delicate, marginal control over her other self necessary for the nuances and subtleties of "romance." Tricky business that. The feelings, the whole process was so foreign to her that she'd had to relinquish control almost completely, while she herself was forced to hover nervously on the outer fringes of their shared consciousness, ready, hoping that she would be able to regain control quickly enough if things went awry. Mary was in truth, falling in love all on her own, unprompted, undirected, and "Mary" supposed she was fortunate in that as it fit so well with her plan. But as the urge to kill grew stronger again, all her good fortune thus far, even her "imperative," seemed nothing more than distractions, secondary concerns, like the need for shelter or status among one's tribe, while her bloodlust was as all-consuming as a drowning man's need for air. That is why she had "suggested" to her other half that it was important she sleep alone tonight, and that David not be expecting her. Mary had simply worked that suggestion into a line of reasoning commensurate with her emotional state. This time, however, she would be better prepared than on her first kill-run. The jogging suit was perfect for the kinds of activities she had planned, as were the tennis shoes David had bought her at the mall (except for color; all the shoes for "women" were either white or light pastels, and the sky-blues she'd finally settled on wouldn't even hide grass stains); and while none of the several "bras" she now possessed bound her as tightly as would have been ideal, she was better off in that department, too, than she had been four days ago.

She even had her exit from the house better planned. The bedroom window, she'd noticed, was equipped with a removable slide-screen, one that adjusted in width to fit the size of the opening and was held in place mainly by the weight of said window resting on its top. Around one a.m., she slipped out that window, taking time to replace the screen so that it looked undisturbed but still afforded a fingertip hold along one side to reopen it. Outside she stood there for a while as the anticipation of killing again coursed through her like a physical thing, made her skin pull up into goose-bumps, same as if she had just emerged naked from a stream and been struck by a cool breeze. Then she shuddered. The night was filled with possibilities: A dog nearby, in the field to the west. Some cattle further away in that direction, just barely "touching" her, like, a spider-web dragged across her mind. A raccoon out near the barn . . .

No. No. And no. Too much resentment had been allowed to build, too much restraint forced to bear in her dealings with the Carol-woman and Mark, both adversaries, both alone with her for the taking. She needed human prey tonight to make up for some of that. Maybe the killing of someone like one of them would help assuage the keen sense of loss she felt, the feeling of having been deprived of something that was rightfully hers.

She knew, however, that among Mary's kind the taking of a human life was forbidden, and the whys-hows-and-whose were relentlessly, almost obsessively pursued. She didn't understand it, failed to comprehend at all the notion, so basic in man it was almost instinctive, of "inter-responsibility," yet it was there: kill or harm one and you somehow damage them all.

And while so few of them having knowledge she even existed was an advantage, she still needed to think things through and take every precaution she could. One way of doing that was to make her kill as far away from where she slept and fed as possible.

For the first thirty yards, as she moved down the driveway, then across Forrester Road and into the same field she'd "arrived" in, she was noiseless as a mist. Even the stray dog, which by now had come up out of the west field and onto the far edge of the lawn, approximately one-hundred feet from where she walked, was not aware of her passing. Then she settled into the same ground-eating lope as last time she'd hunted, knowing this time that she could maintain the pace for hours if need be, now that the soft, disgustingly tender feet she possessed with this body were protected by shoes.

In something under seven minutes she had reached 223, which ran parallel with Forrester but a little over a mile further south. She had passed through two wheat fields, another planted in soybeans, and a small woods to get there, and now, in the light of a moon just two days past full, she stood in the backyard of the house Emily Stevens had lived in over a century ago, the house Mary had set out cross-fields to visit, with her sheet music, the day she had disappeared. There was a stirring deep inside "Mary," something like a gasp of recognition without sound, and she clamped down harder on her restive other self.

The house was unoccupied now. But even if her senses had told her otherwise, she would have moved on. Too close.

She was familiar, now, with the concept of hitchhiking (although she did not know that is what it was called), having witnessed a young woman doing just that on a crime/detective show two days ago. She also knew, or thought she knew, by the leering glances of the man who had picked the girl up and by other more subtle clues, that a woman doing it, especially at night, would generate exactly the kinds of notions in the male mind that could be used to her advantage, the kind that would make it easy for her to get him to a secluded, unobserved spot. That, plus the fact that riding in an auto could very quickly carry her far away from here, made the concept (not the word) of hitchhiking seem just about ideal. Boldly she jogged to the front of the house, across the highway, and stood facing oncoming, east-bound traffic with her thumb out, even copying the girl on the television's provocative stance.

The very first auto (*car*, David would use *car*) to come along slowed, then stopped, and if she had ever doubted the effect of her current appearance on males other than David, the raw desires that touched her mind as the man rolled down his passenger-side window and said, "I'm as far as Sylvania. Will that help?" laid those doubts to rest. But the man was nothing like Mark, for whom she had built up a great deal of resentment and kill-hunger. He was shorter, with a belly and a receding hairline, and closer to David in age. She would have had difficulty transferring all of her hostile rage and frustrations onto him.

98

"Oh! she said. "I was looking for someone younger."

The man's face, which was very much like a baby's face except for stubble and bad skin, had been carefully shaped into a mask of neighborly concern. Now it twisted into something more in line with his inner feelings – indignation, then hate, and a desire to hurt her in some way. "Oh yeah?" he snarled. "Well, fuck you bitch!"

His car leaped forward with a squeal of tires, and "Mary" jumped back. But before it had gotten more than ten yards she reached a decision. "Wait!" she called out. The brake lights on the ' vehicle lit everything with an eerie glow of red as she ran to catch up. "Wait," she said again, leaning in the window. "What I meant was I was expecting someone younger. Someone I already know who drives this route often at night, and I thought you were him. Sorry. But actually, I would be extremely grateful if you would take me instead." She tried to make the word sound as suggestive as she knew how, because suddenly, after the aggressive, threatening way his thoughts had lashed out at her, she found it very easy to transfer most of her hostilities onto this man.

"Yeah?" he growled. But already the general cast of his thoughts was swinging away from the malevolent towards the lecherous again. "Well, hop in."

Once inside, the man asked her where she was going, and having nowhere else in mind, she very quickly said, "Sylvania."

The man grinned and winked at her. "Sure." Then he told her his name was Lee Redding, and all the while his eyes were on her crotch and the outline of her breasts beneath the clinging material of her jogging suit more than they were on the road.

She told him her name was Emily.

"Hey, sorry 'bout my temper back there," he said after an awkward silence. "It's just that I'm of an age where somethin' like that hurts, y' know? Seems like the whole world is lookin' for someone younger, girls especially, and I'm-here-to-tell-you that I can do everything, ev-er-y-thing, better than I could fifteen years ago" – he winked at her again, let his eyes roam her body one more time, knowing full well she was watching – "if you get my drift."

For someone with mind-touch abilities it was impossible not to get his drift. It was so blatant, so dominant over every other emotion that she decided subtlety was a waste of time. "You mean, by 'everything' . . . sex?" she said with just the right amount of shyness.

Lee blinked, then did a slow grin. "Amen and you better believe it!" He paused then, giving the appearance of someone whose mind is working faster than it was designed to go, a cogitative runaway careening wildly around an icy mental curve.

"'Course that's the opinion most girls have. What I would value a whole lot more is the opinion of one particular girl, one that's truly beautiful, maybe the most beautiful I ever seen."

She groaned inwardly and her desire to rip this man moved up a notch. But she played his game. "You think I'm beautiful?" she asked with round eyes.

"Absolutely."

"And . . . my 'opinion' would mean that much?"

"More than you could know."

She pretended to be mulling it over, wary, but tempted. Meanwhile, she could hear his heart going, *ba-bump, ba-bump.* "I . . . did feel something the moment I saw you, Lee . . ."

ba-bump, ba-bump

"There's a nice place the other side of Valor. A motel. We could –"

"Oh! No! We have to be further away, where people won't know me. Besides, I prefer the outdoors. The moon, the stars . . ." She reached across and playfully ran the tip of a finger up and down his forearm. "If you know what I mean."

ba-bump, ba-bump, ba-bump

They drove on mostly in silence. Every once in a while he would toss out a compliment, kind of like bread crumbs to lure an animal, as if he were afraid she would lose interest otherwise. Things like, "Your hair is gorgeous, y' know? Better than any movie star's." Or, "Geez, how come someone built like you needs to jog? (*Because of the way she was dressed, she presumed, although she wasn't entirely sure what "jogging" was even with Mary's stored knowledge to help her*). And she pretended to be thrilled with every word, as if to the rest of the world she was an undesirable. Never once did he ask about her, about who she was, what she did or why she happened to be out hitchhiking in the middle of the night; although he did manage to work in a good deal about himself, including the fact that he was distributor's rep for a company that sold "performance-related auto parts" and was "damned good at it." Still, there were lots of silences, and as they passed through Valor, then Adrian, she began to wonder just how long it would be before even a man as stupid as Lee obviously was would begin to question the likelihood of all this good luck he was having and become suspicious. So when they got as far as the hamlet of Palmyra and she spotted a sign reading Raisin River, she said, "Oh, Lee! I just love rivers; they're so romantic!" and looked at him expectantly.

At first, acute intellect that he was, he said, "The Raisin? Hell, it's not much more than a big creek around here, though it does get good-sized over ta – " Then he caught on and changed in mid-sentence to, "'Course size doesn't matter much. It's a nice, clean river hereabouts, and I bet there's lots of cozy spots to view it from if we just take a side road or two."

She smiled at him, pleased.

It turned out there were a number of places close by, all fairly isolated from prying eyes; but while Lee was only concerned that it be hidden from view, she knew that it also had to be out of earshot of any nearby houses, in case he screamed.

They finally found such a spot off a gravel road where a lane of some sort obviously meant for tractors, "Lee" told her, turned at right angles off the road proper just before the latter crossed a single-lane bridge and paralleled the river for the depth of the cornfield on that side. Between the lane and the river's edge was a tangled, wooded strip approximately fifty feet wide. It was exactly what "Mary" was looking for, and as Lee hesitated out on the road, she reached across again, this time placing her hand on his thigh. That decided it. He even backed in, something she suggested but for wholly different reasons than those he assumed. Still, even his assumed line of reasoning, which was far less threatening than the truth, caused him to balk for the first time that night, because it spoke of experience and suggested that "Emily" had done this sort of thing before.

"Say . . . how do I know you don't have AIDS or somethin'?" he asked once he'd shut down the engine, forgetting for the moment all about being charming. A regular chorus-line of crickets that had momentarily been silenced by the car's arrival resumed their chirruping. An owl hooted somewhere off in the distance. The engine block ticked and clicked as it began to cool . . . but "Emily" just sat there, smiling at him in the moonlight, and said nothing. Then, after a discomforting length of time, a new sound was added to the night: *zzzzzzzt*. She of the inscrutable smile was slowly unzipping the top of her jogging suit, somehow managing to create the impression that the act itself was something rare and astounding. When she'd undone it all the way she shrugged out of it with an economy of motion that was uncanny. Beneath it she wore nothing but her bra and –

"Do I . . . look like I have AIDS?"

ba-bamp, ba-bump That was good enough for him.

She opened the passenger-side door, slipped out and shut it again with such an economy of motion that he must have found himself still staring at the place where she had been. "C'mon," she called from outside, and he eagerly clambered from the car.

"Uh!" The sound escaped him unawares as he turned to walk around the car's front end, because he almost bumped into her and it must have startled him, no doubt wondering how she could have possibly gotten around from her side that fast. In fact she "sensed" something like that, along with the return of fear. Humans were such turtles! But then it didn't matter because she took his hand, lifted it and pressed the back to one of her breasts, holding it there just long enough to say in a husky voice, "Down by the river." Then she was leading him by the same hand in that direction and he would have followed her anywhere.

The tangled strip between the lane and the Raisin River was virtually lightless, cut off from the moon and stars by a canopy of leaves. And yet "Emily" led him unerringly through it, never once stumbling or colliding with anything. She could "feel" him on the verge of commenting on that fact when, just a few yards short of the river, she let go of his hand. He reached for her again, suddenly in desperate need of the reassurance of her hand, but she wasn't there.

"Emily?" he called out in a voice meant to sound more confident than he was.

Nothing. Crickets and frogs.

ba-bump

"Emily, c'mon. What is this, a game?"

Some crackling in the underbrush to his right.

ba-bump, ba-bump

"Em –?"

A low, rumbling growl that sounded like it could be anywhere. It was the kind of sound that belonged in a jungle, not here, and its presence threw him into a panic. He started to grope- run in the direction of the car, and she'd never been so "connected" with any human's mind!

Whhump! Something knocked him down before he'd taken a dozen steps, slapped him to the ground via a blow between the shoulder blades. It was like being hit by a truck. "Huh-*UH!*" he gasped, lying there, trying to recapture some of the air that had been driven from his lungs. Then a dull but rapidly growing burning sensation low in his abdomen made him want to get up anyway. He made it to his knees before he realized he'd fallen on something sharp – and that "something" was stuck into him! It was a stick the diameter of a pencil and about half as long; it must have been protruding at the perpendicular from a longer branch, and now it was protruding from him! He felt a wave of nausea as he forced himself to yank it out.

It came out easily; it must have been in less than an inch, thank God, just enough to –

The rumbling growl again, closer. The image of a black panther flashed across his mind – "Mary" could "see" it in her own – and he scrambled the rest of the way to his feet. "Em – Emily?" he whimpered for no apparent reason. Of course it wouldn't be her; the thing had probably already –

"Oh YEAH?" a voice boomed. "WELL, FUCK YOU BITCH!" but it wasn't a human voice. It was the kind of voice his panther might use if it could talk, all throaty snarls and dripping with evil, and that is when Lee Redding realized it was Emily, and that she must be a werewolf, something he'd always halfway believed in . . .

"Oh, God, Emily. I'm sorry! I didn't know! If I –"

Something enormously strong grabbed him by his belt and shirt-collar and propelled him forward so fast his frantically scrambling feet barely touched the ground. His sense of direction during his first panicked run, before he'd been knocked down, had been true. It had carried him within twenty feet of the car. This second, "assisted" run brought him the rest of the way. Unfortunately. *"Uhngh!"* His face slammed into the door frame at about fifteen miles per, and his nose moved sideways with an audible crack to accommodate this new and unexpected intimacy with his Ford. Both his lips split too, but because of the pitched-forward angle his nose took the brunt of it, and he didn't lose any teeth – or consciousness. Maybe it was the pain that kept him lucid. It came in waves that made him want to scream. So did the blood, in sheet-waves that –

He was yanked back away from the car, roughly spun around to its front, where he was left standing in the open lane, hunched forward, while his smashed nose worked like a spigot, filling up the puddle that had miraculously formed between his feet that looked purple-black in the –

"Fuck you, bitch," the panther-voice said. Only this time it wasn't as coarse or as loud as before. He peered out through pain-watered eyes, and there she was, only a few yards away, not looking like a werewolf at all. Looking just the same, as a matter of fact, except for the fact that now she was absent the bottom half of her outfit as well, and stood there in only her panties and her bra – and he didn't understand.

"Memm . . . Memily?" he said, and that didn't sound quite right either.

"Actually it's Mary," she answered back in a much more human voice, walking toward him at the same time. She was enjoying this immensely. It was like being both the hunter and the prey at the same time, the knowing what he was thinking, the feeling his fear . . .

It didn't make sense. None of it made any sense to Lee, and he was terrified. "W-why?" he asked, still feeling he was going to die.

"Because you made me angry, Lee. You shouldn't have made me angry."

"Jesus, I'm sorry. I never meant . . ." Then, seeing her up close, the softness of her skin, her woman-sized limbs, it suddenly hit him. "Wait. You're not alone in this, are you? You couldn't do this" – he waved a shaky hand at his face – "you're not strong enou –"

Steel fingers grabbed him beneath his armpits, waltzed him around with his feet off the ground like he was an inflatable doll. It was all done with muscles five times as strong, pound per pound, as his own, the kind an apes possess. But of course Lee didn't know that; all he knew was that he was suddenly lifted high, swung in an arc and slammed with controlled force against the car's hood, where he was held in place as "Mary" shoved her face inches from his own.

Her eyes, even in the half-light, were the eyes of a blue-eyed beast, gone rabid. "That . . . .makes me angry," she snarled. It was the voice of Satan.

"Oh, shit," he moaned, and she plucked him back off the car, set him on his feet again.

"Now . . . if you don't want to make me angry, you'll do what I say."

He nodded in a daze of fear, pain and rough treatment.

"Take off your shirt," she ordered. Human voice again.

Mechanically, he obeyed.

"Now, clean yourself up with it. The blood."

He did that too. Surprisingly, his nose had shut most of the way down, bleeding just a trickle now, and his cut lips had stopped altogether.

"Now, say you're truly sorry and deserve to die."

That is when Lee Redding began to cry. He didn't say anything, didn't plead for his life. He just stood there and cried.

"Oh, there, there, Lee . . . don't do that! We're almost done here, and then you can be on your way. Just . . . give Mary a kiss and all this will be behind you." She held out her arms.

Somehow, even as he still cried, he thought he saw a ray of hope in that. Sniffling, trying hard to control himself because he wanted so much to please her, he shuffled forward. When he was quite close she leaned in, tenderly kissed each cheek, then his chin . . .

"Lift up. It's beginning to bleed again. Your nose."

He titled his head backward because he didn't want to make her mad.

Then his eyes grew wide, and he screamed a short, barking scream. Maybe not a deer's hide, but a throat as soft and exposed as Lee's . . ? Child's play even for "human" teeth.

As the remainder of his life's blood poured out through his torn jugular in pints and quarts, Lee Redding stared at her with such a grievous look of disappointment and surprise that for just a moment "Mary" felt as if she'd done something wrong.

ba-bump, ba-bump, ba----

After early-breakfasting on Lee Redding's heart and a portion of his liver, "Mary" hid the body in the tangle beneath a pile of underbrush and small logs. Then she stripped, washed herself in the river, got dressed again, minus her bloodied underwear, and approached the car. The keys were still in it, something she'd taken careful note of before she'd buried Lee.

She'd also taken note of Lee's driving, and David's before him. This vehicle seemed less complex to operate than the latter's truck, which had an extra floor-pedal and required all sorts of complicated movements David called "shifting." Just turn the key, put it in "D" and go. On the third try she got it started, although it took her a minute more and a few surprises before she got the lights on. Then, a bit jerkily, she pulled onto the dirt road, knowing full well these silent back roads were the only ones she dared try to negotiate, but also knowing that the further away from the kill-spot Lee's car was found, the less likely it would be the body would be discovered right away. Finally, about a quarter-mile from where the first gravel road Lee had turned onto joined 223, she abandoned the vehicle.

Once out on the highway she stood facing the westbound lane and stuck out her thumb. The man who picked her up wasn't even from Michigan; he was an "Ohioan" and was on his way up north to spend a three-day weekend with friends. "Mary" was comfortable with that. He wouldn't be likely to hear the news even if the body was discovered and therefore wouldn't make any connections between it and a hitchhiker he'd happened to pick up at three in the morning. All the way home, until she asked to be dropped off, she behaved like a lady.

X V

Friday is a day with two faces. If you are loved or believe you are loved, if your life is in order and has meaning, then Friday is a time of hope and great expectations. Friday is the weekend almost here and unlimited potential. But if you are alone it underscores your loneliness. If you are depressed and your life is empty, those failures of the spirit are, by contrast with all the eagerness and joy around you, made all the more unbearable.

In the Rigert household Friday's split personality wore the faces of father and son.

Building upon the single word "too," as in ". . . please tell me you at least think you love me too?" David's hopes were soaring from the moment he got up on Friday morning. Then Mary sent him off with a kiss and the admonishment that he should ". . . come back quickly so we can resume this business of falling in love," and it was Mr. Bluebird's-On-My-Shoulder all day long. Then, late that evening, they made love for the first time and the weekend looked like the last day of school before summer vacation did when he was ten, only rosier.

On the downside there was Mark. Friday was Mark and Jenny's senior prom, and while that might not immediately seem like such a bad thing, events on one of those nights that are supposed to be pure magic in a teenager's life have a way of swelling all out of proportion, assuming too weighty a significance even for someone less disturbed than Mark. For Mark they plummeted him to an all-time low that would have him by the end of the night embracing wholeheartedly an idea he'd only half-considered till now: the taking of his own life.

He'd never wanted to go to the dance, had in fact insisted that Jenny deserved to spend Prom Night with someone who was "whole." But things had started off better than he expected once they got there. He'd even managed to get outside himself to a degree and relish the fact that Jenny seemed to be having a good time. He'd even begun to entertain the notion that with Jen maybe love was enough, that maybe the absence of a limb really didn't count for that much. Then some of his friends began clamoring for a square dance.

It was almost a tradition with their class, this acknowledgement of their Midwest, rural roots, and most of them got a real charge out of it. It was as if aside from the fun, the inclusion of a square dance or two was their way of saying, "Hey world, look at us! We're rap, hard rock and Beyonce', but we're together enough to be proud of being a little bit country, too." Someone had brought a record with some calls on it, and before Mark had time for second thoughts he and Jenny found themselves head couple in a squared off "set" consisting of three other couples, all of whom were close friends. Jenny at his right, was looking up at him and her face was all flushed with happiness and excitement. There was something (gratitude?) else there too, that he would have done anything not to extinguish

"Honor-r-r your partner-r-r-s-s-s . . !"

Because it was basically a beginner's record, there were some preliminary moves, some walk-throughs which served as a warm-up and which, in Mark's case, gave him a false sense of confidence. Then they began in earnest. The first dance was an old stand-by, "Red River Valley," and Mark made it as far as the point where the Hank Williams imitator bid everyone "Allemande-Left!" Now allemande-left is a fairly simple move, basic to all square dancing. It is also a move which, once called, will invariably be repeated several times during the course of the dance. For the man it consists of turning to the lady on his angled left, his "corner lady," taking her right hand in his own, and pulling her past, then around him, so that each walks in a short circle. He is then back facing his own partner, ready to take her left hand in his own.

But Mark didn't have a left hand.

He made it around his corner lady fine, but when he got back to Jenny he had nothing to offer her. There was split-second of confusion, a momentary break in the rhythm of their steps while her eyes registered a voiceless "Oh!" Then, undaunted, she grasped his empty coat sleeve. The idea, in allemande-left, is to more or less "pull" oneself past the hand one is grasping, that persistent pull never abrupt. Gentle yet firm. With the pull on Mark's empty sleeve the jacket of his rented tux, which didn't fit him all that well to begin with, shifted to the left. The open lapel came within an inch of sliding completely off the skeletal protuberance of bone, where clavicle and scapula met, which was all that comprised Mark's armless, meatless left shoulder. He could feel the sleeve, yet he continued on, moved towards his next outstretched hand with the same kind of nightmarish, distorted perception of time and speed an accident victim often experiences as their car plunges out of control and seemingly in slow motion toward the inevitable collision. And all he could think was, *I shouldn't have come here. If this thing happens, if they SEE . . .*

The next hand swam into view. Chrissy Beal's hand. Chrissy, SWEET Chrissy Beal. Her RIGHT hand. *(You were always such a good girl, so kind, I–)* He took it with no less gratitude than if hers were the hand of an angel sent down to deliver him from all pain and suffering in this world and the next. And he was caught. Because all her hand could do, all it was ever meant to do, was pull him on past – and to keep him from reaching up with his *own(ly)* hand and adjusting his coat.

Jody Denbroeder's hand was next. Her left. It was as if his empty sleeve had a sign on it: PULL HERE FOR MAXIMUM HUMILIATION. PULL HARD. He tried to shrug away. He tried to expand the muscles on the right side of his back, the way a bodybuilder expands his lats, so the coat would fit more snugly. He – *(shouldn't have come. Why was he here? They would all SEE)*

Jody Denbroeder, his executioner, took hold of the sleeve, and with a happy, winning smile, PULLED HARD. The jacket slipped from his left shoulder, slid down his ribs. *(The shirt is ripped savagely from the hunchback's torso, so that all might see and shudder at his deformity.)* Unlike the thicker fabric of his jacket, the shirt beneath did nothing to camouflage the sharp angles of pure bone. Like twin knife blades beneath a sheet, the knoblike projections poked at the cloth in a grotesque, stick-man parody of a man's shoulder, for all to see and remember, each time they looked at him. Forever.

With a hot flush of shame that made his cheeks and ears feel as if they were on fire he allowed himself to be pulled on past an open-mouthed, panicked Jodie Denbroeder. Linda Muir was next, with her right hand extended. *(Brave attempt not to notice, Linda, but you see. That's why I can never –)* He took the hand in a farewell grasp. Which brought him back 'round to Jenny. His Jenny. The only one who could see and not be repulsed, because he had made her see, once, a long time ago, made her run her fingers over the hard ridges of bone, the empty, puckered flesh . . . and she'd looked at him, looked at his deformity even then the way she looked at him now, through the eyes of love. Eyes that read and understood immediately what he was going through.

"Mark, I'm sorry. But these are your friends, Mark. It doesn't matter. They care for you." She reached up – he was a whole head taller than she – and gently fixed his coat. The music still played, the Hank Williams-voice still did the calls; but in their set all motion had stopped, and the noise seemed a distant thing as if everything were coming from several rooms away. So quiet he could hear the wisp and crinkle of her dress as she moved in close to him, pulled his head down and whispered in his ear, fiercely, "And I love you," then kissed him.

He tried hard to swallow something, some emotion that was unswallowable. Twice, unsuccessfully. It was as if everything he felt or ever could feel were lodged in his throat. Dear Jenny. HIS Jenny. *(Yes!)* His mo–

And that is when it happened. "Mom, I –"

Jenny paled. She paled because she had grown up with him, traded dreams, secrets and fears with him since the age of five. She knew him as intimately as he knew himself, and in the knowing, she knew that this apparent slip of tongue was much more than that. He stared at her helplessly. He couldn't take it back. Why, God, weren't you ever allowed to take something back, really take it back so that it never happened? He glanced around him in confusion. They were all watching him, his friends. They looked so sad. Then he turned back to Jenny. "Jen . . ." he choked. "Jen, I can't do this! *You* do this!"

Then he bulled his way across the room, bee-lined for the nearest exit, oblivious of the fact that his path cut straight through the middle of three other sets of square dancers, hopelessly throwing them off cadence so that there was nothing left but to reform their squares and wait out the finish of the song and the beginning of the next. And Jenny, after a moment, followed him.

The east wing at Valor High School was comprised mainly of two large gymnasiums, the boy's and the girl's, which on this night had been transformed into a single enormous room by rolling back the massive folding wall that separated them. It had then been done in suspended paper clouds, Styrofoam planets and stars and some fairly impressive lighting effects to the theme of "The Sky's the Limit." There were, however, several smaller rooms along that wing's back corridor, and it was to the semi-darkness of one of these that Mark fled. There was a plaque on the door that said "CHORAL," and the room itself had a tiered floor with each ascending level curved 'round into a partial circle so that its focal point was the one small corner area which remained at ground level. One entered the room at this lowest level and upon doing just that, Jenny paused to allow her eyes to adjust to the gloom.

"Mark?"

No answer, but she could sense his presence and finally she could make him out up on the highest level. Even in the partial darkness there was a certain rigidity to the way he stood, with his back to her, staring at the night beyond the room's single window.

Finally, "Why, Jen?"

She didn't answer immediately. "Why what? The jacket was just a simple mis–"

"Why do you think you still love me?"

She was quiet for a moment. Then she said, "I can't explain love Mark. I just do, that's all." She paused again, this time longer; and when she went on her voice was stronger, more assertive. "It's . . . because you're part of me."

He snorted. "Yeah, the crippled part."

"No! The best part! You are part of me, and you can't, you won't take that away from me unless it's not true!"

He wanted to turn around and face her, but he didn't. Still, he could see her there in his mind's eye. Her arms would be rigid at her sides, her fists clenched. She would have that brave-yet-frightened look on her face, like up in his room when she was fourteen. God, God . . .

111

"Will you, Mark? Will you take that away?"

He squeezed his eyes shut, as if not seeing could absent him from the whole confrontation. "I don't know," he answered weakly.

Silence.

"But it's true, isn't it? You're part of me and I'm part of you?"

"I wish it weren't."

"Why?"

"Come here." He listened to her footsteps, two at each tier-level, sometimes three, where he'd taken them at a single stride each, and it struck him that even the sound of her walk was something so dear, so essential to his life that losing it would be like losing another part of himself. Then she was there, the warmth, the rightness of her snuggled against his side. The crush of her breasts against his ribs, the way her hips pressed and fit against his own . . .

That was it: she fit. She fit so Goddamned-wondrously-can't-survive-without-her well . . ! She was right – spiritually, emotionally, even physically, they were part of each other. He started to cry. He didn't know he was going to cry; it just sort of happened, standing there holding her, thinking about how truly connected they were and about how for her sake it couldn't remain that way. Big, silent tears, one after another like off a conveyor belt, running down his cheeks, dripping from there onto his left lapel because he had turned his head away from her. If it had been anyone else but Jen they probably would not have even noticed, here in the semi-dark. But her hand crept immediately to his cheek.

"Oh darlin' . . ." she murmured with infinite tenderness. And they were nine, and he'd talked her into following him across a high beam in the barn and she'd fallen and broken her leg. ("It's all right, Mark. It wasn't your fault".) Even as she lay there in absolute pain.

"I'm – " He fought for control of his voice. "No! I'm part of you all right – a tumor! A fucking tumor and it's got to come out!"

"No, Mark, you're –"

"You know what a tumor is, Jen?" he cut in, deliberately loud. Do you?"

"Mark –"

"It's a sick, diseased part of something, a part that has to be removed or it'll destroy the rest!" His voice, which had risen steadily not only in volume but in emotional intensity, was suddenly flat and quiet. "That's what I am, Jen. I'm sick" – he reached up, tapped his head – "up here."

"Mark, you're not. You're just upset. Let me hold you."

"Jenny, I called you 'Mom' out there! And we both know it was more than –"

She cut him off desperately. "Let me hold you! *Please!*" He hesitated, fought it, but only for a moment. Then he allowed her to pull his head down onto her breast. God, it felt so good –. and it was what he really wanted anyway, wasn't it? What this was all about?

"I'll . . . be your mother, if that's what you need." There. She'd said it. In answer he made a half-sobbing, half-groaning sound, the kind of sound one might make as an arrow imbedded in their back is finally removed. Then he slid to his knees and buried his face against her abdomen.

She ran her fingers through his hair. "Shhhh. Shhhh. It's all right."

Then she was on her knees, then sitting back, and his head was in her lap, his arm curled around one warm thigh beneath the crinkly material of her dress as she rocked him.

"I've always been in a way, haven't I?" she said soothingly, almost as if she were talking to herself. She rocked him some more. "It's okay. I don't mind. I guess I wanted it that way . . ."

His hand slipped along the softness of her inner thigh. She breathed in sharply, and that is when he came to his senses. It was wrong, all wrong. She couldn't play both roles.

"No! It's all screwed up!"

"But it's okay. I w-want to be everything, Mark. Just love me! Just let me love you!" The words were all rushed and tumbled and shaky, and he should have known even in his own torment what he was doing to her. "F-for you, anything, Mark. For you, my life."

No. "No!" He pulled away from her. Those words, those never-forgotten words . . ! They were the basis for everything beautiful and right between them. They would not be used to change it into something unnatural. Suddenly he was strong and in rigid control of himself. "No, it can't be this way. In the long run you'll end up resenting me, wishing I was more of a man." He stood up. He could see it all clearly now, what

113

had to be done. "It's all too one-sided, Jen. You looking out for me. You pitying me, comforting me, listening to me complain . . ."

She reached up for him, caught at his finger. "You're wrong, Mark. I need you as much as you need me. Come back down."

Carefully, gently, he extricated his hand. Just as gently he said, "You don't need me; you just think you do because you've never given anyone else a chance." Despite the gentleness there was a certain detached finality to his tone that was frightening, even to him.

There was a long silence then when neither of them spoke, but in the half-light he could see her shaking her head back and forth, denying him voicelessly. Finally, with the same soft compassion-minus-the-passion immutability in his voice, thus giving it the ring of a judge passing sentence, he said, "We're not going to see each other anymore, Jen. There's more wrong with me than just a missing arm, a lot more."

That is when she started to cry. Softly at first, while he stood by helplessly and watched, then more fiercely, with more abandon, as if there were a slow yet total surrendering inside to something overwhelming strong. Finally she turned away from him, buried her face in her arms and her whole body was wracked with sobs.

He knelt, then lay down beside her there, on the topmost tiered step, put his arm over her protectively and murmured, "I love you, Jenny. That's why it has to be this way."

She twisted away, sobbed even harder with a helpless *uh-uh-uh* sound that was almost convulsive and that spoke of whole worlds of loneliness and pain. He remembered thinking later, on the way home, that this was the sound she would have made giving birth to their child and that only then would he have been able to make it better.

("It's okay, Mark,") his mother's voice said. "It was for her own good."

He was back in his bedroom. They'd come home early. The night of her senior prom he'd dropped Jenny at her doorstep at 11:01. She'd kissed him, told him that she understood even as fresh tears rolled down her cheeks, and now he was lying in the darkness, alone.

Alone? No, not alone. *She* was there. What did it matter that it was all in his mind, his weak, aberrant, infantile mind? His mother was still there, sitting on the edge of the bed, and her fingertips stroked his brow.

"But it hurts," he whispered. "*She* hurts." He turned on his side in the darkness and rested his head against her hip which, tonight, seemed more substantial, more like solid flesh and less like his pillow folded over for that purpose.

(*"Shhh. I know it hurts. But all that will be gone soon. As soon as you come back to me."*)

"How?" Did he ask that aloud or only think the question?

(*"All you have to do is WANT to badly enough . . ."*)

"You're dead! I can't! He was sure he'd said that out loud. He needed to say that out loud. He pushed the pillow away from him, but it didn't make her go away this time. Her voice, some voice, went on in his head: (*"Come back to me. In my womb, where nothing can touch you. I'll have you all over again!"*)

"No!" he whispered harshly. "It's sick!"

(*"I'll have you when you're eight. Jenny will be waiting for you – and this time I won't let you lose your arm."*)

"It's –"

But she was so strong and he was so weak. And if it were true, if it were true . . .

(*"'TIS true, Mark. But I canno' have you unless you come to me, REALLY come to –"*)

He froze.

(*Who. . . ?*)

Her words had never rung so clearly in his mind, so separate an entity from the rest of his consciousness. It was almost as if their origin were outside himself. Something else about them, too, something . . .

And then he thought he knew what it was. Up until now he'd never "allowed" her voice to suggest an awareness that suicide was what these "conversations" were really about, simply because he couldn't quite come to terms with her as his mother knowing and not trying to dissuade him. Now she had evinced just such an awareness. Or *he* had. His mouth shaped itself, in the darkness, into a grimace that was meant to be a sad but gallant smile but somehow fell short of either sentiment. He wanted to be with his mother, be part of her . . ? He wanted to crawl back into the womb . . ? Death could accomplish that; death was like the womb – no worries, no fears . . . Shielded, protected from the rest of the

115

world and at peace. At least the possibility of starting over. (*"Yes, Mark, yes! Come back to me, darlin'! I'll have you all over again! I'll have you when you're eight!"*)

Mark lay awake for a long time that night. He was still awake when, downstairs, Mary invited his father back into his own bed, although he could not hear exactly what words were being spoken. The heat registers in an old farmhouse are excellent sound conductors, though, and he heard enough: Soft murmurs. The peculiar creaks and groans that particular bed made when subjected to a second person's weight. And then . . . other noises, hushed yet urgent, that built, eventually, to a fevered pitch. Noises that told him even more clearly than his mother's "voice" that his place was no longer in this world, where she was forgotten, betrayed . . . and where his father had found a new life that didn't include either of them.

XVI

On the evening that he and Mary made love for the first time, David came home from work to find her crying. She had read all in that single afternoon the novel *Somewhere in Time*, which he'd given her two days ago, and he should have known it would hit too close to home to not affect her that way, especially the part where Richard finds a 1971 penny in his pocket and is immediately snatched back through time away from Elise, just as the two of them are celebrating the wonder and joy of newly discovered love. Snatched back irreversibly. David felt selfish and guilty, because his main reason for giving her the book had been the magic way Matheson was able to weave romance into every single element of the idea of a man and woman thrown together from two different times. It said a lot of things more eloquently than he could ever hope to, and he'd never once considered the fact that it would also be the cruelest reminder of her husband, Jim, that he could possibly engineer.

"Hey, Pumpkin, hey . . ." he soothed as he put his arms around her, calling her for the first time by one of the pet names that till now had been solely reserved for Pamela. "I should've known. I'm sorry. And don't feel bad. It doesn't have to be that way. In the book neither of them loves again, but in the real world that's just not –"

"I want you to burn my dress," she said into his chest. "Burn everything else too, or . . . or at least hide it where I'll never stumble upon it because –" Then a great, wracking sob cut off the rest, and he rocked her. They were sitting on the edge of his bed, exactly where he'd found her when he'd come home. The bedroom door had been shut, and he'd had to listen very closely after knocking to know that anything was wrong, because most of her crying had been done softly and to herself.

"What? Why?" he asked, momentarily stunned. Then he understood and his heart leapt with guilty joy.

"Those . . . those poor people!" she said, fighting for control. "If . . . if I am torn from you now, David, I" – a shuddering breath – "I would die!" She had pulled back, and now her eyes, still with tears in them, searched his face imploringly, looking for some assurance there. Instead she caught a glimpse of his guilt. "And poor Jim!" she went on. "Of course I think o' him too . . . But David, in all my year-and-a-half with him I never once felt the scope o' love I feel for you right now! I could no' bear to go back!" Then she threw herself against him so fiercely it was as if no amount of closeness would suffice. "I love you, David! I-love-you-I-love-you-I-love-you!"

"I love you too, Mary," he said, choked with emotion. "And I'll . . . 'no' give you up either. Ever."

She smiled at that through her tears, at the solemn way he copied her brogue. Then they were kissing again, and it was a good thing his mouth was thus occupied, because if it hadn't been he would have shouted with joy, something enough unlike his normal self that he was afraid it might cause her to have second thoughts. That she should love him, actually choose to be with him, when a week ago she'd been half mad with despair to return to her own time, seemed the most miraculous circumstance of all in a week filled with miracles.

The rest of the day was lost on him. He was in a daze of happy confusion. He knew that she fixed an excellent meal for them, doing amazing things with a pot roast and a few vegetables. He also knew that while she was in the kitchen working on it he pretended she was his wife – and that gave him more pleasure and excitement than seemed reasonable. But if anyone had asked him even a day later what else, specifically, they'd done, what they had talked about, he wouldn't have been able to tell them – other than the fact that Mark had come home from the prom early and he'd tried to talk with him, find out what was wrong. But even that, in retrospect, seemed vague, since Mark had been his usual uncommunicative self and had gone to bed almost immediately. And somehow it seemed impossible to worry that much when he was close to Mary, almost as if he were under some kind of spell.

The only moments absolutely clear in his mind were those as she told him she loved him. And those beginning with the moment at half past eleven when she said, "You'll no' sleep on the couch tonight, will you? We would both end up on it, and that would be foolish with a bed to share in the next room." It wasn't long after that when his ranked list of what was most miraculous about the week had to be revised yet another time.

She insisted they undress each other. It was all done slowly, deliberately, and with much wonder and awe. Everything was new again. It was as if he'd never seen a woman's body before, nor she a man's. There were moments, a number of them, when he was so overwhelmed by her carmine beauty, so caught up in her sexuality, that his five senses seemed not enough to take it all in.

On her part there were sighs and soft exclamations of delight as she lay bare then explored each new part of him – and he'd never been made to feel that way before, so thoroughly, reciprocally appreciated.

There were caresses and murmured words of love. And when he cupped his hand *there* she shuddered, arched up against him, and their eyes locked. "I . . . I was never able to look Jim in the eye! No' before, during or after!" she told him during the brief pause which had to follow. "'Tis true! 'Tis true! You possess me body and soul!"

Then it was time, and as he lowered himself into her it was like all his life, everything he'd ever felt or done, was simply a preliminary for this moment. The pleasure was almost agonizing. She was a liquid furnace garnished in red, and the feel of her, feel of them, sliding, melting, melding into one caused him to groan out loud. She, too, groaned beneath him, a soul from which some awful burden had just been lifted.

After that it was if they were in each other's minds as well as each other's bodies. It was perfect. It was perfection building, building . . . reaching for something beyond perfection.

The feral lights in her eyes came then receded, came then receded. She dug her nails into his back. Hard. He kissed her mouth just as savagely. The tempo increased. It was like making love to something wild. They were abandoned to it, lost to it, when finally simultaneously, climax caught up with them and she arched up against him so violently that her hips came off the bed, carrying his weight with them. It seemed to spin out forever; if it had lasted any longer his mind would have poured out with everything else.

Afterward, after they had held each other, she said, "I . . . had no idea it could be like this. I mean, it never was, and . . ." She looked at him with a child's light in her eyes. "Will you think me wanton if I tell you I could do this again and again, every day and more? Would that shock or repel you?"

He laughed. "Neither. It would make me a very lucky man!"

She looked relieved. Then, possibly encouraged by his laugh, something mischievous crept into those eyes. "Did you know that you went cross-eyed there at the end, David Rigert? Just for a moment but . . . definitely cross-eyed!"

He laughed some more. "I probably did. But what I'd like to know is, was that before or after your own turned completely around in their sockets so that you looked like Orphan Annie?"

She poked his ribs then kissed the spot. Then, cautiously: "Who is 'Orphan Annie'?"

"Oh . . . just another redhead I know."

The mischief vanished. She was serious again. "Should I be jealous? Is she my competition?"

"There is no competition. And if there was, you'd win it hands down!"

She studied his face a few seconds longer. Then she said, "Oh, David . . !" And they made love again and this time it was all Mary, instead of nine-tenths Mary. But that was okay; she was too caught up in the moment to say or do anything that might reveal her "other" self's presence. "Mary" could afford to let go the reins for a few minutes; she had gotten what she wanted from the experience. Now, for the first time, she was seeded. And that, of course, was of preeminent importance to her "imperative."

XVII

Why is it that two scientists living on opposite ends of the Earth and never having communicated will suddenly begin research along radically new yet amazingly similar lines, when nothing in their shared discipline nor in recent developments would indicate that was the direction to go? How is it that two authors, unbeknown to each other, will suddenly decide to do a fictional treatment of the same subject – Leif Ericson's discovery of "America" in the ninth century, for example – when nothing in current events, the media or from any other source, including their publishers, would indicate the time was ripe for such a story? Or why is it, with a husband and wife, that one will begin humming a tune that is, at the same moment, playing in the head of the other, despite the fact that nothing in their shared environment could possibly have precipitated the coincidence?

Strict pragmatists would claim that in each case there has been something overlooked, some "catalyst." Something perceptible to at least one of their shared five senses. And from there it is merely a logical sequence of thoughts and associations that have led to the "coincidences." They would insist that ideas are not free-floating entities, that they have no means of transference separate from those aforementioned five senses. They would also scoff at the idea that two (or more) people can truly be "on the same wave-length," that thoughts can, under the right circumstances, be broadcast from one mind to another either intentionally or unintentionally.

"Mary," of course, could have set them straight on a few things. In so far as the world goes, she was the ultimate broadcast machine. They would have been appalled. And if they had possessed even half the imagination Professor William E. Haroldson – he of Astronomy 101 – possessed they would have been just a little afraid as well.

Under the right circumstances. For renowned psychics like Edgar Cayce and Peter Hurkos the circumstances must obviously and frequently have been right. For the professor, too, they were right – but only in a very special, very limited sense. There was something in his chemical makeup, in the patterns of his brain waves, that made him, during the low-alpha stages of sleep, receptive to "Mary's" mind, though he did not know it. He, in a sense, shared her dreams; only for him they were nightmares.

This morning, as he hobbled down the steps and into the kitchen where his wife Flo already had a pot of coffee brewing, he knew he'd had a particularly vivid and disturbing nightmare. Trouble was, he could only remember fragments of it now that he was awake. He remembered distinctly, though, how alone he had felt during it, and that frightened him.

There were only two things these days that really frightened the professor; his arthritis and being left alone. The former because it signified a loss of control and in his mind a diminishing of his ability to be lover and protector to his Florence. Ankles and hips, ankles and hips – and now his toes too! It didn't matter how cockeyed smart you were, you couldn't fight something like arthritis.

The second, the fear of being left alone, was in reality a fear of no longer being loved, which up until the dreams had simply meant a world without Flo. But in the dreams he had been part of a *world* without love, an emotionally cold, cruel world that was Earthlike yet at the same time as alien as the moons of Jupiter. He was part of it, a citizen of it, and the part of him that was still himself could not have felt more hopeless if he had been permanently turned to stone yet remained sentient.

At least he thought he knew where they were coming from, what prompted the dreams. They had begun just about a week ago, about the same time he'd allowed someone in one of his Astronomy 101 classes to "lure" him into yet another episode of wild speculation concerning the existence of an alternate-Earth. He'd spoken of cataclysmic disruptions in the evolution of man during that class period, and in the dream he'd seemed to have actual knowledge of two separate species, one very similar to what Homo erectus might have been had he not become extinct, the other . . . not us, not Homo sapiens. His dreaming mind had simply elaborated on the theory, concocting the emergence of a second form of human once ol' Sapiens had been removed. But it had done more than that; it had contrived a whole social milieu, a worldwide pattern-of-thinking/mode-of-life to fit this "two-kinds-of-man" world. It had painted in the background, in a psychological sense, and it had painted it as stark and forbidding as anything Salvador Dali, Marx Ernst or any other surrealist had ever produced; and now he was remembering portions of it, perhaps with more detail than he would have preferred:

The one species was primitive, animal-like in their physical powers and predatory to the extreme. The other was advanced, possibly more advanced than Sapiens, but absolutely cruel. The more intelligent species used the less advanced one. He wasn't sure how, but he got the impression they were regarded more as a form of livestock than as a people in so far as rights and humane treatment were concerned. In other words, they were expendable.

There were other impressions too. One of them was of enormous "preserves" where the primitives were allowed to roam free – but were never truly free. Another was of unspeakable atrocities, experiments . . . and of an almost Godlike power over the life sciences, especially biology, as a result of those experiments. Then there was the more general yet equally disturbing impressions, so all-pervasive in his dreams that he seemed to breathe their mood along with the alien air: bloodlust, countered by blind ambition; savage instincts versus calculated self-serving cruelty; an inability to love and/or the ability discarded . . . They were all felt-dreamed-sensed in pairs. Always two sides to the same coin, as if in his dreams he was both species simultaneously. That frightened him, too, because it was significant in some ominous ways relative to his waking self, if he could only remember . . .

"G'morning," Florence said, setting his coffee and a bowl of hot, steaming oatmeal in front of him. He had seated himself at the kitchen table without so much as a hello, and now she nudged him with her hip in a playful but reprimanding way before turning back toward the stove. He threw an arm around her and hugged her close for just a moment. "Morning." She smelled of powder and flowers, and wasn't it better to think of things like that then to struggle to recall details of a dream which once remembered would probably only disturb him more? She had smelled that way for every one of the forty-seven years they had been married, and he still felt a welling of love and sense of security every time he smelled the smell. "Puffs" facial tissues smelled kind of that way, like Flo did, and for some inane reason he remembered the time not so long ago that she'd been away for a week, staying with her sister immediately following his brother-in-law's death. By the third restless night he'd had to move the box she always kept on her nightstand to the pillow next to him. After that he'd slept like a baby, and he realized his line of reasoning was not inane after all. The dreams, just like her absence, made him feel vulnerable and alone, and the smell of her just now had simply reminded him how much he –

Suddenly he froze. If Flo had been looking at his face then, instead of straight down onto the top of his head, she would have wondered if he'd seen a ghost. As it was she felt him stiffen, and by intimation imagined she could also feel the icy chill that traveled up and down his spine.

"What?" she asked. "What's wrong?"

He didn't' answer right away. The knowledge *(knowledge? Yes, knowledge. I know – THEY know –)* had hit him with such force and surprise that it took him several seconds to remind himself it was only another fragment of the dream, come back to him in the peculiar way that bits and pieces of nighttime chimera sometimes do – not when we try to remember them but of their own accord when we least expect it. It did little to reassure him, though.

They know! a voice inside his head was shouting at him. About us, about our world . . . and they're *waiting!*

"Honey?"

This time her voice tore him from it. "Uh? Nothing," he answered in a shaky voice. "Something from a dream, that's all." He hoped she didn't push too hard for more, at least not right now, because he needed to remember the rest. And maybe if he let it all just percolate for a while instead of saying any of it out loud and risking mixing it up or maybe even driving it away completely, he would remember. He would know the answer to a question that filled him with more urgency and dread than anything born of a dream had a right to: *Waiting for what?*

XVIII

"Mary," who in a manner of speaking was both humanoid species of which the old professor dreamt, knew the answer. She knew what "they" were waiting for. They were waiting for another one-hundred-and-seven years to pass. They were waiting for The Gate between their world and this one to once again be open. They were waiting for her to be "fruitful and multiply" so that her genetically altered body might deliver them sons – and then for those sons to sire more sons, and so on and so on, until there were at least several score of them ranging in age from early twenties to late fifties, each carrying a set of very special genes passed on from her, each ready to do his part when the time came.

"Mary" knew other things as well. Things about herself and the world around her, and if she thought about those bits and pieces of information at all, she did so with mixed emotions. She knew, for example, that her gender was perceived as a handicap – in both worlds – and that with reference to her goal of rapid and prolific spread of certain dominant genes especially, herself as a male would have had an enormous advantage. She was at best a "second choice," simply because the mind and body that fate had sent them had been female – and she resented that fact.

Yet, on the other hand, she also knew that she was a triumph of cryogenics, genetic engineering and a dozen other life sciences so advanced they could create or "grow" a being with the strength and savage instincts of one species, the cunning and ambition of another, and the outward appearance of yet a third. She was a wonder, a phenomenon, guided by the preserved, altered brain of that latter species, which was not even of her world, in such a way that she could be sent back to its planet and function undetected.

She knew the odds were heavily against her living long enough to see a successful conclusion to the long-range plan her presence here had set in motion, and yet she was supremely confident that the special physical/mental gifts of her progeny would accomplish it. They would be Olympians and senators, heavyweight champions and world leaders – and sometimes both. Where awestruck reverence for their physical powers would not take them, their political savvy, made infallible through their ability to "touch" peoples' minds, would.

They would have the power and influence necessary to make sure this world's sciences could, and would, keep The Gate open – at least until it was too late to close it again.

And then there were the things she did not know but would have liked to have known, starting with what, exactly, The Gate was. How did such factors as the "matched resonance on mirror worlds," "galactic spin" and "relative positioning of "wormholes in space" combine so that on a cyclical basis the matter of one world "kissed" that of the other across the light years, thus enabling one to step from one world to its twin?

And what of herself? Who was she, really? The genetically altered, cloned body that was a new, improved model over another named Mary Donegal, "taken" one-hundred and seven years ago? That she could accept. But what of her mind? That she could think with a brain frozen, worked upon and having belonged to someone else seemed impossible. Was she Mary, then, and her present consciousness extant only as an especially strong alter-ego belonging to that girl's mind? Who was *she*, "Mary"?

Then there were the more practical questions, whose answers could play a vital role in the accomplishment of the plan: How could she better control the killing instinct that ruled her completely on a regular basis and placed her in needless risk of discovery? What was love, compassion and empathy, that she might better demonstrate those ways of emoting in front of David without being forced to allow Mary so free a rein? What made the rare person (she was aware of one even now, in her dreams) sensitive to her alien mind, and was there a way to dampen whatever signals it was that she was sending out? In between her efforts to learn as much as she could about this planet and her interactions with David, "Mary" thought about those things. Which is not to say that she worried; absolute ruthlessness and any real self-doubt are mutually exclusive. If there were questions, problems, she would overcome them. If anyone or anything posed a threat to the implementation of her plan, it would die.

Mary only felt one-hundred percent when she was with David. No, that wasn't exactly true. It was more like ninety or ninety-five percent. She had only completely been herself since coming here on two occasions: One was during those precious moments last night when they had made love, not so much the first time as the second. The other had been for only a few seconds duration and hadn't involved David at all. It had occurred on Wednesday afternoon when she'd suddenly found herself in the kitchen, comforting a crying Mark with no idea how she'd gotten there. The rest of the time, being with David brought her about as close to her real self as she could get, and now she thought she understood why. For as long as she'd been here, in this age, she'd been marginally aware of her "other" self. No shock at the discovery, separate from the shock of her dislocation. No sudden revelation. Just a gradually increasing awareness that didn't seem to have a real beginning, so that there had never been a point at which she'd cried out either aloud or to herself, "My God, I'm possessed!" But she was possessed, possessed of two minds, and the one always kept a calming, restraining hand on the other's metaphorical shoulder. She was the one with the shoulder, and she felt weighted down, sometimes even crushed.

Ninety-five percent herself . . . Fifty percent . . . Zero percent . . .

One-hundred percent.

She was beginning to see a pattern. The "hand" came down hard each time she was seized with a desire to tell David he was really in love with two people, one of them evil. It became lighter, she was more herself, the more circumstances demanded selflessness, a giving disposition and love – and the thing that made her believe she was onto something pivotal here was the feeling that this relinquishing of control was done reluctantly, begrudgingly . . . and possibly fearfully. It was something that she might use to de–

NO!

– sooner had she thought these things than she felt herself fading again, the "hand" coming down extra-hard, the way it did when –

Then she screamed inside (it was all that was allowed her) as, for a hairs-breadth of time, she saw "Mary's" mind, knew what she was about to do. She screamed not only at the horror of it but because she knew for that one awful moment that she'd been here, face to face with the beast-woman, before, knew that terrible things had been done, *would* be done, and that she would remember none of it separate from "Mary's" mind because her own consciousness was about to be shut down completely. Hope was an illusion. She could only fight back when she was allowed a part of herself to do it with, and "Mary" could take that away so quickly and cleanly that when it was given back again she couldn't remember a thing. Not even the screams

Does a mass murderer, a psychopath, ever scream inside, terrified of the monster that is himself? Mary did. But not frequently or for very long. Because most of the time she couldn't even remember.

XIX

David glanced over his shoulder from the kneeling position he was in to see if his ears had served him right. They had. Carol's 2009 Chevy Malibu had just pulled into the empty church lot; cars that old developed a sound all their own.

The first thought that crossed his mind after that was in the form of a question. Would she or would she not somehow sense that he and Mary had made love last night? It sent a flutter of alarm through his insides and made him feel defensive. He continued his digging at the roots of a juniper bush slated for transplanting and did not get up or turn around.

Her footsteps approached slowly, coming to a halt directly behind him. From there it would have been easy to give him a good swift kick in the rear-end. Or notice the way his hair was thinning on top or that his back and waist were not quite the lean, mean parts of a wrestling machine they once had been – and decide he wasn't worth half the heartache he knew he was putting her through. In a way he wished something like that would happen. But Carol wasn't the kind who hurt people when they were vulnerable, he was. She also wasn't the kind to be so easily influenced in matters of the heart by something as fleeting and shallow as physical appearances.

He was.

"Tell me I've lived my whole life in vain, David," she said behind him, no preliminaries.

He cringed. Then he did stand up. And turned around as well. "I can't."

Her eyes widened in mock surprise. "Oh? But you have! You already have! You're falling for her, and no words are required to tell me that!

Why else would you let her stay so long, believe her ridiculous story about time travel and wear such a pained expression every time you see me? You're falling for her! And if you do that, I've lived my whole life in vain!"

He studied her face. This was something that had been building for a long time. "I'm not the measure of your life," he said quietly. "I can't be."

"No? What is then, Nick Reeves? All the children I don't have? The café . .?" With each question her voice rose a note. It was half an octave higher by the time she was done, yet it did not sound shrill or hysterical; Carol could never sound hysterical.

He shook his head. "I don't know. Something inside. Jesus, Carol, talk about some heavy guilt . . ! Besides, even if I deserve it, I don't –"

"Guilt? You feel guilty?" (Not hysterical, but with enough suppressed emotion to make him wince.) "Well, I absolve you of all guilt, David! To–this—point. Tell me you don't, never did and never could love me and you're off the hook completely!"

And of course he couldn't, because it was happening again. Every time he was away from Mary and in Carol's presence he saw such qualities there, like the straightforward kind of courage she was demonstrating now, that he couldn't bear the thought of severing his life from hers any more than he could have from Mary's.

"But if you can't tell me that . . ." she went on, seeing that he could not and allowing a note of tender triumph to creep into her voice, "then you should feel guilty. Because you're throwing away something that could have been beautiful – for both of us."

She paused then, her eyes never leaving his face. The air, hot and still this morning, roused itself into a short-lived breeze that blew a strand of honey-gold hair across her cheek. She didn't brush it away, and it could have been twenty-five years ago, before he'd given his ring and his love to Pamela. Then her eyes did leave his face. They sought the ground, the distance behind him, anywhere but straight on as she added, "You can also feel guilty, very guilty, if you, Mark and . . . "Mary" don't show up for Sunday dinner tomorrow at two o'clock at my house. I'll have worked all morning fixing a huge meal, paid Janet's sister ten bucks an hour plus tips to be Janet, while Janet is me, at the café . . . and I deserve a chance to be judged side-by-side with the competition on poise, personality and –"

"No, Carol. It would only end up –"

"Not from me . . !" she cut back in anticipating his objections. "If there's any . . . unpleasantness or sniping it won't come from me! You *know* I can handle it! I'm just curious to see if she can."

"Still, no. I just don't think it'd be right."

"Guilt," she repeated then, still not looking at him but saying much with the stubborn set of her jaw, seen even in profile. "I will be making all those preparations, taking the day off . . . everything else I said, assuming you'll all show. If you don't . . ."

And that was the end of it. She turned and marched away from him then, like a soldier who has made his report and is now relieved of all personal responsibility for what it contained. The ball, her body language said, was no longer in her court.

After watching her, somewhat in surprise, until she'd pulled out of the driveway and was gone, David turned back to his juniper bush. Today would see the conclusion of his work here at the churchyard. It had turned out well. He'd come in substantially under what he'd bid for the job and was turning back the difference to the congregation rather than adding it to his profits. He'd thought a few days ago that he'd be feeling pretty good about himself right about now. He'd been wrong.

X X

Professor Haroldson and his wife Flo had lived in the same updated Victorian on a tree-lined side street in Saline for the last twenty-two years. It was only a short drive into Ann Arbor and the University from there, yet it offered at least the illusion of escaping each day to a simpler, more tranquil, small-town way of life. The professor liked that. So did Flo.

Then, too, both Detroit and Toledo were less than an hour away, while Detroit Metro Airport was only thirty minutes. And Valor . . ? Unfortunately, Valor was only a short distance as well – thirty-seven easily hitchhiked miles, to be exact.

But the professor didn't care about that. Valor was just a name on the map, a place on the road, like Onsted, Adrian and Tecumseh; and right now it was less than that, because he was dreaming again, and in his dreams such names weren't even a part of the same universe. He dreamt of killing, and consuming raw, strange creatures that were neither mammal nor reptile.

He dreamt of bloodlust and the possession of enormous strength. He dreamt alien dreams; and he did it to the accompaniment of Flo's vacuum cleaner, because this was Saturday, and on Saturdays he got to doze on the couch beneath the morning paper while Flo cleaned the upstairs.

It was the absence of noise that finally woke him. Not just the fact that the vacuum was silent, but the "presence" of absolute, claustrophobic silence that was an entity all its own, the kind that closes in on you should you happen to wake up for very long at, say, three in the morning.

Nothing. Nothing but the tick . . . tock of the pendulum clock on the mantel.

"Flo?" he called out, raising himself to a seated position.

Nothing. The house was all hardwood floors and throw-rugs and ninety years old; there should have been noise.

He got up and moved to the bottom of the open stairway, put a liver-spotted hand on the mahogany rail. He felt uneasy after his dreams. His insides seemed to be wanting to creep up closer to the protection of his ribs, and that was a bad sign. "Flo?"

No answer. But this time he thought he heard movement, subtle, furtive movement directly overhead, like maybe somebody was tiptoeing across their bedroom, and now he was definitely spooked because Flo wasn't the kind to play games; she would answer if there wasn't something wrong. "Flo?" he called again when he was halfway up the stairs.

And then he heard it. A tiny, "tinny" voice, a little squeak of a voice, saying. "Help me." Not a terrible voice, not exactly the kind of voice to freeze one's blood or cause one to become nauseous with fear . . . Unless you are old enough to remember the original 1950's make of *The Fly*, old enough to forever associate that kind of voice with a fate worse than death. Unless you've been suffering from bad dreams, dreams in which something alien and cruel knows you are there, dreaming of it. Unless you are smart enough to realize no sane intruder, none with anything but the worst of intentions anyway, would answer you in the first place.

He finished the climb upstairs the way a condemned man might take the last two or three steps leading to the gallows. For Flo. For Flo and for no other reason.

The door to their bedroom was to his right off the top of the stairs, and it stood open. And for just a moment hope peeked its head through the cloud of dread fear that still had him sick inside, because there was Flo, all the way across the room, sitting at her vanity. True, there was a strange frighteningly beautiful woman standing over her, with the fingers of one hand laced none too gently in Flo's hair; but at least his wife wasn't sprawled dead or unconscious on the floor – which for some reason was exactly what he'd expected to find. If only he could catch her eye in the vanity's mirror! If only it hadn't been tilted up, he could –

"F-Flo?" he called out, stepping into the room, moving closer now and wondering, oh wondering if an old man's strength would be equal to that of a young woman's. He outweighed her by at least sixty pounds and that was something . . .

"You've been stealing my dreams," the woman said in a more normal but still threatening voice. "I want them back."

Something inside the professor wilted then, and all his courage leaked out of him as if his character were a sieve. No. It couldn't be –

"Your wife agrees. You canno' hold onto other people's DREAMS!" And with the last word she released her hold in Florence's hair, shot that same hand beneath his wife's chin, while her other grasped the top of Flo's skull as if she were palming a basketball. Then she twisted. Violently.

The head came around till it faced the professor directly. The body remained facing square-way. It was done with a minimum of resistance, a minimum of crackling – which should have told the professor that she'd been dead all along, that her neck was already broken before he'd entered the room. But it told him nothing, because he was too far gone in shock, too busy gasping his wife's name to think clearly.

And what "she" did next pushed him further over the edge: She made Florence's poor mouth move. Like a marionette's. Like a female Howdy Doody, complete with blood trickling from both corners of her mouth to form the same, grotesque marks of delineation on either side of the chin. She made her say, in the tiny, tinny voice, "Yes, husband, yes! Give back the dreams!"

The room spun just a little in front of the professor's eyes then. The floor tilted, tilted back, like something in a fun house. But he didn't' care, didn't even give much notice. All he cared about was becoming dead, like Flo, as quickly as possible.

He didn't care, either, that fingers like steel springs, fingers possessed of an inhuman strength he was all too familiar with in his dreams, closed round his wrists *(how did she get –)*, pulled him stumbling to a far corner of the room where they let go briefly, leaving him standing in a daze in front of his desk. He didn't care at all.

Until he heard a sound, a peculiar, cold, metal-on-metal sound – *tsssiinngg* – that was the sound of his Japanese bayonet, his one and only souvenir from the year-and-a-half his father had spent in the Pacific, being drawn from its steel scabbard. Until she growled, in her own octave, "We'll just make it look as if it's your work! All of it! Killed her then stabbed yourself!" Then he did care, and he began to fight. Not for his life – something told him that was futile – but for Flo. People would know that he'd loved her, that there had been nothing about her that could inspire this from her own husband. If he had to die, it would not look like a suicide!

He fought silently and as expected, futilely. She was barely even bothered by his puny strength, was behind him somehow, hanging onto both his wrists, pulling them wide apart as if it were her intention that he be crucified. Then her right hand slid further, seized his own and turned it up to a supinated position. The bayonet's grip was slapped into his open palm, and though he fought even harder, now that his left hand had been momentarily released, she forced his fingers closed on the wood and steel. Then she half-nelsoned him with her left arm, rendering that side of him helpless again.

"All right, then . . !" she hissed into his right ear. "On the count of three!"

He tried everything to rid himself of the bayonet, shake it off; but her hand, clamped over his own, kept it there as easily as he might with a three-year-old child.

"One . . !"

In desperation he threw his feet out from under him, forcing her to support all his weight. She merely back-pedaled several steps to the edge of the bed and sat with him in her lap.

"Two . . !"

"Oh God –" he managed to gasp. And then, before he was ready, before he had braced himself completely, she cheated him of his last few moments of life. The blade came round and though he struggled mightily to resist, his hand came with it. It was like trying to ward off, with your hand, a car that has jumped the curb and is pinning you to the side of a building. He screamed as the cold steel entered his flesh. Then he made another sound – *guHHH!* Then, between the white hot explosive pain of his heart being skewered and the knowledge that he was dead, there was no more room for sounds.

"I cheated just a bit on the count," 'Mary" said as she squirmed from in under him, careful not to get any blood on her Adidas shorts or top.

135

"Hope you don't mind." The professor's head lolled lifelessly to one side from where he'd collapsed backward onto the bed, and his wide-open, surprised eyes took a last, permanent snapshot of the room's wallpaper, framed between her long, lithe legs. If he did mind, he was too much of a gentleman to say anything.

Part III

Alliances, Hangman's Knots and Choices

"After loving you so much, can I forget you for
eternity, and have no other choice?"
-Robert Lowell (1973)

XXI

The first thing he saw when he entered the room was something he didn't want to see. It was her shoes, Mary's shoes, on the floor at the edge of the bed. One of the several pairs his father had bought her. They were side-by-side with his father's shoes, the ones he wore when he wasn't working, the penny loafers, and they sort of leaped out at Mark as soon as he entered the bedroom. Side-by-side, the way the two of them had been, on the bed, last night.

He hadn't wanted to focus on anything in particular, because there was too much about his parent's room that had changed, and seeing all the changes made it more difficult to feel his mother's presence and he needed to feel his mother's presence right now . . .

This was it, the final commitment. Once he took the gun he was destined to use it. Destined. He'd already tried to imagine changing his mind at the last minute, and the thing he absolutely could not imagine was sneaking back in here hang-dog fashion and putting the gun back, so he'd come into the room unfocused, half-closed eyes because that was the best way to feel someone's presence. And he'd found Mary's shoes.

Their presence was like an amulet, an African gris-gris, keeping his mother at bay. But not his father. As he stood there in the middle of the downstairs bedroom his father was all around him. On the never-dusted bureau was a whole stack of westerns by Louis L' Amour and Loren Estleman, and next to that an oversized volume titled OUTLAWS OF THE OLD WEST: A PHOTOGRAPHIC GUIDE. His father was an avid fan of any and every facet of the land beyond the Big River. His Big Plan, up until the accident, had been that Mark would land some kind of football-related job out in Arizona or Colorado after college, and that he would follow him there.

Next to the books were some bottles. Some aftershave from Jenny from two Christmases ago, still unopened; a five-year-old bottle of scotch, ditto; some Absorbine Junior, well used; and a bottle of Corn Huskers Skin Lotion, an item that had appeared there only since Mary had arrived.

Across the foot of the bed lay one of the summer undershirts he regularly slept in. Until today, it or one just like it had been left out on the couch all week.

Damn.

And on the table on the far side of the bed, a table that was always kept dust-free and neatly arranged were Mark's football trophies – those that wouldn't fit into the cabinet in the living room anyway – and his picture with his father's arm around him. This was going to kill his dad. If *(not if)* he did it, he would take a little bit of his father with him.

He glanced at the shoes again, and the undershirt *(No it won't!)* and moved toward the bureau to get the gun.

It was gone!

A quick search of the rest of the drawers plus the shelves in the closet had panic welling in him like a trapped animal. Then he was back again, groping frantically among the socks. It was gone! It had always been in that drawer – always! It had been there when he was ten, when he was fifteen . . ! Last week . . ! And now it was gone! A whole gamut of emotions ricocheted inside his skull, sometimes colliding with each other, but he was only vaguely aware of them: rage, confusion, despair . . . The mental equivalent of a hurt whimper . . . But mostly he just stood there, stunned, out on his feet, like a fighter who should go down but won't or a prisoner who has tunneled secretly for five years during the middle of each night and finally breaks through to what he thinks is freedom only to discover he's in another cell, with the warden right next to him, saying, "We've been wondering when you'd make it this far . . ."

Finally he was aware again, and the thing he settled on was a kind of hurt bewilderment. *He knows, or at least he suspects. Why didn't he at least say something?* "Geez, Dad, geez . . ." he said aloud to no one, to the ceiling with his head titled back. "The gun was for you!"

The gun was out of consideration for his father, because his father would be left with the mess. He'd thought it all out very carefully. Which was better, the .38, stuck far back inside his mouth - - clean, not much mess, but he'd heard of cops who'd tried to "eat the gun' and botched the job – or the twelve gauge he'd had since he was sixteen that was up in the closet right now *(he hoped)* and that his dad maybe hadn't thought of? Not so neat, but no chance of surviving either, if he did it the same way, with the barrel-end up against the roof of his mouth. A nauseous shudder ran through him and he knew it couldn't be the shotgun; if he put the shotgun in his mouth he'd gag and throw up. Billy Cassandra's dad had fixed that for him. That's the way he'd gone out, in the Cassandra's family room. There had been blood, brains and bone fragments, even pieces of his scalp, everywhere, splattered all over the ceiling and the wall behind him. And who had had to clean it up? Not the cops. Not the people with the body bag either. Billy had cleaned it up, because he was the oldest and his mom had tried to and gone right into hysterics. Billy. Today's chores for a young man of responsibility: clean your room, unload the dishwasher and scrape your father's brains off the family room wall. Billy used to be both a fun and funny guy; he wasn't either of those things anymore. He couldn't do that to his dad.

Let's face it, he couldn't do it to himself either.

With the .38 he'd even planned how he'd put a plastic bag over his head because he'd heard that was the "cleanest" way.

Why couldn't his father at least have said something? It would have to be the barn then, and the rope. Visions of his father taking him down off the rope, his neck elongated, his tongue bulging out, his dad's voice groaning, "Ohhh, Marky-boy! Why'd you do it, son?" over and over again, made his eyes fill with tears, and he knew he was losing his nerve, that maybe he would have to go on living as a cancer in the sides of both his father's *and* Jenny's lives forever.

"No!" he shouted. "I'm doing it!" But it was only words, and he wasn't at all sure anymore. He backed up, sat down heavily on the bed and put his face in his hand, feeling sorry for himself. Why did it have to be so hard? Why couldn't he have just walked in here, got the gun and not been reminded of all these things? He lay back crosswise on the bed, let his arm sprawl out sideways as he stared at the ceiling. The back of his hand brushed against a pillow, and a bitter sardonic smile thinned the corners of his mouth. And where was she? Where was she now? Where was that cool, comforting hand on his brow that he knew must be of his own invention but that he'd come to believe in these last few days?

He only whispered her name, so as not to embarrass the larger portion of him that had suddenly become such a realist. "Mother?" And she was there. Just like that.

("I'm here Mark. Your mother's here.")

He wasn't even startled, just . . . surprised. The same kind of eyebrows slightly raised surprise he might feel as the host on *Jeopardy* tells a contestant, "Sorry Mrs. Jones, China is not the world's leading consumer of rice." *Oh, you're here?* Then, almost as composed: *Wide awake, middle of the day and I'm not even dreaming. I'm crazier than I thought!* But on a deeper level almost desperate with relief, a little boy running to her arms, burying his face there for comfort.

("Come to me, Mark. BE with me. In the barn, tomorrow; it has to be the barn and the rope.")

"But –" This time fully aloud.

("He'll get over it, Mark. He has the other; he has Mary. I only have you.")

"But what about how slow it will be? With the gun I –"

("I'll be there with you; I'll hold your hand.")

And that, really, was the final persuasion. Not what she said but the fact that he was talking to her out loud now. He lay there, next to her, weighing all his options again. It came down to this: Life as Mark the Freak, Mark the Tumor, the original ain't-life-a-drag kid . . .or the warmth and acceptance he felt with her. Suddenly he felt very sure, very confident again.

"Maybe it won't be too bad." Then, with an air of the gallant. "Promise me you'll be there?"

("Come back to me. I'll have you all over again. I'll have you when you're eight.")

If part of him wondered at the fact that her response, all her responses, were just a little unfocused, a little abstracted, he either didn't notice or completely ignored that part. He focused instead on how alluring she sounded. How downright eager. He sighed heavily, a sound that was both wistful and resigned. It would be the barn, then, and the rope.

Had Mary possessed more curse words, stored within her memories of an era twelve decades past, "Mary" would have used them all. This could cost her. This could complicate things. She had taken the gun with her on her little jaunt to Saline only because she was fascinated with it, with its killing power, and not because she actually needed it. If it turned out that those special psychic emanations, so on a wave-length with her own, that she'd sensed coming from Haroldson had led her to a more secluded rendezvous, she would have used it, just to see what it could do. As a whim. How was she to know that Mark would pick today to muster the courage to finally steal it from his father's bureau? He was supposed to be at work till six!

Now, as she stood among some trees to the east of the house waiting for him to leave, she knew she had some "corrections" to make. First, she had to come up with a suitable explanation for her absence (although she was fairly sure Mark would keep that piece of information to himself, under the circumstances). Second, she had to put the gun back, because David would discover it gone soon enough, and even if he believed her denials – after questioning Mark first – it just might put enough suspicions into the boy's mind to make him want to stick around for a while. And last, she had to keep Mark convinced, through his "mother" that the barn and the rope were his salvation, and that would not be easy. It had taken all her powers of suggestion, once she'd come home and sensed his presence there, to make the dead woman seem real enough in broad daylight to convince him of that. It was an idea he resisted and feared.

("*Yes, Mark, yes,*") she willed the word/concept at him again. ("*The barn and the rope!*")

XXII

That evening, as a strangely subdued and quiet Mary sat next to him on the couch, reading a text on American government, David found himself feeling introspective. Carol's mid-morning visit to the churchyard formed the bulk of what he kept turning over and examining in his mind. That and the questions it raised anew concerning his feelings for Mary. He didn't believe for a minute that it was possible for a man to be in love, really in love, with two women at the same time. If he thought he was, then one or both of the relationships were suspect. And yet, when he was with Carol and away from Mary, the feeling was a lot like rediscovering a rare and wonderful book first read in your youth and marveling all over again at how perfectly it suits you. Or like the welling of pride and affection he used to get when Mark was introduced onto the playing field. Was that love? Was enormous admiration and affection for a woman love?

Question: Did Carol appeal to him on a more sensual level? Could he have made love to her? Answer: Yes, most definitely. Then what was it he felt for Mary? Next to him the girl in question gave her head a toss and brushed back a mass of autumn-red hair a man could get lost in. Then she looked up at him with knowing, loving-eyes, and it was almost as if they were on the same wave-length, the same erotic/romantic wave-length. God. What he felt for Mary was some kind of magic, a sensual, sexual spell, and that should have been enough. After all, any man who finds a woman who can affect him that way on a daily basis is a lucky man, isn't he? But it wasn't enough. Because tonight, with Mary so immersed in her book, so subdued, and with memory of his feelings when he'd spoken with Carol still fresh in his mind, he found himself questioning that relationship.

Another question: Did his feelings for Carol change; were they diminished in any way when he was with Mary? And what about the reverse, his feelings for Mary when he was with Carol? Even in his present mood his answer was in the form of a rationalization: respect, admiration, a lifelong affection were not the kinds of sentiments apt to suffer much with absence, whereas physical attraction and a direct line to the libido were by nature heavily dependent on the flesh. Even rationalized, he wasn't particularly fond of his answers.

Magic.

("She's dangerous, you know.")

So beautiful . . . Girl of his fantasies . . .

The caved-in bedroom wall, the feral light . . .

He was suddenly acutely aware for the first time in a week of just how preternatural the circumstances of their meeting and falling in love really were. Even if the "magic" consisted of nothing more than that, it was still heady stuff, romantic stuff. Time travel? Ethereal appearances from thin air? Maybe it was good to be examining it in a different, more objective light. Thinking that, he decided to broach the subject of dinner at Carol's tomorrow.

When he was done Mary was quiet for a while, looking at him through guarded eyes. Then, playing her Irish lilt and cadence to full effect, she said, "Would you enjoy seeing two grown women fight over you, then?"

"That won't happen," he assured her. "Carol promised – sort of."

She made a deprecatory sound - - *phhh* – with her lips and said, "It will! It just won't be overt! But the undercurrents will be vicious, David! The woman thinks I'm part o' some ruse, and that's not likely to change! I . . ." She turned her eyes away, back to her book. "I think you need to make a choice."

Her posture, the way she gripped her book and stared at it with a fixedness of purpose that threatened to burn a hole in the page told him it was useless to push things further right now. Sometimes a little time is the best argument anyway. Still, he felt exasperated, and when he got up a few minutes later he said, "We can't isolate ourselves. That's not the answer." Then he went upstairs to try the same proposal on Mark.

Mark kept looking at him funny – and not just now. The looks he

145

was receiving now reminded him that several times during supper he'd glanced up and caught his son staring at him in the same puzzled yet expectant way. The idea of the dinner tomorrow seemed to catch him by surprise, as if he had other plans, but he agreed to come so David didn't really think it had anything to do with that. Then it was back to the funny looks. He lingered, pretended he was studying the layout of the room. Actually there was little to study; it was as stark and devoid of personality since the accident as a new prison cell. All the sports pictures, the travel posters and the knick knacks were gone, stored, David knew, in the attic. "Is . . . something bothering you Mark? Is there something you want to talk about?"

Again the look, like he'd forgotten the boy's birthday. "I don't know, is there?"

Their eyes locked. After a while David said, "Not unless we communicate. I mean, you may have a problem, but I can't catch it through osmosis. I get the feeling you think I can read your mind, and I can't. Now . . . I ask again, is there something you want to talk to me about? Jenny? Your future? Something about me? He hesitated. "Something about Mary? Anything at all; I'm here for you."

Mark shook his head and his eyes dulled over. "I guess not. Maybe . . . Maybe some other time."

David studied him a few seconds longer then went downstairs. He'd been short with him. Maybe not in content, but in his unwillingness to play whatever game it was Mark wanted him to play. Sometimes you had to play games with people you loved, and David Rigert, NCAA Champ, had never been good at playing games.

Exactly one half-hour later, as David stood at the bathroom sink brushing his teeth, Mary crept up behind him, slipped her arms around his waist and molded her nightgown-clad body to his back. The crush of her breasts against his ribs was just beginning to make him feel plugged into something far more vital than himself when she murmured in his ear, "Whither thou goest, I will follow." His libido was only so immune, not to mention his male ego. They made love and it was just as extraordinary as the first time. Then, no longer quite so anxious to analyze and scrutinize his feelings for her, he went to sleep. Having just purchased some additional "vaginal insurance" against tomorrow's dinner at Carol's, "Mary" should have, too. But just then, her "two selves" heard someone calling.

As he lay listening to the telltale bed in the room below again this second night, it suddenly dawned on Mark why it was his father had taken the gun but hadn't voiced any of the concerns and suspicions that act would seem to imply. It was because subconsciously his father knew Mark would be better off dead, that both of them would be better off with him dead. Getting rid of the gun was merely token resistance to that horrendous (for his father) idea so that afterwards he might more easily assuage his conscience by telling himself he'd taken steps to guard against it. Proof of that was still leaning upright in his closet in the form of his twelve-gauge shotgun.

Mark didn't blame his father. He knew his father loved him; he just couldn't help him. He couldn't give Mark his arm back, his mother, or enough meaning in his life to make prolonging it a more attractive option than oblivion. He didn't blame his father . . . After all, the decision not to say anything was probably subconscious. He didn't blame him, but it hurt like hell just the same, to know your own father could be an accomplice, even if only by omission, to your death. The hurt was like a steel band just inside his ribs, and even though it had to be psychosomatic, it made him turn on his side and draw his knees up into a fetal position. "Mother?" he whispered into the night. "Mom?" Then his throat tightened closed, and the steel hand moved up and seized hold again, viciously, behind his breastbone as the first tears leaked from his eyes. His single hand clenched into a fist and pounded his mattress. Once. He hated to cry, and yet he'd cried twice in this single week. It added to his misery.

"Mom . . ? PLEASE?" he called out silently. All he wanted was some comfort, some yes, admit it – sympathy. Some compassion. It wasn't too much to ask, especially if he had to wait another day to –

("There, now, there . . . ") his mother's ethereal voice cut through his thoughts, and it had never been so alive with compassion. *("You're a fine boy, Mark. Fine and strong. FIGHT her, fight –")*

Then it was gone. And he'd never wanted it back so badly. Fight who? Her . . ? Who was she? "Mother?" he called out again, this time forgetting to whisper in his urgency.

Nothing. Silence. The silence of the soul. And even if she couldn't answer those questions, even if it meant nothing, the tenderness there, the way she seemed so much more vital . . .

"Mom?"

Silence.

Silence.

And then: (*"Come back to me. I'll have you all over again. I'll have you when you're eight."*) But it wasn't the same. He began to wonder if, with that sweeter, more caring voice, he'd finally really heard from his mother for the very first time. And if so, what was it she was trying to say?

XXIII

Carol Schemansky had bought practical when she'd finally moved back to Valor in '14. "Practical" meant a forty-five year-old brick ranch with less than twelve hundred square feet of floor space, no basement, and Runway Number Two off the county airport ending fifty feet from the edge of her backyard. It was only a mile from the café, though, and through countless hours of hard work and an eventual home improvement loan, "practical" would have been upgraded to "sharp" on any realtor's list by 2016; and had she chosen to list now, phrases like "real class" and "restored gem" would have deservingly found their way into the descriptive literature. But right now real estate values and what was practical were the farthest things from Carol's mind. It was a few minutes before two and she was wondering if she had time for one more quick trip to the bathroom before David, Mark . . . and Mary arrived.

If they arrived.

That last thought did it. Her lower abdomen cramped painfully and she hurried to the bathroom. When she came out a few minutes later with absolutely nothing left in her entire intestinal tract they were climbing out of David's truck. David and Mary. No Mark. Her heart did one last flip-flop, the word "D-day" kept swimming to the forefront of her mind, and she opened the door. "Hi! I'm glad you could make it!" she said. "Where's Mark?"

Just then Mark's car, a 2009 Camaro whose only concessions to its one-armed driver were a steering knob on the wheel and an automatic transmission, pulled up and parked alongside David's truck. David tilted his head in that direction and said, "You know eighteen year-olds and their independence." He looked as nervous as she felt. Mark looked awkward and unsure of himself too, as he got out of the car, the way a kid his age might look coming to his first funeral. The only one who didn't look nervous was Mary. She looked fairy-tale beautiful and like she was at home anywhere, so long as she held onto David's arm the way she did, so possessively . . .

Seeing the two of them together was like seeing David and Pamela all over again. There was that same aura of destiny; and as she showed them inside Carol knew she'd been wrong about her intestines; she could have made one last trip. Too late now.

"We're all French today, by the way," she said brightly as she seated them in the living room. *(Why did Mary have to sit so close to him? As if everything was already decided. Damn her!)* "We're having chicken in white wine sauce, stuffed artichokes and Dauphine potatoes for the main course, with French mushroom soup as an appetizer and orange-almond cake for dessert. So I hope everybody's hungry!"

"Sounds good. Smells good, too!" David offered.

"It sounds extravagant," Mary added. "You shouldn't have."

"Don't be silly. Besides, if I know these guys, most of their meals are probably straight from the can or the microwave, supplemented by massive amounts of peanut butter. They don't take the time to –"

"I cook," Mary cut in. It didn't really sound indignant or anything, but it cut through the life of the room and froze it into a separate five-second block of icy silence just the same.

"Well, yeah," Carol tried to recover. "For right now, but as a rule they –"

"And I intend to go right on cooking, though I'm sure nothing as fancy as all this. Still, I will see to it they have a hearty meal each day."

This time Carol fought the awkward, paralyzing silence that was ringing down on them, as if allowing it would be admitting defeat. She wanted to say, "You bitch. You antagonistic, possessive little bitch!" Instead, she said, "I see. So you're their cook, then. I was wondering what the arrangement was." And before Mary had time to respond, followed up with, "Would anyone care for a drink before dinner? David, I remembered how much you liked the Spumante we had at Christmas. Will that be okay for you too, Mary?" Then, turning immediately to Mark, "And I stocked up on A&W root beer, Mark. I even frosted a mug and have it sitting in the freezer. I'll go get it." As she left the room she noticed the beginnings of a smirk on Mark's face. He was on her side.

But when she came back a few minutes later he was dead, and she wasn't even surprised.

The idea had mushroomed in her mind, that he was dead, while she was pouring the root beer, starting with a tiny grain of absurdity then billowing out like hot gas after an explosion until it was a dread certainty. She didn't even drop the tray when she came back into the room and saw him, although the condition of his neck and face – all purplish and swollen, with his tongue sticking out – caused her to gasp out loud.

"What's wrong?" David asked, concern in his voice.

But when she turned in his direction it was anything but an expression of concern she saw there. It was near ecstasy, an excess of physical pleasure as Mary sat astride him, her dress hiked up and spread over his lap in a false effort to hide what they were doing. But she knew. Carol knew . . .

"Yes, what's wrong?" Mary's voice echoed. But her eyes, her tone, everything else about her, as she leered back over her shoulder at Carol, said, "Cook? I do much more than cook."

Then things shifted focus half-a-degree and everything was as it had been when Carol left. Mary sat next to David very primly on the couch. Mark was alive and frowning a puzzled frown. And David was looking even more concerned than his voice had sounded. Relief, blessed relief flooded Carol's veins, robbing her of all her strength. With it came a brand of shame as well, as if they all knew what she had seen and were repulsed by a mind that could imagine such things.

No! some inner voice protested. *It's not me!. It's* – And that is when she knew for sure that it was Mary. That revelation should have been solace piled upon relief; she was not crazy. Instead it frightened her, frightened her badly enough that she could not even look at the girl in question. She set the tray down on a coffee table, mumbled something about forgetting to turn off a burner and hoping she hadn't ruined the meal and rushed back into the kitchen.

What kind of woman was this Mary? What was she dealing with? Standing there in the middle of her kitchen Carol remembered the other "tricks" her mind had played on her that day she'd confronted Mary at David's house, and she shuddered. "Dangerous" was an understatement.

She thought of David. Of Mark. Could this . . . this modern-day witch (a dread thrill ran up and down her spine) play tricks with their minds, too? She seized upon the idea with a vengeance and drew from it what she needed. Yes! Yes, she could and had! That was her power over David! That was why someone as kind and as deep as he was could abandon what they had, what they had been building, for the lure of nothing more substantial than a pretty face and an inconceivable story about time travel! Well, she would fight it! She would convince him somehow that –

Convince him that what, he was under a spell? How receptive would any rational person be to that idea? She felt defeated again, but determined. How do you fight a witch? Or the red-haired-vixen equivalent of one?

First of all, you keep your guard up.

When she came back into the living room she handed out the drinks as if nothing of any consequence had happened. "If I'd burned the sauce it would have spoiled the whole meal," she lied. Actually, the "sauce" was not even a separately cooked item, it was a baste whose main ingredient, white wine, didn't burn so much as evaporate.

The final ten minutes before dinner were about as easy to live with as an audience's embarrassed and continued silence must be to a stand-up comic whose up on stage bombing, dying a little at a time. The weather, the Tigers' prospects for the first half of the season, and David's next landscaping job were all grasped at lamely, but they failed to get a firm grip on any of those topics and they all slipped away undeveloped, uninspired. Possibly so much tension in the air robbed it of some rare but vital gas needed for the prevention of discursive lethargy. It seemed that way.

The meal itself was better – at least the first half. They had the processes of eating and passing plates to occupy much of the dead air, and it must have been a welcome distraction because they ate heartily, wholly absorbed in their food. David even remarked several times how good everything was. Mary, of course, did not like that one bit. Carol could see it in the subtle tightening of her eyes and the way she chewed her food, and that lifted the latter's spirits enough for her to make one more brave attempt at meaningful conversation, which may or may not have been a good idea.

"What are your plans for the fall, Mark? Are you still going to school?"

Mark shrugged, swallowed the mouthful he'd been chewing on and said, "Guess not. School was just a way to keep playing ball, get looked at by the pros maybe. It wouldn't make sense now, and it costs a lot."

There was silence. Carol refused to bow to it. "But what about advertising? You always said you'd like to have your own ad agency someday – after the football. Now you just start a little earlier. And that takes schooling."

"I don't know. It doesn't seem that important anymore." He shot her a look that was part irritation, part entreaty. "Look. I'm just taking things one day at a time right now. You know what I mean?"

Carol thought she knew exactly what he meant; she understood that look, but she was trying so hard now. "It's just that" – then she was looking directly at Mary for some reason – "that Mark is so talented. You should read some of the papers he did in high school, see some of his artwork. He's really good. He'd be a natural for advertising, and surely you of all people can attest to what a huge role it plays these days, how it's changed things . . ."

Mary set her fork down and stared at her, pretending to be puzzled yet amused. "I – uh – hardly know how to answer that. I mean, from what frame of reference? You sound as if I should ha' some special insight into such changes, and I was just curious as to what you thought that might be."

Carol pressed her lips together. She recognized the corner she'd been backed into, so smoothly, so effortlessly, and she felt like crying out with frustration. And how much of that ease, how much of the whole conversation was merely another one of Mary's 'tricks'? "I'm . . . trying to give you the benefit of the doubt," she practically growled. "On the time travel."

The room grew absolutely quiet again. David and Mark sat paused in mid-chew.

"Oh. I see. And are you succeeding?"

"Not really."

Mary's eyes glittered. "Then, in a sense, I'm being patronized, is that it, Miss Schemansky?" It was a look of triumph only Carol could see from where she was sitting. "In a sense, you're still calling me a liar."

Carol was furious now, furious at the way it would look to someone who didn't know what was really happening. "In a sense," she said tersely, "yes. As a matter of fact, I'll go you one further. In a sense, Mary what-ever-your-name-is, I'm calling you a first class bitch."

Stunned then by the enormity of her words, she turned her eyes downward, not trusting them to look anywhere beyond the scope of her plate. She pretended to be focusing all her attention on the simple process of separating the meat from the bone on her uneaten chicken leg, and the silence hung on for several more seconds. Then David said, "Carol, for Christ's sake!"

But Mary, who was looking at her with eyes that didn't even have to be seen for their savage light to be felt, cut him off. "I want to go home, David. Take me home."

And Carol screamed, "It's not your home!"

"Your friend is clearly no' in her right mind," Mary went on calmly, as if by her composure she was shedding herself of all blame. "I sympathize with that, but I canno' sit here and be insulted this way. She is unbalanced. Surely you must have noticed how distracted she was in the living room with the drinks. How she –"

But she never finished, because that is when a vein in the chicken leg Carol was stripping – one of those red-blue strings of nauseous, slippery elastic present in poultry and fowl that we all try not to think about, try to pretend is just part of the meat – slithered and coiled its way from the meat itself onto her fork with a life and purpose all its own. And from there to the back of her hand. And finally, impossibly long now, round and round her wrist as if it were a headless, diminutive python. She jerked her hand away, made a guttural, *wuUHHH* sound. Then she screamed. By that time her fork was sailing across the room behind her.

David and Mark stared at her in amazement.

Mary's expression was more controlled, more like someone trying to read a sign from far away – focused and intense.

Carol looked at each of them, eyes wide. Then she looked down at her hand and plate. She was standing somehow, with no recollection of having risen to her feet. Nothing. No animated vein. But then, once the element of surprise was gone, she knew that. The knowing itself was enough to make it so. Did Mary know she was aware of that?

"Stop it!" she thundered, eyes fixed solely on Mary now with glaring hatred. "Just . . . stop it! I know it's you!" Then she was addressing Mark and David" "She makes you see things! Puts ideas in your head! She's probably done it to you, too; you just don't know it! Isn't that right, Miss . . . Miss Mary-Queen-of-the-Witches?" She was whirling back on Mary now, and there was infinite contempt and loathing in the way she assigned her that name. "Think about it, David. It's all just so 'magical,' isn't it? She appears from thin air, she's from time . . . you *believe* her . . . Because, after all, you saw it happen! But she's playing tricks with our minds, David! It's all some form of mind control!"

She glanced away from Mary, appealed to both males with her eyes, saw that David had gone white. Mark, too, was more pale than she'd ever seen him.

"I want to go home," Mary repeated, her voice deliberately low, calm and immutable. "She's a madwoman."

"Go!" Carol hissed. "There's a manhole cover out front and the sewer is right beneath!"

"Jesus, Carol . . !" David chided.

"I'll wait outside exactly one minute," Mary went on in the same even, no nonsense voice. "Then I'll stick my thumb out."

Now the man she loved looked from Mary to her then back at Mary again, who, as good as her word, was already up and on her way to the door. "I'll take you home," he said with a little more of himself in his voice, "but I want you to understand it's only because I can't allow you to hitchhike, Mary, and not because I think either one of you is right, here! You coulda' turned things in a whole different direction right from the word go – you know, when she asked you about 'changes' and advertising? – yet you chose confrontation."

Then he turned to Carol. "And you, Carol . . . what did you expect from this dinner? And no matter how much things didn't go as planned, you still over-reacted!" He looked at her in a sad, bemused kind of way that thrust at her heart. "You have more class than that and I know that . . ."

By the time he was finished, Mary was at the door. She paused there long enough to turn around and glare at Carol, not really even acknowledging that she'd heard what David said. It was the same kind of look a cat gets when it is on the inside looking out a window and a bird lights on a low-slung branch just beyond the sill. No, it was more personal. Carol found that she had to turn away from that gaze. Then she left, and David got up to follow. "Everything you see, everything you experience . . ." Carol called after him, desperate that he understand. "Look at it again, see if it's real! Is that too much to ask from somebody who's so ready to believe in something as crazy as time travel?"

He opened the front door, paused in the arch and turned around. For a hopeful half- second Carol thought by the expression he wore that she'd finally gotten all the way through to him. All he said, though, was, "I'll be careful." And, "Mark, are you coming? I think Carol needs some time alone to rest."

Mark was the only one still seated and she put a hand on his shoulder to keep him there. "That's exactly what I don't need!" she said, trying hard to keep her voice from breaking. "I mean, there's all this orange-almond cake for dessert, and if I was to be left alone . . ." There, she thought. Class. If that is what he saw in her, then it was suddenly very important that he see it now, leave her with that perception restored. But then he motioned her over with a tilt of his head and with his eyes. And when she was close enough so that he could speak in a low voice and possibly not be heard by his son, he said, "Look . . . I'm sorry for the way things turned out and for how bad you feel, but . . . the boy's only eighteen and impressionable, and you're not yourself. I, uh . . ." He turned his face away a few degrees, looked past her shoulder instead of at her eyes. ". . . hope you won't say or do anything he can't handle."

And that stung her so badly that the thing she left him with, the last thing she said before practically closing the door in his face, was, "How dare you!"

She would have cried if Mark hadn't been there. But he was there, still sitting, stiff and uncomfortable, at the ill-fated dinner table, and Carol was grateful for that, for the will and the reserve strength his presence forced her to summon. Because Carol hated to cry. She hated it and its implied loss of control, its implied helplessness, almost as much as the boy sitting over there waiting for her did. They had always been of like minds . . .

David's truck turned left off her street at the end of the block and disappeared, carrying David and Mary "home," and there was no longer any reason for her to hover at the door. Was it because she so desperately needed someone on her side then, especially Mark, that she clung there, momentarily paralyzed by the sudden and acute silence after the storm? Or was it simply that she sensed by the rigidity of his back how awkward and uncomfortable this must be for him? For both of them? Whichever, the stillness was the same kind of unhealthy suspension of sound that hangs in the air at a high class restaurant immediately after the waiter has dropped a whole tray of dishes and glassware, only this silence stretched on and on; and as she shifted her weight to take the first steps that would carry her across the room to his side, the floorboards beneath the rug creaked and groaned. The sound was magnified by the silence until it seemed as glaring an intrusion as a scream at High Mass.

She walked through the silence, took her place at the table and studied Mark's face. He pretended not to notice. "You said you liked the food . . ." she said, deciding that pretending nothing had happened was just plain stupid. "How about the live entertainment?"

He colored slightly but said nothing.

"Ringside seats?" she added hopefully. "That oughta be worth something."

The old Mark would have cracked a smile about then, no matter what. This one just sat there looking uncomfortable.

"Well?"

Finally, reluctantly, he said, "I . . . kept waiting for you to dump a plate of food on her head." His face was absolutely serious.

She gave that some thought; it actually had crossed her mind. "Would you have liked that?"

"I think so. I'm not sure."

Her reaction surprised even herself. First her heart leaped with gratitude that he was on her side. But that was short-lived, and in its place came a dawning realization, then anger. "This has been hard on you, too, hasn't it Mark?"

He looked away. There was a quick inhalation-exhalation of air, a voiceless explosive sigh. She recognized the sound. It was the sound of someone determined to show no weakness, no tears, fighting back emotions that are overwhelming. She knew that sound, and the anger turned to fury. Mark was the son she'd never had, the boy who could-have-been/would-have-been hers if only things had gone differently all those years ago, and suddenly she found herself imagining – no, wishing – she was some kind of comic strip hero, a female Popeye maybe, with anvil-sized fists capable of delivering a killer punch – *kaPOW!* – to Mary's chin that would send her skyrocketing to the moon. It was inane and ridiculous, she knew, yet she could imagine in fine detail how grimly satisfying it would feel. She hated the red-haired witch named Mary, not only for herself and for David but for an absolute certainty in her heart that the woman had played tricks with the boy's mind as well. All this in the second or two since he'd looked away and made the sound. And now she didn't know what to do. She wanted to hold him. Instead she laid a hand on his forearm, rested it there briefly, then pulled it away and said, "Do you remember the hospital, Mark? That first night?" And, without waiting for an answer, "You were delirious, I think. In shock. And you kept calling out for your mother . . ."

Now he turned back and there was a look in his eye that could have been something defensive; she wasn't sure. But it was too late now, she'd already committed and so she went on. "You needed to be held. You needed a mother." she paused. "The nurses, everybody, just stood there . . ." She paused again. "And I held you."

The words hung in the air between them like a love offering; to be accepted or rejected as the case may be. Carol had always known or sensed they were pivotal words, that to tell him would change their relationship, either for better or worse, forever. And yet she also sensed that the time was now, that within a very few days it wouldn't matter which way the admission pushed him because Mary would have gotten to him by then and reached a little deeper into her bag of tricks.

"That's how close we are," she went on when she decided she couldn't take the silence any longer. "So you can talk to me without being embarrassed. I mean, my God, you've just seen me make a complete fool of myself, so . . . is she playing 'tricks' with you, too?"

"I knew it was you," he answered after a long silence, although not to the question at hand. "I remember a lot about that night. Too much. And one of the things I remember is the smell of your perfume. I didn't recognize it then; I wasn't recognizing much of anything. But I did later on, and then I knew it was you." He paused then, deliberately. "I was even glad when you changed brands, 'cuz it always took me back to that night" – he gave a shake of his head that was more like a shudder – "so vividly."

Carol flinched, scarcely daring to breathe. In a voice just audible she said, "So it didn't help then – my holding you?"

He frowned, but even with the frown his face was inscrutable. "It wasn't my mother's perfume . . ."

Her face fell. She tried to hide the awful disappointment she felt, but he was looking directly at her and he saw. "But another reason I didn't like to smell it," he added quickly, "was it always brought an image of infinite kindness and compassion." His voice drifted off. "And then I would miss Mom." Then he made a visible effort to lighten the mood. "But that's you, too, I guess. All that compassion; it was coming from you and I sure as hell needed it then, so . . . yeah, it helped."

Through a tightness in her throat she said, "Compassion comes easy if you care about someone. It's still there, Mark. So don't starve yourself."

He shook his head. "Uh-uh. It's addictive; don't you know that? For me it's addictive. Even talking about it is addictive, like waving a candy bar in front of a chocolate freak. So let's get back to your problem; it's safer."

She didn't know quite what to make of that, the way he would open up, allow her to feel close, then shut her out again practically in the same breath. But his expression said, "Don't push it," so she said, "My problem is Mary. And for starters, I'd like to know whether you think she's from out of time."

He worked that over in his mind, and when he didn't' immediately scoff at the idea, Carol's heart skipped a beat. "Out of time? No. But she's not normal, either. She's got . . . something. 'Magic,' if you want to call it that, only I think its telepathy."

Carol leaned forward eagerly, expectantly. She didn't have to ask him to elaborate; that request was written on her face.

He told her about Wednesday then, about the time he'd spent in the kitchen with Mary.

Not everything, she sensed, but enough, including Mary's admission that she was "sensitive" to people's minds and the way she had demonstrated that sensitivity through her awareness of the Evans kids out on the road long before they were within actual hearing distance. It made Carol's heart do far more than just skip a beat. She found herself telling Mark about her own confrontation with "The Witch" even before she was sure that was wise; and it felt so good to have anything, *anything* that was even vaguely corroborative that she told him everything, including all she could remember of her own "visions" on that day, except for the one in which Mary and his father made love. And by the time she was done Mark wore the expression of someone away for the weekend who's just remembered they forgot to shut off the bath water they'd turned on right before they left. It was a frightened, queasy look, which he made every effort to hide; but it was as obvious as a blush.

"What?" Carol asked. "Mark, are you okay?"

He swallowed awkwardly. She could hear his throat click. "Uh . . . yeah. It's just that –" His eyes darted about the room. Suddenly he stood. "Look, I gotta go!"

She stared at him, open-mouthed. "What? Now? You're kidding! We're just getting somewhere! I finally find someone who –"

He started for the door. "I really don't feel that well . . ."

She was dancing along beside him, sideways, in a needy, puppy-dog kind of way she would normally have abhorred. "What, Mark? You said, 'It's just that – ' It's just that what? Tell me. Maybe I can fix it. I –" She grabbed his single arm. It was like his father's: wide and as hard as iron. "I know you're not sick."

He slowed down, although for a moment it seemed as if he might not. For a moment it seemed as if he would merely drag her along with him until she let go. He still wore a dazed, haunted expression. "I am too. Sicker than you know." He tapped a finger to the side of his head just in case she didn't catch his meaning. It wasn't necessary.

"Talking helps," Carol said, trying hard to sound less urgent. "And if something to do with Mary is bringing it to a head . . ."

"No. Thanks, but . . . no." He turned back toward the door and started moving again.

"Why?"

"Because I need to think! I need to be alone!"

Now she was trailing him again, out the front door and across the lawn to his Camaro, and grasping at straws. "Well . . . when can we talk some more? We need to talk, Mark. If she's as bad as I think she is –"

"Tomorrow. We'll talk tomorrow."

"When?" She watched him fumble with his keys, drop them, grab at them and drop them again, then try to insert the trunk key into the ignition. He was genuinely frightened by the things she'd told him – and he was leaving! She felt so helpless, and when he didn't answer, she said, "How about in the morning? Stop by the café on your way to school?"

He nodded his assent, and on impulse – because he looked so miserable sitting there and because she wanted him to know there was a bond between them now – she took his chin in her fingers, tipped his head so he couldn't avoid her eyes and said, "Be there or be square!" And then, "I love you, Mark. Whether you want me to or not."

He made a sound deep in his throat that might have been a groan, might have been a whimper, but was definitely something he'd wanted to keep inside; and she understood the sound, understood that it probably wasn't so very different from the groan of years irretrievably lost she'd wanted to make as she'd noticed for the first time as she gripped his chin that he had a man's set of whiskers now, a man's stubbly beard. Different voices, different lyrics in the mind . . . the same sad melody.

As she watched him back from the driveway she wondered if she'd done the right thing by not telling him about the first of today's little "Mary-induced" hallucinations, the one in which she'd seen him dead.

The drive home from Carol's was made in tight-lipped silence. It was almost as if both of them had to distance themselves physically as well as emotionally from the heat of the moment before trusting their mouths to say anything that wouldn't make matters worse. At least it was that way for David. He wasn't so sure about Mary – and, Jesus, that was it, wasn't it? After what had gone on at the dinner table and what Carol had said at the end ("Everything you see, everything you experience . . . question!") he wasn't sure about Mary anymore!

As he switched off the truck's engine, after having finally made it home through five solid miles of tension, he turned to her and said dryly, "Do you think it was the wine?"

It was supposed to relieve some of the tension, be funny, but it fell about as far short of the mark as his "life's a bitch" comment had a week ago; and all it made Mary do was turn away from him, bow her face and press her forehead to the passenger-side window. To the glass she said, "She's the one person who could steal you away from me."

It wasn't what he'd expected. Her whole "penitent" posture somehow just didn't jive with what he'd been feeling in the air between them on the way home. "She won't 'steal' me," he said quietly. "How I feel is how I feel, and you pretty much know how that is."

"How?" Her face was still toward the window, but it came up some.

"How?" He squirmed in his seat. Damn. Here he was pissed off at her, a little disappointed too, and she wanted him to – "Geez, Mary, I really don't feel like answering that right now. It's kind of hard to tell someone 'I love you' and still be P.O.'d at the same time."

Now she was back facing him. There was a pleased, almost triumphant look in her eyes that she tried to camouflage by cocking her head and saying, "P.O.'d?"

"Mad."

"Mad?" The head remained cocked, the eyes registering just the right amount of surprise.

"Yeah, mad. And don't pretend you don't know what for. Like I said there, you wanted a confrontation. You pushed for one."

Her face changed. Just like that. "So did she."

"Not really."

"What do you call all those horrible names she called me?" She turned red slowly. Her lower lip trembled, and he wasn't sure whether it was part of an act or not. All he knew was that she looked lovelier on the verge of tears than any other woman under the most perfect of conditions. Lovelier and more . . . "holdable." Funny, how strong the urge, the suggestion in his mind . . . Resisting it was like standing aloof with your hands in your pockets while a lost puppy cries at your feet. He could practically feel his arms reaching out to hold her.

"S-so you choose her then, over me?"

"That's another thing," he said with less conviction than he'd felt only moments ago. "You forced me to make a choice – in front of Carol! And that hurt her deeply! I don't ever want to be backed into a corner like that again!" He forced as much sarcasm and disgust in his voice as he could manage. "Leave her now or I'll hitchhike . . ! That's emotional blackmail!"

Then he folded. All she had to do was continue looking at him that way, with her woman/child's lower lip trembling, and say in a contrite voice, "But I love you so!" and he folded. He pulled her across the seat and held her and kissed and stroked her hair with all the sweet relief an addict must feel after taking his first hit of the day. "Don't you see?" he breathed into the carmine sea he loved to drown in. "It's not as cut-and-dried as you want to make it. I can't just abandon her because you came into my life; she's too good a friend! You want me to just close the door on that?"

He felt her stiffen in his arms. God.

"You don't understand," she said, starting to pull away. "That's exactly what love is – man-woman love. It's . . ." Her brow wrinkled. "It's exclusivity! Closing the door on any other possibilities is exactly what it's about! So the one love, the true love, can grow!"

Now she separated from him completely – so he could see her face, he thought. It was serious. Frightened. Brave. Mark would have called it a Joan of Arc face. "I need you to choose, David, once and for all. Exclusivity. And if you can't, I . . ." Add pain, around the eyes, plus a little more fear. "I don't think I should stay here. I think I should try to make it on my own." And suddenly he had an image, as vivid as the sun on a cloudless day, of her a year from now, ten years from now, with all the life gone from her eyes, everything but despair gone from her soul. Behind bars, kept isolated, in a mental institution. An orderly would enter the room every day, leer at her hungrily and say, "How's our time traveler today?" He shuddered, but not just with the horror of the scene, so real it was uncanny. In his mind another scene played as well:

Carol, standing at the dinner table, furious, shouting, "She makes you see things! Puts ideas in your head!"

The world and the sounds around him faded back in. He didn't know he'd been away. Mary was saying ". . . canno' make that choice? Is it me you want or her?"

And feeling the same loss of control, the same sick sense of inevitability the laid-off factory worker with a wife, three kids and a mortgage must feel as he signs papers on the new Corvette he's just got to have, he said, "I'm here, aren't I? With you?" But his voice was weak.

Shortly after that, almost as soon as they got inside, Mary asked if they could spend the rest of the afternoon and evening in Ann Arbor. They could leave Mark a note, she said. It was as if she sensed all the doubts and fears that were building in his mind and deliberately chose the scene of what was possibly their most romantic hours together to offset them. At least it seemed that way to David's newly acquired paranoia. And to some degree it worked. The brief, almost sickening moments when he would become flushed with a feverish dread, the moments when the nightmare possibility that Carol was right seemed most real, occurred with less and less frequency as the evening wore on. The memories that the place held, the way she held his hand . . . the touchingly self-conscious way she even attempted an "Irish" joke of her own to match his 239 bean story from the last time they'd been there . . . All of it combined to lull him into a sense of security, then enchantment, all over again.

They walked with their arms around each other.

They laughed at the antics of small children and cooed at babies.

They kissed again, on State Street.

But none of it, none of it, prevented him from dreaming that night that as they kissed, she changed. That as her head tipped back and her eyelids dropped closed in dreamy passion, she grew fangs. That when she opened those lids again, the eyes beneath them were yellow, reptilian and alien. Or that he tried to kiss her again anyway – was compelled to – and that she tore his throat out as a reward.

XXIV

"Mary" hated the woman, Carol, hated her with an intensity that made her muscles crawl and her belly pull up tight against her ribs the way it did when she was about to spring on unsuspecting prey. Even lying here in bed it did that to her, the hate. Didn't she know? After the visions she'd given her, didn't the Carol-bitch know she could easily tear her limb from limb? Not just choke the life from her but keep on squeezing 'till her eyeballs popped and "Mary's" fingers burst through the soft, putrid skin of her throat and finally met, as if they were closing around soft mud? She would pluck off and feed the woman pieces of her own anatomy! She would –

She would do nothing. Not yet. Killing the Carol-bitch would arouse too much suspicion, be counter-productive, and even though her limbs and hands throbbed with the need, with the power to do so, she would have to wait. Her last kill, the Professor-male, was done on Saturday; this was only Sunday night. She could wait if she had to.

Bitch.

She liked the sound of the word, which she'd heard, now, for the second time today, the first time straight from her enemy's mouth. It was a good word, one of the few in this alien tongue, in that there was something expletive to its very sound, something venomous that allowed it to hold and transport concentrated doses of loathing, hatred and disgust. *Carol-woman, you bitch, David is doubting me thanks to you and for that you will pay!* Her mind grooved on that for a while, on the payback, then it moved on to other things.

David. He'd made no move on his own last night that might have indicated a desire to mate again, and she'd done nothing to force the issue, being unsure in her present dark mood that she would be able to handle a possible rebuff. But the physical pleasure this new, softer body allowed her to feel through his administrations exceeded tenfold anything she'd experienced before she'd been "changed." And further, she could ill afford to miss an opportunity for impregnation; it was the bedrock of her imperative. On her own world, in her old form, she might have clawed the eyes or even killed any male denying her either of those things, especially one weaker than herself. And now? And now, if her hate were an angry sea, then David, who lay sleeping next to her, had just been sucked by the undertow from the shallows into the deep.

And what of Mary? Her other self was a loathsome thing, too, certainly worthy of her hate. Especially now – now that her miserable excess of compassion had alerted Mark last time she, "Mary," had "spoken" to him through his mother. She, too, would be made to suffer. She –

Mark.

Mark.

Concentrate on the task at hand. First things first. Mark she did not hate. Mark she could not afford to hate, wouldn't allow herself to hate. Mark she wanted dead in a most benevolent way. You couldn't play "mother" with hate in your mind. You couldn't re-convince a boy that his death was in his own best interests if the "suggestions," the intrusive mind-words and images, were painted upon a screen of malevolence. Calm yourself, she thought. Imagine that you care. But not too much, because that might open a way for Mary once again.

("Mark . . ?") She called out with her mind, focusing on that other consciousness she "heard" still awake in the room directly above her. *("Mark, come back to me! While you still can! While there's still time!")* She coupled that with an image of Pamela, as she knew her to be from photographs, standing in a cold, desolate place, an airless, dead place. His mother was crying, silently. *("Please don't abandon me! Don't change your mind!")* The spectral image slowly swept a hand to encompass the almost lunar landscape around her, the black empty sky. *("This is death. Death is loneliness, the void . . . I would not be here, I would not truly be dead with you beside me, INSIDE me, in my womb . . !")* Then the familiar refrain: *("Come back to me, Mark. I'll have you all over again. I don't mind. I'll have you when you're eight!)*

She followed this up with a whole barrage of images, visions aimed directly at his fears and though her psychic "hearing" was limited to general impressions, moods, rather than more literal accessing of his specific thoughts, she knew that some of the scenes suggested to his confused mind were devastating. He saw himself again, five years hence. As with the first time she'd given him this particular glimpse at the future, he was filthy, disheveled. But this time something new was added. This time there were other people around – a party of some sort, with his father and Mary at the center. The "beautiful people." The perfect couple. As he enters the room all eyes turn toward him, and his father blushes with shame.

He sees Jenny (merely a female to "Mary;" she senses strong affection for a specific female and his own mind fills in the rest). She is with another boy/man, and she is laughing, having a wonderful time. He is strong, able, and he is holding her, lifting her, whirling her about with his two good arms. The look on her face is that of the earthbound suddenly able to fly . . .

He sees his father's hands. He sees the rest of him, too, but mostly his hands. They are removing one picture, one photograph of his mother after another – from the walls, from his desk, even from Mark's own bureau – and packing them into a box. The box is carried down into the basement and deposited on a mildewed, cobwebbed shelf. And when he rushes to its rescue, snatches up the top photo, it is fading. All the pictures are fading. Not as a whole, as with age, just . . . his mother. She is a transparent ghost now. Soon she will be gone completely. (*"While there's still time!"*) The words echo in his mind. Then: (*"I thought you were coming. I thought I would have you back,*) so sad, so hauntingly disappointed . . .

She worked on him. She worked on him, and she knew he was young, much too young to be able to separate his sadness and self-pity from the visions. She gambled on the fact that by his very youth he would be unable to step outside himself and assess what he saw, felt and thought, with any degree of objectivity. The young were masters of self-indulgent rationalization; a single week's reading, television and dredging through that "other" Mary's memories had taught her that much, and for that reason her visions might still fool him despite what

Carol undoubtedly had said, whereas with the woman that degree of vulnerability was a thing of the past.

The boy above her sobbed, and though "Mary" could not hear it as sound, she was aware, and she smiled.

She worked on him through the night.

("Fading...")

("Before it's too late...!")

(". . .not dead with you beside me.")

It was enough to drive a teetering mind over the edge.

X X V

He dreamed of barns, heaven, and his mother. And of cold, alien landscapes not of this world and of other things that *were* . . . but shouldn't be. But the ringing fit with none of these thing, so he woke up. Mark's first thought after opening his eyes was a sardonic one: Tired. Slept badly. My last day on Earth and I'll be –

Then it hit him – HIS LAST DAY ON EARTH! – and his heart, stomach, everything inside him lurched then reverberated with a high-energy resonance as if it, all of it, were a single string on some monster-guitar and someone had just plucked it mightily. *THRUMMM.*

The ringing continued, but during the first half-minute or so as the initial adrenaline-rush still gripped his body it no longer registered. Then he shut off his alarm. He must have set it last night out of force of habit. Before he decided. Before he'd known that to save a life, you had to take one: your own.

The clock said six-thirty. Monday morning. Final exams week. In an hour and a half he could either be sitting down for a two-hour physics exam, for which he was hopelessly unprepared, or he could be swinging at the end of a rope. Funny. Somehow thinking about it that way helped. Or it could, if he worked it right. All he had to do was try and imagine what it would be like for him any other time, to walk into that classroom knowing full well that the problems on the stapled test papers he'd be handed would seem just as indecipherable, just as intimidating as had they been written in Greek. Yeah, as the guy from SNL used to say, "That's the ticket." Don't think. Don't think about it. Think about all the shit things you'll no longer have to deal with, like –

Should he have breakfast? He should have a really sweet last breakfast of all the things he'd pig out on if it wasn't for the cost, calories and his father's concern over fat intake: about a pound of bacon, ten eggs, fifteen slices of buttered toast dipped in hot chocolate . . .

Suddenly he felt sick. He'd puke it all up. Either right before he jumped from the platform or right after, as he was hanging there slowly strangling. He'd end up choking on his own vomit. Jesus Christ. No breakfast. No more thoughts like that, either; just do it, do it, do it, do –

Calm yourself. Be mechanical. Be a machine; he'd always been so good at being a machine during conditioning drills – the wind-sprits and laps in football, the line sprints and push-ups in wrestling . . . Shutting down his mind . . .

He got through dressing, washing, combing and getting himself downstairs that way, like a machine, without allowing himself to once think about it. But then he had to, when he wrote the note, because –

Dear Dad,
I love you. I've gone to be with Mom. Don't worry there is life after death. I know it, she talks to me
I love you,
Mark

– his dad at least deserved a note; and all he could see as he was writing it was himself through his father's eyes as the latter took him down off the rope. And all he could think about was how his dad would feel, his anguish, if he himself was wrong and his father really didn't believe he was better off dead. The more he thought about it the more tragic it all seemed and the sorrier he felt both for his dad and for himself. Then it was mostly for himself, in spades, under the auspices of sadness for his father, and that was the crack that allowed the damn to break. He stood there, miserable, crying, with not even enough self-pride to try and put a damper on it, and with no one there or anywhere who really gave a damn or understood. Except his mother.

Instinctively he stumbled for her room, for the bed where she used to be at this hour of the morning – and found Mary there, next to his father's place, still asleep.

He'd forgotten about her, about the fact that she would still be there even after his father had gone to work. It was a bitter, bitter shock – insult to injury, really. But it stopped him crying, dried it right up and gave him his resolve back so that he turned around, marched through the kitchen, out the back door and toward the barn – and destiny – with no further need for self-pity. But halfway there he turned around and came back. He'd forgotten his varsity jacket. He'd thought it all through last night and decided both for his father's sake and his own that he didn't want to be up there a whole day, maybe, before someone thought to look in the barn. And yet, because of Mary being there, because his father sometimes stopped home in the middle of the day for supplies . . . and because the school checked up on student absences with a vengeance, he could not wait till later in the day. He would hang the jacket on the barn door facing the house, and in June that would be a sign.

On his second trip out he started getting scared again, started thinking too much about the fact that in a few minutes he'd be dead; and that is when the visions came – again – so real, so strong, of his mother, fading, fading . . . calling out to him. Of Jenny with someone else. All of them, plus some new ones. He didn't even question their coincidence or their power. In fact, he welcomed them. And entered the barn.

XXVI

The man with the gray-blond bush for a beard and the enormous grin said, "Carol-girl, I'd like to order some of that sausage-gravy and biscuits I had Saturday now. Kinda as a dessert . . ?" The man's name was Bill Hedlund, but all the other truckers called him "Big Bill," and lately he was more and more deserving of that title. At fifty-seven and just a tad under six-one, he weighed in the neighborhood of 300 pounds and looked like an older, puffed- out version of Grizzly Adams.

"Uh-uh, I don't think so," Carol shot back at him. Then she glanced at the clock above the door, a bundle of nerves. It was eight-fifteen.

"Why?"

"'Because . . . what's that on your plate?"

(Where was he? Where was Mark? School would have started by now . . .)

Big Bill glanced down at the yellow smear there then back up at Carol and said, "Nothin'. It's Empty."

"What *was* on it?"

(He said he'd stop in. It wasn't like him to –)

"Some eggs, pancakes . . . What's that got to do with the price of milk?"

"It's empty because you ate it, all of it, a big, full breakfast; and any more would just be feeding those chest pains Charlie told me about last time she was in." "Charlie," whose real name was Charlene, was Bill's wife, and she rode with him on more than half his runs now that their boys were both married and lived halfway across the country.

Big Bill turned red. He was a kind-spirited man, the kind who usually saw it as his duty whenever he walked into the place to see he got everybody smiling. But now he felt backed into a corner. "A man ought to be able to decide for hisself how much he eats and when . . ." he mumbled through his beard. "Specially at a restaurant." It was the quietness with which he said it that got everybody's attention. Big Bill boomed his words same as he boomed his laugh, and hearing the man mutter under his breath that way got everybody around him real still. The hush spread like a stink until the only sound in the place was the clatter of dishes from Janet, back in the kitchen. "Just bring me the order," he said.

"I'd rather not." Now all the tension and worry she'd been feeling inside since the clock had first crept past seven-thirty and Mark still hadn't shown joined forces with what was in the air between her and Big Bill and created a pressure behind her breastbones that could have gone either way, up into her throat so that she was choking on her emotion or down into her belly in the form of nervous indigestion. She opted for the latter, willing it downward; she needed her voice.

Bill took a sip of coffee, slow, deliberate, then set the cup down. He squinted up at her, still red. "I been a loyal customer here for how long? Prit-near five years, I think. Seems like that oughta be worth somethin'." He paused. "If it ain't, then . . . I just don't know if I can keep comin' here!"

Her move. Should she hang tough or should she fold? And all the while, a separate part of her was stuck on Mark, telling her something-wrong-something-wrong-something-WRONG-something –

The guy was killing himself, eating this way. And suddenly she knew what she had to do. Killing himself. *Killing* himself. She fought back the panic. "You know what, Bill?" she said in a voice that almost cracked. "I guess it really doesn't matter. Because I'm gonna lose you anyway – from a heart attack –you keep eating the way you do! And because it doesn't matter, I'll *get* you your grease-laden, artery-clogging sausage-gravy on biscuits!" She turned then and stalked into the kitchen. But the first thing she went for once she got there wasn't the skillet, it was her cell phone, still in her purse in her office. It took her several minutes of waiting on hold before she was finally switched through to the attendance desk from Valor High School's main office. "Valor High School. Attendance," a female voice answered.

"Hello," Carol said, thinking fast. "I was wondering if you could tell me whether Mark Rigert – that's R-I-G-E-R-T, a senior – has made it in to school yet."

"Your name?"

Her heart jumped. But only once. "Carol Schemansky. I'm his aunt. I was visiting, and it was my responsibility to drive him today but I overslept. And when I woke up he was gone, so I –"

"Just a moment please."

The seconds dragged by, affording her time to think of half a dozen ways they might catch her in the lie, Mark was so well known at Valor. But the thing that made her sweat most had nothing to do with how embarrassed she would feel, it had to do with a dread certainty she would then be refused an answer. And she had to have an answer.

Then the girl was back on the line, saying, "Mark was not in his first hour class," and Carol knew what real worry was.

"... every effort to contact some member of the student's household if an unarranged absence extends past the second hour, so in the interests of time we ask that . . ." The voice droned on, mechanically, as if the speaker was reading from a prepared script, and Carol caught neither the beginning nor the end; she only caught the sound. And when the sound was done, she said, "Thank you. Good bye."

Not at school. And she knew final exams were going on because Janet's only daughter was also a senior and Janet had mentioned that just the other day. The worry turned sour in her stomach, became something she couldn't live with. She had to know.

First she dialed both David and Mark's phones and let each ring an even dozen times. No answer in either case. Then she heated some sausage-gravy in a skillet, some biscuits in the microwave, and got Big Bill's order together. Then she told Janet she'd be back in an hour, took the food out to Bill, who was looking about as sheepish now as a man can look behind a bushel-basket-size beard, and said, "Here. I'll serve it to you, if I have to. But nobody says I have to stick around and watch you eat it, because . . . because I care about you and I care about poor Charlene!" Then she stalked out the door.

Poor Bill stared after her in amazement. Then he reacted in shades. Pink before the door swung shut. Beet-red by the time she got to her car. Crimson by the time she pulled out into traffic on 223. The place stayed silent for a long, long while after that. Big Bill pushed around the biscuits in his gravy and studied the effect – studied it hard, as if properly arranged, those biscuits might spell out a message that could save his life. But he didn't eat any of them. Then he let his fork drop right onto his plate, so that the handle got all wet with gravy. Deliberately. "Shhhit," he said, making the word sound almost thoughtful. By the time he got his bill paid moments later he'd toned down to a hot pink again.

XXVII

David couldn't get a clear picture in his head of how the job should look when he was done. He couldn't, in fact, even remember what had been glimpsed vaguely in his mind's eye when he'd estimated the price. He'd made sketches at the time, but they seemed as mute and foreign to him now as the menu at a French restaurant. They no longer spoke to him or grabbed his imagination, nor did the land itself, which was extremely unusual – doubly so considering the fact that this particular plot of land climbed at a steep twenty-percent grade all the way to a wealthy man's house. He loved working with sloped ground; there was so much you could do with it, especially when cost was not a problem. But today he looked at the land and drew a blank.

Well, not exactly a blank. He saw things, remembered things . . . they just had nothing to do with the landscaping business. He remembered his dream last night, in which Mary had turned savage. He remembered everything Carol had ever said to him. He remembered hearing Mark moan in his sleep this morning, around six, and the peculiar way his son had stared at him last night, for the second night in a row, when he thought his father wasn't looking; and felt the same exact sense of crippling panic a man who has just bet his entire life savings on a single race must feel as the announcement goes out that all bets are now final and the race track windows are closed: Helpless. Impotent. Swept along toward the falls . . .

What if he'd thrown it all away? What if Carol was right? And even is she wasn't, he was hurting her and hurting Mark, anyway. Was it worth it? Was it fair? How much were they hurting, and how much of someone else's pain, especially his son's, could he afford to pay? With Carol that was a complicated question, with a lot of variables. But with

Mark it shouldn't be. With Mark the betting window was still open, and maybe he could cut a deal. A man should be able to talk with his son about anything; all he has to be willing to do is play the other guy's game. He resolved then and there to meet Mark for lunch; the kids only went half-days during finals week. That decision alone made him feel more optimistic, more relieved somehow than he'd felt in days. They would talk things out. He would park next to Mark's Camaro in the school lot, get there by ten-thirty so there was no possible way he could miss the boy.

He went back to work then on dismembering by chainsaw a diseased elm he'd already felled, thankful that his temporary employer at the top of the hill had no way of knowing he didn't have the slightest idea what he would do with the yard beyond that. The next time he looked at his watch it was only eight-thirty.

XXVIII

He couldn't tie the rope! He couldn't tie . . . the fucking . . . *rope!* It was so unfair! Even in dying his deformity reached out and robbed him of his dignity, turned the act itself into something pathetic and absurd! *He* was pathetic and absurd, beside himself with frustration and rage! It spilled out in animal sounds, little whimpers, groans and snarls that were disgusting and that he wanted to stop but could not. Mad dogs sounded the way he did now, must feel the way he did now! He wanted to scream and bang his head against a wall and keep on banging and screaming until he was dead! But he could not; Mary might hear him and interfere, so he had to dissolve inside, with nothing more clamorous than a groan.

It had been that way for more than an hour when it suddenly occurred to Mark to use his feet. He'd been trying to tie the hangman's noose using his knees to hold and align the up-and-down curves of the inch-thick rope while, with his single hand, he did the wraps. But the rope's very thickness made it stiff and hard to bend without generating a strong torque on the parts higher up that were supposed to be kept in line. When he gripped it between his knees he couldn't hold it strongly enough – and when knelt on it on the floor, the floor itself, plus his own legs, got in the way of the wrapping. But with his feet . . .

He finally got it tied by clamping it between his bare right foot and the skin on the inside muscular bulge of his left calf. He found he could apply more pressure that way than between his knees and still have clearance on all sides to do the wraps. Next he had to re-adjust the other end of the rope where it was tied to a horizontal beam which decades ago had helped support a second floor, a "mow," across the north half of the barn. He had to climb up on top of the John Deere to do that, just as he had when he'd adjusted it the first time in order to give himself slack to fashion the noose. It had to be just right, so that when he jumped his feet couldn't touch the ground, and yet not so high that his father couldn't easily reach him, and here is where he ran into another problem. The rope's original purpose was to support and operate a hay-fork, a suspended iron claw somewhat like the four-taloned foot of a giant eagle that grasped, penetrated, lifted and transferred kitchen table-sized clumps of loose hay from wagon to mow in a time before the stuff was baled. It could lift and deposit the hay elsewhere because its rope ran up and through a strong wooden pulley at the barn's apex before coming down again to be hitched to a team of horses or in later years to a tractor; and the pulley itself was then able to be moved back and forth the length of the barn by means of a sliding metal track, from which it was suspended. Although the hay-fork had long ago been taken off, the rope and the pulley itself still worked freely and smoothly. But it had never been moved on its sliding track from the position it was in now. Not once in Mark's entire lifetime. And that position was far enough away from the Deere, the only thing left in the skeletal barn to jump off of, that the length of rope required to reach the tractor would also be long enough so that, when he jumped and swung, his feet would hit the ground. He had three choices.

He could try to break free the grip of two decades of rust and slide the whole contraption closer, something both he and Jenny pulling together had failed to do as recently as last summer when he'd still had two arms, fun in his heart, and a desire to build her a swing . . .

He could try to find something high enough to stand on and jump off of that could be carried or dragged to a spot closer beneath the pulley – but he knew no such item existed within the shell of the barn or any closer than the house, and it was probably between eight and eight-thirty by now. Mary would be up. He'd have a tough enough time even explaining his presence (*although by now she might have looked out and seen his car; damn, he should have hid the car*) let alone why he was sneaking a kitchen chair out the back door . . .

He could move the tractor. It would make noise and Mary might come out and check, but it still seemed the best of the three choices. Number one was impossible, and just to make sure, he yanked and

179

pulled on the rope as hard as possible in the direction of the tractor. The second choice didn't appeal to him because it carried with it the greatest risk of attracting Mary's interference – and of his losing his nerve. If he left the barn today, still alive . . .

He would go off the tractor. He'd always envisioned it that way anyway, and last night those visions had seemed particularly clear. It seemed right, more like the completion of a cycle, somehow. It had always been part of the problem, it and the chipper working together to –

First he got the rope with the noose swinging back and forth, back and forth, in as wide an arc as possible. Then he got the keys from their shadowed nail, high up on a beam. Next he climbed up onto the John Deere's seat, depressed the clutch and turned the big beast's engine over. It started first try; it always did, and the sound – ornery, powerful and malevolent – turned his insides to water and dropped him smack, dab into the terror and anguish of that day eight months ago once again. He gulped a single, enormous gulp of air, as if it were going to be a very long time before he would breathe again, and let out the clutch.

It took a great deal of maneuvering in the limited space, back and forth, back and forth, to get the Deere close enough. When it was accomplished he shut off the engine, let out his air (he'd been holding his breath the entire time) and listened. The wind soughed and moaned its way through the cracks and gaps in the walls, and the loneliness of the sound frightened him. Would death be that lonely?

No! Mother –

Then it occurred to him that if Mary had heard the noise and came to investigate, it would be much better to meet her with a lie before she stepped into the barn and saw the hangman's noose. But he was so frightened, suddenly, by what he was about to do, that he couldn't move. The time was upon him; his hour was at hand. And when he did move, it was to climb onto the front end of the tractor and reach far out for the rope as it swung back in his direction with just enough momentum left to carry it within his reach. He took it in his hand, stared at it awhile in a contemplative sort of way, then put the noose-end around his neck and cinched it up tight.

His heart was beating rapidly.

Would it be cold in the grave? He didn't want to be cold.

"Mother...?" he said aloud.

And, *"I'm here. I'm here with you. Jump. Jump into ME!"*

His insides were so watery. He hoped he didn't shit his pants while he was hanging there, the way he had when he was caught in the chipper. Once was enough.

That helped. That brought is all back clear. Relive that day and it would be easy to –

Suddenly it was as if all the sadness, all the self-pity and despair he'd been feeling for the past eight months came back on him in cumulative form so that the weight of it was more than a person could bear and still remain alive. He knew that. He could see that, now, *("So alone . . . Without hope . . . Waste, such a waste . . !")* that death was the only answer. And he stepped up to the edge.

XXIX

The thing for Carol that made it seem most like a nightmare – even more so than the mad frantic glimpses she had of Mark hanging there – was the way "Mary" leaped onto the tractor. The kind of effortless, weightless jump a cat makes onto a high windowsill, the kind you can't help but replay in your mind in slow motion because it's so amazing. Only with "Mary," with a human being leaping that way, it went way beyond amazing and approached the realm of the surreal and the terrifying.

Surreal. Things had been that way ever since she'd left the café – a sense of unreality, of sure and imminent doom so strong that by the time she was a half-mile onto Forrester she was flying its graveled surface at better than sixty miles an hour. And then she got there and heard the sound of the tractor out in the barn at a time of day when she should be hearing nothing, and that was surreal too, because it turned her face toward the jacket and somehow – maybe by the way her pulse leapt – she recognized it in her heart for what it was – a death flag.

The time it took her to cover the fifty yards between her car and the door where the jacket hung was nonexistent, a blank. She was at her car, then she was at the barn's south door, pausing there to finger the fabric of something that was both familiar and cruel, even merciless in what it represented. Then she stepped inside, into the stuff of which nightmares are made. It came at her like falling through a bad movie – sights, sounds, impressions bombarding her at a run-amuck speed that was almost kaleidoscopic in its effect:

Mark wearing a mask of absolute pain and despair, allowing himself to deliberately lean forward off balance, over the tractor's edge. There was a noose around his neck, and by expression and intent he may as well already have been dead.

"Mary," off to the left and behind him, just inside the larger, sliding doors on the west wall, where he could not possibly see her. She is shouting, "No! She is making you jump! She –the bad part of M –" And that is good, a Godsend, because Carol's own voice is momentarily frozen in her throat by what she sees, and this other, strangely truncated, choked-off and unfinished voice is enough to make him fight to regain his balance, as if he has been pulled from a trance.

And then, just as it seems he will win his fight for equilibrium, this same, wild-eyed "Mary" snarls like an animal, like there is a leopard or a lion caught beneath her skin, and she leaps – and the leap . . ! The leap . . ! The tractor is close to seven feet high across its front end, the part that on a car would be called the "hood." The snarling beast-woman covers the vertical distance, plus at least fifteen more in a horizontal direction, in a single enormous jump, and lands on top of the tractor without even being forced into a crouch! She lands standing up, the way a puppet on a string might land after so ridiculous and inhuman a jump, but certainly no living, breathing human being . . ! She is behind Mark now, on the tractor, snarling and showing her teeth. And then she pushes him off!

Two thoughts pass through Carol's mind like cognitive heat lightning: One, that Mark is as good as dead, that even if the sudden and abrupt snap as his fall is broken by the noose doesn't kill him instantly, he is far too heavy for her to ever get off the rope in time. And second, that she, too, is as good as dead. "Mary's" leap is proof of that – that she has no chance at all against this . . . this *thing* that is a monster in human form. She will be torn to pieces. And yet it never even occurs to Carol to run, any more than it would if Mark were her own, any more than if he were eight, instead of eighteen, and her own. "No!" She cries, and rushes forward.

Slowly, slowly, Mark reaches the "end of his rope" . . . and does not die. The amount of actual drop is small, less than two feet, and the snap is not as violent as Carol imagined it would be. But still it is weighty, oh so very weighty, and any normal young man would have surely died. But Mark's football and wrestling days, the thousands upon thousands of neck-bridges, have served him well. He struggles, kicks, then, still in slow motion, reaches above the noose, grasps the rope with his only hand and pulls. It is obvious he wants to live now, that he whose purpose for being there was to take his own life will not abide by murder.

Carol is almost under him now. His thrashing, bicycling feet are only eighteen inches above the ground, his thighs even with her own chest if she crouches. If she can just get in close and hug and lift –

"Mark! Stop kicking! I'm going to lift you up-*PUHHH!*

Abruptly she is slammed against the west wall ten feet away, so hard and fast she doesn't even realize she's been hit. Till "Mary" rises into her blurred, diminished field of vision like the undead from their grave. Then the still-functioning portion of Carol's brain, the only part not silently screaming for air because all of that precious commodity has been driven from her lungs, realizes the bitch-monster is merely picking herself up from the floor after having delivered a full-body block that would have done the best offensive guard – ever – proud. Darkness frames the edges of what she sees and eliminates her peripheral vision altogether, because she is on the verge of blacking out. She fights it.

"I'm going to tear off your woman-parts and feed them to you!" "Mary" rasps in a snarly, malefic voice that is in itself a defilement, and draws back her hands, fingers bent into claws.

Something bumps the beast-woman from behind. Just a bump. She has forgotten, in her rage, about Mark, that Mark no longer wants to die. And Mark has been busy. He is strong, strong enough to lift and hold most of his weight by the grasp of his single hand higher up above the noose in a crude, partial one-arm chin. He is strong and he is determined to live, and as the natural swing from his fall brought him back again, within a few feet of the tractor, he kicked out, pushed against it for momentum. After arcing away, the next swing brought him closer, close enough to almost swing a leg up on top. Almost. Then he shoved off the Deere's metal side a second time, off the engine block itself, and this time, quite by accident, he shoved at an angle and that is what sent him into "Mary," on his lopsided outward arc.

She whirls around, sees at a glance what he is about, and will not allow it. She has worked too hard for this, stayed awake nights "talking" to him endlessly. She –

– grabs him around his legs in the same way Carol meant to, only for the purpose of adding to rather than relieving the downward pull. It is too much. Mark is strong, but not that strong. He can't hold the weight of both of them, not with one arm, and as all that weight settles into the noose he begins to choke. His eyes cloud over, and –

Thunk!

– that is too bad, because Carol has just hit a triple for him off "Mary's" head, with a wood 2x4, and –

Thunk!

– now she is hitting a home run, just for him, and he ought to be –

Then the weight comes off his legs and half a moment later she is lifting, lifting . . .

Breathlessly she exhorts him to ". . . rope off of you! Hurry! Don't know how long I can hold you like this!" She feels him struggling to do just that, and the moving and thrashing make him even harder to hold.

"Hurry-hurry-hurry-hurry!"

"'kay!" he barks finally, and it is exactly that, a hoarse bark. She is now able to set him down, and between fits of coughing and gasps for air, his eyes fix on the length of timber lying on the barn floor, next to "Mary."

Carol's face is bloodless, haunted. And afraid. "She may not be dead," she says, and grabs his arm, tries to lead him away. "Hurry!"

They stumble and stagger to the door, mostly because of him, and, once, he looks back, because he still doesn't fully understand. Then they are in her car and she is reaching across him, frantic to lock the passenger-side door, roll up that window. Fumbling with her keys . . .

"My God, what is she?" she moans as she tries to start the car. But it is old, years past its prime, and slow to catch hold. She pauses, tries again, and both pairs of eyes bore into the turning key as if by force of will alone they can make the engine fire. Then it does fire and they are rolling forward on the horseshoe drive, picking up speed, spraying gravel.

"What is –" Carol starts again, but the rest is lost in a scream as they receive an answer. Of sorts.

Krrrump! "Mary" is on the hood, on all fours. Her head is down, and she is glaring at them through her brows the way a homicidal old lady might glare over the tops of her bifocals. Her hair hangs on all sides

185

like so much red moss, and from three separate strands of it there is a steady drip of blood. They both know what she is. She is something not of this world, something human in form yet not human. A female, yet the antithesis of that gender's every nurturing trait. She is, as Carol has suspected for quite some time, a bitch-monster.

Thump! "Mary's" hand slaps the windshield directly in front of Carol's face with sledge-hammer force. The glass spider webs, indents half an inch in a jagged plate-sized circle and Carol slams on the brakes at that same instant.

"Mary" shoots off the front end.

And then, instead of backing up or going around, Carol guns the Honda, heads straight at her, lying sprawled there on the gravel drive. And just before they are on top of her, "Mary" rolls sideways out of the car's path. They shoot on past, out the driveway and onto Forrester. When they look back she is still kneeling there, still wearing the teeth-bared expression of a beast, and she is screaming something that is definitely not a wish for their continued good health.

It was a long time before either of them said anything after that – anything sensible that is. With each breath, Carol inhaled then exhaled huge quantities of air long after any accrued oxygen debt should have been repaid. She was hyperventilating, Mark suspected, and he wanted to tell her that because it was causing her white-knuckled fists to cramp unnaturally around the wheel, making her steering erratic. Additionally, every once in a while she would half-moan, half-mutter to herself, "Where was your dad? Where was your *daddd!*"

Finally, on the outskirts of Valor, he asked if they could pull over for a minute, and when they did she turned to him and, between breaths, asked, "Are you okay? Do you need a doctor – for your neck?"

"No," he answered. "I'm all right. Th-thanks to you."

Her lower lip trembled then, making her look vulnerable in a way he'd never known she could be. Then her face screwed up as if she were about to cry and still in shock himself, still very much in need of human contact and the normalcy that comes with it, he twisted in his seat, leaned closer and reached with his only arm to comfort her. And that is when she hit him. One solid blow with the edge of her doubled-up fist, against his chest, hammer-style, then another.

Then another and another, her left hand joining her right now, raining blows in a furious tattoo, and furious was as good a word as any for what was on her face as well, for the way she was shouting at him and crying at the same time: "How could you? How could you? Don't you ever do anything like that again! Don't you ever, EVER do anything . . . like that . . . again! You –" Then she stopped, abruptly, and her hand flew to her mouth. And in that moment Mark remembered something, remembered it distinctly and in vivid detail that made all the difference: He remembered the one time his father had been really rough with him, actually hurt him in a physical way. It had been when he was nine, a year after his mother had died, and he had run across Forrester, which was considered busy back then if two cars passed in the same hour, without looking. But there had been a car. He should have heard it even if he had not seen it, and it had blasted on past him, horn blaring, so close he could have stuck out his tongue and licked the side window. His father, who had been witness to it all, had walked up to him, pale and tense. "Are you all right?" he'd asked in a tightly controlled voice. And when he'd said that he was, those big hands had reached out with lightning-like speed and grabbed him by either shoulder and begun shaking him. They had shaken him and shaken him, and their blunt fingertips had dug into his shoulders hard enough to hurt – the shaking itself had hurt – while the "Don't you ever, *ever* . . !" verbal tirade which had accompanied the shaking had seemed to be made of thunder. He'd been too young back then to realize all that fury was because his father loved him so much and was so afraid of losing him.

Carol stopped hitting him, looked at his eyes, which were wide with shock and surprise, and her hand flew to her mouth. "Oh . . ." she groaned. "Oh, darlin' I'm sorry! It's just that I –" And then she put a hand on the back of his neck, pulled him close so that he was leaning in toward her and his face was nestled beneath her chin, against the soft skin there. She rocked him to and fro gently, murmured in a half-whisper, in a soothing, pleading mother's voice, "I thought I was going to lose you. I thought you were going to die and there was nothing I could do! Mark . . . Mark . . . promise me you'll come to me, come to your father, if things are that bad . . ?"

Shock and surprise. It had been there alright, in his eyes. But it was a different kind of shock, a different kind of surprise from that she imagined. It was the shock of discovery, the surprise of revelation; and what he'd discovered, what Carol had revealed to him in these last few minutes, made it easy to say the words and mean them. "I promise." He could have stayed there, pressed up against her neck, up close to where he could feel her pulse, for as long as she would have had him and not felt the least bit embarrassed, not felt that he was weak, disgusting or regressing back into some infantile childhood at all.

X X X

While Mark and Carol were busy cruising the sloped, winding streets of Maple Hills, Valor's only really well-to-do neighborhood, because the latter only remembered that his father was starting a job somewhere within its confines, David was cruising Valor High School's parking lot looking for his son's car. He'd left the job early, around nine-thirty, because he couldn't concentrate, couldn't shake the uneasy feeling Mark's covert stares last night and his own dream of Mary gone savage had left him with. And now that feeling was of almost panic proportions again, the way it had been before he'd decided to come here, because the car was nowhere to be found.

The first thing he did was march straight in to the school's attendance office, having learned the proper channels one day a year ago when Mark had decided to try his luck at skipping school. He wished that was all Mark was doing now, just . . . skipping school.

As luck would have it, the student-aide Carol had spoken with earlier had an exam herself at this hour, so that connection was never made. But her replacement, a heavy-set girl with a breathing problem, was helpful in other ways, first very quickly verifying the fact that Mark had been absent from school all morning, then, on David's request, checking to see if Jenny was also absent (she was not), and, finally, calling both his home and the Big Boy Restaurant where Mark worked from her desk phone.

No answer after a dozen rings at his house, no knowledge of his son's whereabouts at the Big Boy, and now David had a very hard time remaining calm. Even harder when he arrived home, which was the only "next step" that made any sense to him, and saw Mark's Camaro sitting in the driveway – and his varsity jacket hanging on the barn door. And, finally, the noose. By that time in fact, even the idea of remaining calm was an impossibility. Although he didn't actually do it, looking up at that noose had him aware of how a person might just pass out if what was presented to their senses was traumatic enough. The barn floor tilted just a little. Things grayed. Then he was sprinting for the house.

But the house was empty, too. No Mark. And to make matters worse, no Mary. He fought hard against making a connection there, but his gut made it anyway; and for a while he simply wandered from room to room, feeling helpless and sick. Then he thought of Carol, thought that she was probably who Mark would turn to if he were in trouble, needed an adult and couldn't reach out to his father; so he called the café, found that she, too, was mysteriously absent, whereabouts unknown . . . and another unwanted visceral connection was made.

Mark. Mary. Carol. The noose. Mark-Mary-Carol-The-Noose. Mark-Mary-Carol-The-Noose. The words, the names, wobbled and spun in a warped, sickening manner inside his head, as if his whole mind were a dark, spinning coin that never fully came to rest and these were the sounds it chittered and clattered endlessly.

. . . hated the Carol-woman,
("No, I –")
– hated her even more vehemently than after Sunday's dinner. Because now something new had been added, something quite simple really, that was very, very potent. It was called pain. It gave her an immediacy that threw all caution to the winds, made her not care for her masquerade, for her imperative, for anything but swift
("No! Noooo! Oh God, please –")
violent revenge. Give the sweetest, nicest old lady a bump on the head, clobber kindly old Grandpa's thumb with a hammer, and even they will see red, at least feel the urge to lash out, as readily as the rest of us. Cause a tiger or some other beast equally savage a like amount of pain, and you had better hope they are in a cage.

"Mary" was not in a cage. And the pain in her head from the Carol-bitch's wielding of the 2x4 wasn't the whole of it either. Somehow the trauma had "weakened" her – not physically but mentally, yet, incongruous as it seemed, with no real diminishing of her cognitive powers. It had weakened instead that portion of her mind able to "touch" other minds, the same portion which kept Mary so tightly under control, "sleeping" most of the time. It had awakened that other more human half of herself so that, for "Mary," it was a constant, conscious struggle to keep control of the reins. She was still the stronger by far, but there was resistance, a certain balking. It was the mental equivalent of having to run a course that had changed, suddenly, from flat to a mild yet persistent uphill slope, and along with her throbbing head, it made "Mary" mad enough that drool spilled from the corners of her mouth.

As she set out cross-fields with a sense of direction unimpaired,

(*"Stop! You CAN'T! You –"*)

the tug of Mary's resistance was there with her. Good. Let her resist. "Mary" hated her as well, and at least this way she would suffer maximally. She, "Mary" would kill them both, the Carol-bitch

(*"– won't! I'll kill –"*)

and Mark. The boy gently, by strangling, so she could put him up on the rope again and make it look like –

(*"US! I'll kill US!"*)

But with the Carol-bitch, she would kill her a little bit at a time, make good on the threat regarding her woman-parts made in the barn. And then,

(*"NO!"*)

when she was dead, she would bring her back, along with Mark, in the Carol-bitch's own car and butcher her.

(*". . . Thy kingdom come, Thine will be done . . ."*)

and bury most of the body, and feed

(*"Guhhh...Goddd!)"*

the prime cuts to David, telling him it was steak.

He remembered driving like this once before, dead, or at least so numbed with shock and loss that looking outside himself at the road, operating his hands and arms in order to steer, was like being inside a metal robot, inside a tiny control room in its head, with its eyes *(not YOUR eyes)* as the only windows. The other time had been after a call from the State Police ten years ago to tell him his Pamela was dead, killed on the same 223 that figured so prominently in their lives still today, when a semi –

Ten years ago! And now his son had attempted suicide and the woman he'd fallen in love with had had something, maybe everything, to do with it, was, in fact, a human monster.

Dead? Numb? Not so much of either, that other time, that he hadn't had to stop the car halfway to the county morgue and throw up. He wondered if he'd' have to do the same this time, before he reached Carol's house. No. That merely physical crisis had passed. A wave of nausea had risen then ebbed again as soon as he'd hung up the phone. It had been fifteen minutes after he'd called the café before it had even occurred to him to call Carol at her house. In the meantime he'd been trying Jenny's number over and over, because by now she might be home on a half-day and might know something. But the line had been busy, so he'd called Carol's and at first he hadn't believed her despite the evidence of the noose. Then denial had given way to enormous guilt and a debilitating sense of shock that left him sick and weak, the way he'd felt nine years ago the time Mark had just missed getting hit out on the road right in front of the house – because he'd almost lost him.

His feelings about the other half of Carol's news, the part about Mary, had been walled off and shut down completely at that point, because somehow to think of her at all, to doubt that part of the story, seemed disloyal. It would have been the final straw that broke the camel's back so that he never would have been able to forgive himself.

But now, after he'd had some time to think, to agonize over the fact that his obsessive behavior toward Mary was probably a factor in Mark's attempted suicide – and was certainly the reason he hadn't recognized the warning signs – he finally allowed his thoughts to turn in her direction. And the first thing that came to mind was something he'd read a year ago with, even then, a detached kind of horror. It was in the Sunday magazine supplement to the paper, and it was the supposedly true story of a KGB agent planted in this country while still in his teens. Said agent had grown up, established himself within the community, married, had children . . . . all the while never wavering from his original, secret purpose, that of spying for Mother Russia. People trusted him; his wife and children loved him, and thought he loved them back; and no one ever knew, until his wife found out quite by accident. The story had been done from her perspective, and David remembered trying to imagine how shattering so profound a betrayal would be. He'd been unable to, not completely. In fact every time he'd come close his mind had skipped sideways from it in the same way he'd never really been able to imagine how he'd be able to cope if Mark should suddenly die; it was that terrible. It was *(You wake up early, turn sideways in bed just in time to see the inch—and-a-half fangs, the needle-sharp eye-teeth recede beneath your wife's gums)* that terrible.

X X X I

It was 10:40 on a Monday morning. At 10:35 David had finally reached Carol at her house, shortly after Mark and the latter had at last given up a desperate search for him that had covered all of the Maple Hills subdivision and its surrounding areas. They had just unlocked the front door, in fact, when the phone had rung, and it had seemed almost a miracle to Carol that it was him. Miraculous, too, was the all-encompassing, weak-in-the-knees magnitude of relief she felt upon first hearing his voice, despite what she had to tell him.

Now, five minutes later, as her initial sense of deliverance wore off, she was experiencing a different, darker sort of emotion. Call it prescience, a sixth sense, or a plain-old premonition of danger. "Mary" was nearby, she was sure of it. She was as sure of it as had she heard her voice, calling to them from outside the house. Close, very close. Carol could sense her presence as a non-photic darkening of the atmosphere. And with this shadow on her soul came a certain thickness to the air itself, a trapped, claustrophobic feeling so that she found herself laboring to breathe. She shouldn't have come here; she should have gone to the café. But Mark –

Mark suddenly sat upright on the couch opposite her. What she was feeling must have registered in her face. "What? What's wrong?"

"Shhh. I thought I heard something." Substitute the word "felt" for "heard."

He listened. But not like a near-adult in broad daylight. He listened the way a little boy left alone in the dark listens, eyes wide. Because he could feel it too, couldn't he . . ? Then, as if reading her mind, he said, "She's ten miles away. And she can't drive. I heard Dad say so."

Their eyes met. So much whistling in the dark, and they both knew it. But it was up to her to act on the feeling. "I've got a gun upstairs," she said finally, and rose from her chair. She kept it in a drawer next to her bed. It had been David's idea, a gift in fact, over a year ago, because her house really was quite isolated, with the neighbor on the left a whole field away and the one on her right never home because he and his wife owned a party store. She had never fired it, but with no children in the house had always kept it loaded and she was thankful for that now, as she crept up the stairway, reluctant to put that much distance between herself and a fellow human being but equally loath to ask Mark to come with her because then he would know how frightened she was. The gun. The gun was her security, her instant protection, and as she reached the top of the stairs it loomed large and wonderful in her mind's eye.

Turn right, into the bedroom . . .

Walk across to the nightstand . . .

Almost there . . . Almost there . . .

Her hand, reaching out for the drawer, stops. Something wrong. Some –

The window, too late she noticed the window. The screen has been knocked out, *torn* out - - here, on the second floor! And she knew that "Mary" was in the room with her.

There is a low growl, purely animal, purely bestial, behind her, and her hand shoots across empty space for the drawer; but before her fingers can do more than lightly brush the handle she is grabbed by the collar of her blouse and yanked backward like a ball on a string. There is no time to cry out, there is no means; that portion of her collar not bunched in "Mary's" grip is pulled tight against her throat with all the force of her hundred-and-thirty pounds being suspended from it, and all that is forced out is a compressed *Akkk!* Then she is spun around as easily as she might turn a hollow mannequin. Her collar is released and she is seized again by one wrist in a grip inhumanly strong, inhumanly quick in its purpose. And now she is face-to-face, eyeball-to-eyeball with the bitch-monster.

Her eyes . . ! "Mary's" eyes . . !

The late Robin Williams used to do a bit in one of his routines on Qaddafi, the Libyan madman, on how the man's appearance was initially so deceiving – clean-cut, regular features, even handsome – until you looked into his eyes. And they were saying, *"Helter-skelter! Helter-skelter!"* "Mary's" eyes were like that, too, now that she was her true self, now that she was in her beast mode. Insane. Utterly devoid of compassion. Dead, in some fundamentally inhuman way, yet animated, even blazing with hate; and just like Qaddafi, it was the contrast that made them the more terrifying: beautiful face, beautiful features . . . and those hell-crazed eyes.

Carol gazed into those eyes now and knew there was no hope. She opened her mouth to warn Mark, scream for him to run, but before the first sound was more than air expelled from her lungs, "Mary's" free hand seized her throat and would not let it pass. "Cry oot now and I kill the boy!" "Mary" hissed in a venomous whisper, made all the more alien and therefore merciless by the unprecedented thickness of her brogue. "I will run him doon with ease! And you . . ? Too dead ta stop me!"

Carol had no choice. The amount of sound she could make would have been negligible, and after seeing "Mary" in action she was sure the part about running Mark down was absolute fact. She nodded her head as much as the hand at her throat would allow.

"Good. Good," "Mary" said more calmly. "Now, down the stairs with you. And if there's trouble, I vow ta make you watch as I tear off his other arm!" This time, however, there was no long "u" in "down," and for some reason that alone made her sound a little less insane. Carol allowed herself to be led from the room by her wrist and her throat.

By the time they reached the stairs, both of them walking sideways now like partners in some grim, sadistic dance, Mark was there, halfway up. All parties froze. Then: "Let her go." From him. And the look in his eyes was the one he used to wear right before he stepped out onto the wrestling mat.

With a flourish "Mary" released Carol's throat. Between gasps for air Carol caught what she thought was a flash of glee in the beast-woman's eyes. "Done," "Mary" said. "I allow her to breathe . . . you move off the stairs." The hand hovered close by Carol's throat again, and as the two of them took the first step down, Mark backed toward the bottom an equal distance. And so their sideways-backward dance-of-the-hostage continued, this time with the addition of a third party who always kept a uniform distance, until all three of them were downstairs and in the living room, where they'd gathered yesterday before the ill-fated dinner. Then, as if sensing that Mark was merely bidding his time so he wouldn't have to attack uphill, "Mary" said, "Just so you know that pouncing upon us now is futile and will cost her dearly . . ." And as her voice trailed off, the hand that had been at Carol's throat shot down and caught the latter's other wrist with animal speed, raised it up until it was eye-level, never once taking her feral eyes off Mark . . . and with a sideways flick/twist of her own wrist no more strained than had she been casting flies in a trout stream, but a hundred times more powerful, broke it nearly in two – broke it so completely that the hand itself was now canted in the direction the open thumb spreads, the one direction a normal hand will absolutely not go, at a sixty degree angle. Bone gleamed white beneath the skin, threatened to break through on the little finger side of her wrist where, before, half of Carol's hand had been seated. It was the ulna's distal end, uncovered and fully exposed but for a single layer of skin. And through it all, rattling back and forth on itself as if the pain and horror of the moment were trapped and encapsulated within a tiny universe all its own was the scream. Carol collapsed toward the floor as far as "Mary's" hold on her wrist would allow, still screaming, and with an inarticulate growl, Mark took several steps forward. But "Mary" stopped him with, "The other hand too, is it? You decide."

Then, from the same mouth and after gazing a full moment at Carol's wrist: "No more! In the name of Holy God, I canno' –" And: "Mark, run!"

And finally, with a look of dismay, surprise, and seemingly in direct conflict with what she'd said just the moment before: "Advance and she will pay for every step; run and she dies!" Then a short pause to let that much sink through, before she finished with, "So now . . . will you listen to my plan . . ?"

Does a mass-murderer, a psychopath, ever scream inside? For Mary, the answer had changed. Abruptly. As abruptly as being hit over the head with a 2x4. Changed from "not frequently or for very long" to "constantly." Or almost constantly, because even an internal scream cannot go on forever, must at times dwindle to a groan or a whimper, just the way a burn victim's must, though his agony is ever-present. But even with the burn victim there is always a limit past which there is only unconsciousness, while for Mary, whose anguish had little to do with actual physical pain, no such limit existed. She was trapped inside her mind with a monster, and there was no longer even temporary escape. From the moment "Mary" came around after being hit by the 2x4, Mary was there with her, overruled but wholly, horribly aware. Horrified in a way a wife and mother might be if she were to suddenly come awake with vivid and total recall of having murdered her husband the night before, while not herself, and yet not be able to stop herself, not able to do anything but – yes – "scream inside," as she rises from the bed *now*, takes up the knife *now* . . . and heads for her children's bedrooms.

Mary fully remembered, now, the killing of the deer. She remembered how "she" had murdered Lee Redding and Professor Haroldson and his wife Flo, whom he had loved and who had loved him back. And she remembered what "she" had tried to do to Mark; and as she ran along with "Mary" cross-country to visit Carol at her home, no longer capable of being "squelched," of being banished to an oblivion of non-awareness, she resisted, pleaded and "screamed" all the way.

It broke a piece off her soul to do what "she" did to Carol's wrist; and for a moment, just a moment, she fought her way to the surface. Then she was overpowered again as easily as before, and "Mary's" guard was up, and dear God, she shouldn't have wasted what might have been her only chance, because now "she" had Carol and Mark in the car with her and was on her way back to David's, where "she" planned to kill them both!

XXXII

Carol kept forgetting not to look at her hand. And each time she looked, the sight of it made her nauseous all over again. Or maybe it was the pain, because that felt as if each of the bones in her wrist and thumb, especially her thumb, had been drilled hollow and filled with an expanding gas – and that was when she kept it perfectly still; when she moved it or they hit a bump it really got bad. She glanced at it now, resting palm down atop her left knee, while the forearm to which it was attached ran along the same thigh. Ordinarily the fingers would have had no other option but to point straight ahead from that position, but with the injury they were, in fact, aimed more in the direction of her other knee and that was distinctly weird. Yeah, it was the sight of it that made her nauseous. It couldn't have looked more beyond saving, more estranged from the rest of her, attached so crookedly now, than if it had been cleanly amputated and handed back to her in a glass jar.

Or, too, maybe it was the sure, sick knowledge that "Mary," who was wedged into the Chevy's back seat next to her, still gripping Carol's good wrist while Mark drove, was going to kill them both as soon as they got to David's house that kept her ill. That and knowing there was precious little she could do about it . . .

She should have warned Mark back at the house just as soon as "Mary" had ordered them outside and into the car. But the pain from her wrist had been too fresh then – she'd practically been gagging on it – and maybe . . . maybe she'd just plain been too afraid. For her other wrist, for what might happen next; and that, too, made her sick, because now what could she do? She calculated the odds of her being able to slow "Mary" down enough so that Mark could scramble from the car and run for it at one of the two remaining stop signs between here and David's.

199

Not good, practically none at all unless she could find a way to prime him ahead of time. She would –

The grip on her good wrist relaxed just a little, shifted, then clamped down again harder than before. Like steel, she thought. God! Inhumanly strong!

Her eyes moved toward the spot. Her captor's hand was no larger, no more powerful-looking than her own. A shapely, feminine hand powered by a forearm also unremarkable, except for the fact that it was covered perhaps a bit more generously than most women would have preferred with a fine down of red-gold hair. "Means she's hot! Hair on the arm, an animal in bed!" she heard her ex-husband, Nick-the-body-puncher, say. Which was totally inane and insane, becau–

Like steel . . . yet flesh and blood. Or maybe flesh and blood OVER steel! The last thought shook her to the core. One of the most frightening movies she had ever seen had been *The Terminator*, the first one, back when she was a kid, and that's what that walking nightmare had been, a hydraulically-powered steel robot covered over with flesh so that it looked human. It, too, had come out of time – the future, not the past, but definitely from another time – and it had been unstoppable, had just kept coming and coming . . . Her gaze traveled up the arm, up the shoulder to "Mary's" face, which was looking at her now with a cold, speculative smile. Carol shuddered. Ice-cold eyes, too. Inhuman eyes.

This was it then, the unexpected answer to an oft posed question from her youth. An internal question, asked once each year when her family visited the zoo down in Toledo, and she would watch the tiger watching *her* with those glacial eyes: What would it be like to be thrust suddenly on the same side of the bars as it? But even the tiger paled by comparison to what "Mary" might be, and she had to know; not knowing was clouding her thinking. "What are you, a machine?" she blurted out, knowing there wasn't time to be anything but bold.

"Mary" stared at her, amused. "You would like ta think that, wouldn't you now? You in your mechanical world. 'Twould be an excuse for having been fairly beaten!" The tone, the noticeable sneer which accompanied the word "mechanical," was all the answer she needed. Relief flooded Carol's veins with enough physical effect to cause her mangled wrist to throb briefly with increased pain. "Then what makes you so strong?"

Again the sneer, more profound than before. "What makes you so weak?"

After that Carol was silent for a while. But her mind was frantically working, searching for a way to warn Mark. And by the time they had reached the first of the two remaining stop signs, where Airport Road meets Woerner, and had stopped then got rolling again, all she'd been able to come up with was pig Latin *("Arkmay! Extnay opstay, UMPJAY!")*, and if she couldn't do better than that, maybe she deserved to get her other wrist broken. Or worse.

Think.

Another mile down the road and she knew it was going to be pig Latin, and she prayed that it would confuse "Mary" for long enough to at least give Mark a few seconds head start. She also prayed for herself, because in an almost literal sense she was about to throw herself between the tiger and its prey. She prayed that whatever "Mary" did to her would be quick and painless, then quickly revised that as she realized at least half of the wish was at cross-purposes with her original intent.

Think!

She'd never felt so afraid in her life. Too much time to think, now that it was decided. Not like the barn where everything had happened so fast. What were her alternatives? There was a gas station at the next stop sign. Houses, people . . . At David's they would be alone.

Knowing instinctively that "Mary" hated her far more than she could ever hate Mark, Carol also knew that she would likely pay with her life for anything attempted at the sign, whether Mark managed to escape or not. But at least he would have a chance. At David's, with no one else around, they would have no chance all, and "Mary" would kill them both anyway. So what it all boiled down to, really, was the fact that by dying five minutes sooner she might be able to save the life of someone she loved.

THINK!

Plan it all out.

And pray.

And try to ignore the pain in her wrist, the cramping sensation in her belly, which was fear working its liquid metamorphosis on her bowels. Then David passed by in his truck, going the other way and everything changed. She could no longer think, no longer plan, and her prayers were all for nothing more noble or self-sacrificing than the lovely vision of brake lights, as glimpsed through a Chevy Malibu's rear window.

Mark had seen them, too. And he'd never felt so alive. His body was singing to him again the way it had before the accident – and it was a good song, an adrenaline-laced song that made him feel as if he could snap the steering wheel he gripped in his single hand as easily as "Mary" had snapped Carol's wrist. It also made the absence of just one arm seem almost insignificant as far as handicaps go, and that was something to file away for future delectation, just in case he got through this thing with the rest of him pretty much intact. But the funny thing was, he didn't even care (that much) whether he got hurt; it was Carol who mattered. God, she didn't deserve –

Had he done the right thing, getting into the car? What "she'd" done to Carol's wrist, the scream itself, had frozen him. And then he hadn't been sure he could stop her in time before "she" did the other.

He glanced in his rearview mirror.

Yeah. He followed.

Yeah!

Ba-bump. His adrenals kicked up a notch; it was like a turbo kicking in, and that outdated time warp in the back seat didn't even know. Probably. To her cars and trucks probably looked alike, including his dad's. Just one more horseless carriage.

"She" would pay for what "she'd" done to Carol! Between himself and his father, they would make her pay! The thing was, though, how was he going to shake her loose from Carol?

Think. You've always been good at thinking on your feet.

And while he was still thinking, they came to the next stop, the one where Airport meets Woerner Road, and the idea hit him just as they came to a complete standstill. Very carefully, with as little movement as possible that might betray him from the back, he reached across his lap for his seat belt/shoulder harness. But somehow there was an extra tension in the air just then, something akin to the last few seconds during the defusing of a bomb, and it translated into a held-breath kind of silence that made the click when he fastened the belt seem as loud as a stomach-rumble in church despite the fact that he tried to cover it with a cough.

"Why are you doing that?" came "Mary's" voice from the back seat.

Think-fast-think-fast-think-

"I'm fastening my seatbelt. Because you never gave me time to switch off the parking stabilizers over the front wheels and the gage shows they're burned through. And if that's got the modulator hot enough and we hit one of those potholes on Forrester the wrong way . . ." He let his voice drift off, as if the rest were all too obvious, and when she said, "Can you switch them now?" he could have laughed out loud, because he knew she'd bought it.

"They've already burned through."

Silence from the back seat, during which he noted with satisfaction that his father's truck was keeping at a distance. Then, "I sense aggression in your mind. Agitation. If you're lying . . .". And the hairs on the back of his neck stood at attention. "Are there . . . restraining devices back here, too?" This after a lengthy silence.

"No." He tried shaping the lie into a half-truth this time so that he could at least imagine himself believing it. "Just the bottom halves. I don't think Carol ever had them fully installed because she lives alone and nobody ever rides back there." And amazingly she seemed to accept that. Or maybe not so amazingly, considering the fact that the only visible object for comparison, from where she sat, was the shoulder harness portion, which attached to the A-pillar and looked so dissimilar to those in the back, which were set much lower and practically hidden in a plastic sheath.

"Then I'm thinkin' you'd better drive smoothly, Mark Rigert, if you want this one ta keep her other hand!"

Okay. Fair enough. He'd drive smoothly all right. All the way down Woerner to County Line, where the last stop sign was, then north on County Line to Forrester. And on Forrester

Ba-bump

he actually did manage to avoid the pot-holes, which were the only truthful part of his story. No, that wasn't entirely correct. Because he'd implied there could be an accident, and

ba-bump, ba-bump

as his body clarified its tones so that it was singing to him more sweetly than it had ever sung before . . . and as they completed the last leg of their journey, slowing finally to turn into the familiar driveway . . . he floored it suddenly. And with all the power the little car could muster on such short notice, hurtled the three of them directly at the big maple standing like a monolith smack in the middle of their front yard.

XXXIII

David had been slowly cutting the distance between himself and Carol's Honda from the moment he'd turned onto Forrester, so that by the time Mark was braking for his turn into their driveway he was less than three car-lengths away. Close enough to see exactly what was happening and to cry out in horror when instead of making that turn, the car in front plunged off both the road and the driveway and bee-lined straight for an enormous old maple growing in their front yard, spraying gravel and clumps of sod as it went. But it wasn't so much the impending accident itself that had him groaning, "Oh God, no!" With so little distance to accelerate after having slowed for the turn, they would hit the tree at something less than twenty miles per hour. It was what "Mary" might do to Mark and Carol within the confines of the car before he could get to them, as a result of it. If even half of what Carol had told him over the phone was true and "Mary" was provoked to a significant degree, she might try to kill them both. And remembering her feral eyes first time he'd ever gazed into them, the caved-in handprints on the bedroom wall and the snarl behind closed doors, that portion of David's mind that was purely logical told him "halfway" true was a distinct possibility.

He'd known for example, from the moment he'd passed them on the road, that they were unwilling travelers. Hostages. You could tell by the way Mark's eyes had followed him, almost hungrily, and by the fact that the boy hadn't waved or reacted in any other more animated way, although David was sure he'd been recognized. But what he didn't know, didn't understand, was how "Mary" was keeping them hostage. By what means? Was it a knife? A gun? Even after everything Carol had told him – and despite his own logic – it was almost impossible to imagine her with either, let alone accept the fact that maybe she didn't even need a weapon, that maybe her hands were enough. Finally he settled on a gun, became convinced it was a gun, the gun he'd bought for Carol, which "she" had somehow managed to wrest, because everything else seemed just too savage, and –

– all of that vanished, all the rationalization, all the possible scenarios played out in his mind to keep the true horror of the situation at bay, as the car angled across the driveway and toward the tree. *Hit* the tree, with a sound like a five-ton mule kicking a three-ton garbage can. Bodies flew. Carol's and "Mary's." David could see them clearly through the Malibu's rear window. But not far. Only in quarter-circles – up and partway over the front head rests as if they were practicing deep-water dives off a dock, then back again like toys on a string, at the same moment the car was bouncing backwards.

At the same moment Mark was half-turning in the driver's seat, reaching back and jabbing his open hand, thumb and forefinger spread, into "Mary's" face.

Also at the same moment, David's truck was shooting across the driveway, brakes grabbing hard as he skidded to a stop behind them. He was out of the pickup and around the door so fast it seemed merely a continuation of the skid.

Mark was out of the Honda with equal speed, reaching back for Carol with the kind of urgency one usually associates with bombs and live hand grenades.

She made it. She made it out at about the same moment David got as close as the Chevy's rear bumper, and he kept expecting the roar of a gun, for one of them to slowly crumple just before they were safe, and – oh, Jesus – it seemed as if he were slogging through waist-deep mud to reach them. But what he did not expect, what no amount of warning could have prepared him for, was what tumbled out behind them. Tumbled, like a cat that is mad enough to stay and fight, dumped from a burlap bag.

"She" landed on all fours, shoulders hunched, back arched, a carnivore's snarl in her throat and worse than that on her face, in her bloodshot, violated, watering eyes; and even though she wore Mary's clothes – denim slacks, a blouse, tennis shoes that David had bought for her – this was not Mary. This was "Mary" (*"I'm... not the same Mary I was . . ."*) and he was properly meeting her for the very first time, and in his worst nightmares he could not have imagined how terrible that would be.

The girl he'd been ready to give his heart to after ten years of emotional hermitage scuttled sideways in a stooped over, bobbing-up-and-down gait that brought to mind every pathetic ape-man and man-ape in every land-of-the-lost movie he'd ever seen. But with incredible speed and a coiled-spring resiliency that had it as far removed from pathos as a spider's dance across its web towards its prey – speed that cut a half-circle around Carol and Mark, effectively cutting off their retreat. "Mary's" head, hunched deep between her shoulders, swiveled from David to Carol and Mark, then back to David again; and Mary's beautiful features, Mary's face, was as hideously out of place there as had he discovered it instead on the end of an earthworm. Then the neck lengthened, the shoulders came down, and some semblance of the Mary he'd known before came back into that face. "You canno' send me away David." (Visions of the mental hospital, the leering, lustful orderly, flashed in his mind, but he thought he knew their source now and he rejected them.) "Where would I go?"

"Dad –" Mark interrupted, and she whirled on him with an explosive, demonic *"SHHH!"* that was like the pressure-release on a steam engine. Then she turned back to David, her contenance settling again. "These two will tell you I've been bad." She paused. "I'm not bad, David. Just . . . 'disturbed.'" Her face wore all the right lines and angles for supplication, and for someone standing further back it might have conveyed that emotion. But David was close enough to see the eyes, those helter-skelter eyes.

Silence. She was waiting for an answer, ready to go either way. That was when Mark interrupted for the second time. "Dad . . . she did this," and pointed to Carol's wrist. And from that point on there was no turning back. With a squeal that was halfway between a pig and an ape "Mary" leaped at the saboteur of her lies, covering the dozen feet between herself and Mark in a single bound, and slammed an open palm against his mouth with enough force to send him backpedaling, as if by strength alone that which had been said could be unsaid and contained again within its original source. But Mark bit the hand, the meat at the base of her thumb, just as he slammed up against the Malibu, and she let go a millisecond before those steel fingers of hers had time to close and punch holes in his cheeks. Save some cheek, sacrifice some nose, though, because now that same hand shot out, grabbed the back of his neck, while the other one spun him around so quickly that he didn't even have time to tighten the appropriate muscles to resist. Then he did resist – futilely – as the bitch-monster played her rendition of "Whatever-Happened-To-Your-Face, Lee-Redding?" on percussion by slamming Mark's face down against the top of the car hard enough to break his nose.

The blood was her applause, and had there been time enough to notice, she would have felt slighted, because there was far less of it than with Lee; the whole performance, in fact, was less fluid, less convincing than with Lee Redding, because Mark was so much stronger. But she never got past the initial spray, because David yanked her off his son from behind with an arm around her throat and a white-hot band of anguish around his heart. He knew they would have to fight, and it would be like hitting Pamela if she had gone mad.

He backpedaled across the yard then, clamping the arm harder, thinking maybe he could cut off her air enough to make her black out and he wouldn't have to hit her. The chances were good, he thought. Regardless of her strength, she weighed one-twenty to his two-hundred, he was behind her, and –

She bent forward, did the equivalent of a sit-up in the vertical rather than the horizontal plane, and she did it with such power and ease it was as if there was nothing holding her back at all! David travelled over her shoulder in an arc and headed for the ground.

It was his wrestling instincts that saved him then. During the middle fifteen years of his life he'd been thrown – and thrown others – countless thousands of time. Being flung to the ground, or a mat, was as familiar to David as being upside-down is to a champion diver, and he half-turned in mid-air while at the same time allowing the arm around "Mary's" neck to loosen and shift. Instinct. Purely a wrestler's instincts. But the end result was that he came down on the side of one knee rather than on his back like a less experienced man, still in the process

208

of turning; rolled from there onto the other foot and at the same time snapped down hard with the arm still encircling "Mary's" neck. Her own forward momentum pitched her, face down onto the dirt and grass.

It was then that he heard, unobstructed, the same sound he'd heard only once before, from behind his closed bedroom door. "Mary" was on her hands and knees, glaring at him through the tops of her brows in the same maniacal way she'd glared through the windshield at Carol from atop the latter's car earlier that day. And she was growling. And that sound more than anything else – so bestial, so purely carnivorous – jarred David to his very core and made his stomach and intestines feel as if they were scrambling to change places, because there was no rationalizing it away this time; it had come from her, the beast-as-woman, and she was as much an animal, as deadly, as the panther she sounded like.

"You could ha' been father to this world's rulers!" she rasped between growls, and that was worse yet, hearing the human words, that sweet Irish brogue, metamorphosed into something that was all razor-blades, gravel and venom. "To the death, David!"

Her legs had been gathering beneath her *(with secret animal cunning, David thought)* as she spoke, and with a sickness in his heart that went beyond fear, he rose to both feet and assumed a wrestler's stance to meet the charge.

When it came, it was vicious, fast and low to the ground, and all he could do was get low himself and meet it – and from somewhere outside himself, yet inside his mind, he could hear his old high school coach shouting, *"Sprawl! Sprawl!"*

Sprawl: shooting the legs backward while tying up your opponent's arms, shoulders and head with your own, a defensive move to prevent said opponent from grabbling one or both legs and dumping you – but no defense at all against teeth. The moment David sprawled he felt wet heat, then searing, bruising pain in his right trapezius, just below where that muscle runs up into one's neck. It very quickly escalated to something unbearable, and if it hadn't meant his life – and Carol's and Mark's too – if it had been "just" a match, even for the championship, he would have given in to it and allowed the agony to cloud his mind. But he could feel her head trying to turn, her bite shifting, seeking out a more lethal hold further up on his neck, up near the carotid, and when he felt her left hand come up against the side of his head and push it sideways with consummate ease *(God, STRONG, she's –)* thus leaving his neck fully exposed, he used that prying, pushing force against her to help him "duck under" both arms and shoot for her legs. Scoop . . . then lift. Dump sideways, riding your opponent down. Double-leg takedown – two points. Except that part of his shirt and part of himself went with her, leaving behind a shallow, blood-filled crater, and if she didn't turn and, instead, went down on her back there would be other, more serious holes in his anatomy, maybe some clawed-out eyes as well, because he would be falling into her embrace. But in that, at least, she was still human. She twisted 'round to break her fall with both hands, and David let her, coming down astride her back; and if he could just ride her that way, keep her face down where she couldn't reach him with either her hands or teeth till *(When? Till he woke from this nightmare? Till his Mary came back into this demon-thing beneath him and told him it was all a cruel mistake?)* she exhausted herself, then maybe none of them would have to die.

But he couldn't ride her. All those books, all those Tarzan movies were a lie; you couldn't keep your place on the back of a lion or a tiger, or any other beast ten times as strong and a thousand times more savage.

"Get the half! Get the Half!"

Coach again, yelling at him from his past to slip in a half-nelson. Hard to hear, though, even inside his head, because "Mary" was snarling again, growling like an outboard engine – and this time Coach was wrong anyway; she was shaking him off the way a dog shakes off water, and –

"Wait! Not a half, a FULL!"

– he was sliding off to one side when he got the full-nelson – arms under her arms, around the back of her neck, fingers of either hand interlaced – and cranked it hard. "Get outa here!" he shouted at Mark and Carol. ". . . truck! Get help!"

Good ol' full-nelson! Wonderful full-nelson! Nothing could escape a good, strong full-nelson. You could break a guy's neck with it; that is why it was illegal. Tarzan took out Kerchak, King of the Great Apes, with a –

"Mary" arched her neck, forcing his fingers apart, then shot her arms forward, thus effectively breaking the unbreakable hold as easily as shrugging into a coat. Then she reached across, caught his right wrist with her left hand before it could be withdrawn from beneath her arm and pulled up with what felt like tons of force, levered down with her upper right arm against the bend in his right, twisting at the same time, and d-r-a-g-g-e-d him off her back as surely and irresistibly as a dockyard hoist.

She was on top of him now, face to face, with his right arm pinned to the ground. Then his left was sought out, grappled with and overpowered – not easily, though, not even with her inhuman powers – and her face, her teeth, were descending on his neck.

Closer. Taking their time, those teeth. Hovering now, prolonging the –

No! Something happening! Something in those eyes! Forces, warring . . !

Thunk

Wide-OPEN eyes now, wide-open maw; half "Mary's," half –

Thunk

But closer anyway. Rushing at him. Falling, really . . .

Falling . . .

THUNK

Death always comes as a surprise. None of us really believes he or she will die, otherwise it would all be madness, despair and surrender. You are walking to the grocery, thinking about the special meal you will fix tonight because it is your six year-old's birthday – and three miles away a raggedy old pickup is speeding its drunken occupant toward a rendezvous with death, your death, four minutes from now at the intersection of Square Lake and Coolidge. And you never even know; nobody tells you these are the last few minutes of your life . . .

You are only fifty-one, discussing a career change over dinner with your wife, one that will mean less stress and healthier hours, and the saturated fat contained within that final exra-big mouthful of French fries you are eating will kill you two days from now by adding the last fatal micron to the thickness of the plaque lining your coronary artery, thus robbing the heart of critical blood and oxygen. And you take that bite anyway, because nobody told you you are going to die . . .

You are killing your enemy, because now he knows who you really are and in the knowing can be of no further use to you. Victory, how his blood will taste and feel, how *alive* you feel . . . all of this is in your mind as a boy named Mark stumbles like a bloodied wooden soldier toward his father's truck, seeking the instrument of your death. And you do not know.

He opens the door, the sound of it registering on your ears but not your mind because it is you, after all, whose province is killing. Then he reaches across the truck's seat to the far floor for a metal box marked TOOLS; reaches inside the box for something Mary's stored memories would have labeled "screwdriver," had she/you seen it. Long, slim . . . finely chiseled on one end, it never occurs to you that –

No warning. You didn't know. And –

Thunk

one minute later, as the tool that is as much a part of this world as kill-pouches and bared fangs are of yours is driven to the hilt between your shoulder blades, you still don't know that your death is imminent, only that the pain is as if something has reached up beneath your ribs and is tearing your heart loose from its moorings despite the fact that the wound itself is in your back.

Then your heart is torn loose as the weapon is wrenched free again, and –

Thunk

– surprise! Now you know! You are dying! You are as good as dead, and though you can no longer move physically, your mind retreats from the knowledge and the pain, crawls away, seeking out the secluded, hidden place all truly wild things crave when they die. A place –

THUNK

– alone, because alone you would not have felt the third and final blow. But you are not alone, and if death itself comes as a surprise, so too does the knowledge that your "other" self, your more human self whom you have always loathed for her weakness, is the stronger in the face of it. Braver. More fierce, more tenacious in the way she clings to life and identity than yourself at your killing best. And in dying it is you who is the victim – victim to her stronger purpose, Mary's purpose. This is her death, and it is she who will set its mood, decide when to let go. All that is left is to lie back and know that she – her kind – have won.

Your enemy knows, too. The one named David, whom you were about to kill, rolls your shared soon-to-be-corpse off himself and onto the ground, and you are far, far back from your/her eyes, sinking farther, helpless, while she is in them, shining through. And he knows. He can see her there . . .

Gently he cradles her *(our!)* head, and it is not what you want, it is her wish fulfilled.

He brushes the hair from her brow, strokes her forehead tenderly.

(No!)

(the imperati–)

(N–)

()

Mary smiles up at him. At her David. Feebly. There are tears in his eyes, and that must not be. She must reassure him somehow that she will not die. And failing that, let him know that it is she and she alone here with him now. "I . . . have a joke," she half-whispers, half-wheezes, though she intends her tone be bold and brave. "'Tis very funny." She swallows, or tries to. Her throat is as dry as last year's bones. "There was this . . . Irish girl . . . and she falls in l–"

Death always comes as a surprise.

EPILOGUE

Traveling Backwards Through Time

7 May, 2127; 7:29 hours

As the crow flies, Medford, Ohio is exactly equidistant from Valor, Michigan and Gatlin, Tennessee. Not that that fact alone holds any special significance for anyone still alive on this planet. But it could have. *Would* have if things had gone differently some one-hundred and seven years ago on a farm just outside the northernmost of those three towns. As it was, though, the only thing unusual about Medford, Ohio was the months-long dry spell it was suffering through, while towns and communities as close as forty kilometers in all directions were enjoying plentiful rains.

The only thing special until today . . .

Today, at just an hour past sunrise, the air directly east of Kamui Fish Farm's North Atlantic Saltwater Tank Number Three began to shimmer and move in visible waves, like the air above hot pavement glimpsed at a distance. Then it stopped and returned to normal. And from that "normalcy" there suddenly appeared the front end of an enormous machine, rolling forward on equally enormous treads. Appeared. One moment it was not there, the next it was. And as "Aki" Yamashita, who was chief caretaker of Number Three, stared aghast, more of the machine, which reminded him of the "tanks" men had fought in as recently as sixty years ago, emerged – from the open air. It was almost as if for it and it alone, for the machine, the air was an opaque womb from which it crawled on treaded feet, or some monstrous

215

larva emerging from its equally monstrous cocoon. Something like that, something to do with the birth process, eggs, emerging life, played through Aki's mind almost immediately, possibly because his life's work was the raising and breeding of fish. Then, as he ran back and forth at a safe distance, rattling off a hodge-podge of both Japanese and American expletives and gesticulating wildly with his arms, the single word *invisible* obliterated everything else that had been in his mind, and that calmed him. Invisible was easier to accept than "something from nothing." The thing was emerging from invisibility; somehow Science had created an invisible machine, and that was why he could see through the open air where the rest of the machine must obviously be.

With some confidence now, but with equal parts trepidation and awe, Aki half-circled the visible portion of the machine, which was lengthening now at about the same rate of speed a baby crawls, and picked up a stone. He then tossed it gently, carefully, at where the rest of the machine should be – and felt the first wave of vertigo and superstitious dread hit him like everything that had ever frightened him in his entire life all at one time. Because the stone bounced off . . . nothing. It passed *through* its normal trajectory and clattered to the pavement well beyond the width of the visible machine!

But the show was not over for Akira Yamashita because next the machine's rumbling, engine sounds, of which he'd hardly been aware until now, stopped abruptly – and were followed immediately by the *crrunk* of multiple tons of metal alloy dropping onto concrete. All forward progress stopped. The visible portion of the machine was canted now, like a four-wheeled lorry minus its back wheels and Aki was forced to backpedal all the way to his original, somehow more frightening "something from nothing" interpretation. He now believed it had not been invisible at all, front or back, but had *(simply!)* been in the process of emerging from . . . "someplace else." And the "gate" to that "someplace else" had closed, effectively cutting it in half.

That fact alone was almost more than he could deal with, would have him forever and till the end of his days skittish and afraid to walk alone where he could not see other men walking too. But the thing that would make even his sleep unsafe, filling his nocturnal hours with terror and night sweats, was what he saw only now, inside the machine.

The bisection was perfect, as perfect as the bilateral cross-section of a mackerel, ripe with eggs and preserved behind glass, that he had been required to study as part of his training for this job. It cut across treads, across an inner and outer shell and some form of resinous packing in between, across chambers . . . and across the machine's driver.

To Aki, it was as if everything had happened at once. He'd tossed his stone. The machine had stopped and tipped onto the ground. And the words "cut-in-half" had leaped to the forefront of his mind at the same moment his eyes were drawn – inexorably, it seemed – toward a spot high up, where something like the cockpit of an old-style jet was just emerging. Two forearms hung there. Hairy . . . muscular . . . Each gripped, each was *suspended* from a brake-lever not unlike those used to steer the small, treaded tractors and dozers with which he was familiar. Blood dripped in a steady tattoo from their severed ends, where the clean-sawn, bone-whiteness of radius and ulna were clearly visible. It dripped, too, from the half-legs, balanced on booted feet atop what was once part of a floor but was now merely a ledge, dripped from where those legs had been severed from their owner just above the knee. One of the half-legs, not so perfectly balanced as the other, did a slow topple off its shelf and onto the ground. *Kalomp-THUD.*

Aki sank to his knees and began conversing with his ancestors; and when the other caretakers found him a half-hour later he was judged to be in a trance of sorts. He had also reverted to that form of Pidgin English so common to the foreign born, where there is no use for the articles *a, an* and *the.* "Gate . . . close," was all he would tell them. "Gate *close!*" And then he would smack the little finger side of each palm together in front of his face. *Whap. Whap.* Which was as good an explanation as any the investigative teams that poured over the area in the first few days that followed could come up with. The only thing of note that "science" revealed which the average citizen could not have learned through careful observation was the fact that the machine's outer hull was of an unknown alloy – and that the muscle-density of both severed forearms, and the legs too, was closer to that found in the great apes than in man; the hominoid creature driving the machine must have been inhumanly strong. DNA testing and detailed analysis took a little longer and raised more questions regarding evolutionary theory and man's kingpin status in the grand scheme of things than would ever be answered. How could they know more than that? How could they know of failed imperatives, matched resonances on twin worlds, red-haired beauties and the power of love to both save and destroy? They were only scientists.

19 October, 2059: 17:00 hours

The backhoe struck something hard and unyielding, and Raymond Grebbs clambered down off its seat to see what it was. And finally knew why the man who had sold him this land, along with the antiquated farm house, barn and sixty acres directly across Forrester Road from it, had asked for his promise that he never build in this particular field, a promise Grebbs had kept these past fifteen years, until he'd gotten word that David Rigert had passed away last spring, out in New Mexico, where he and his wife had moved back in '43.

The hoe had managed to pull off one end of the makeshift coffin without crushing it completely, and from where Raymond stood, the high-button shoes and long dress almost hid the fact that he was looking at the feet and legs of a skeleton.

Almost.

Raymond switched off the backhoe and immediately marched across the road and into the house, where he phoned the police; and one week later most of the country knew about "Mary Out O' the Earth," which is what the media eventually dubbed her. Or thought they knew. But how much of the essence of a person can there really be, left over in a few bones, some scraps of cloth and seven cryptic words carved on the lid of a coffin? They knew only this: That she was buried in a homemade coffin, made watertight at the seams through ample use of a type of latex caulking not generally marketed past the early 2020s. That the condition of the pine boards from which the coffin was made was of dubious help in determining a burial date, because of their many layers of varnish – but that the relative dryness of the bones themselves put the death at somewhere between thirty-five and forty-five years ago. That said bones were uncommonly dense and strong, and were not only the bones of a young woman, but an exceptionally healthy, active woman at that. That enough remained of her clothing and shoes to be positively identified as of a style worn approximately 140 years ago, not forty – but that the amount of deterioration was far more in keeping with the dates suggested by the bones. That she had and still did have long, lush red hair. And finally, that wood-burned into her coffin's lid was the following inscription:

Mary
Sweet Irish Angel
Whom I loved

The story was a natural for the InterNews people. First there was the air of mystery lent it by virtue of the obvious contradictions within the physical evidence itself and the fact that no positive identification or cause of death was ever determined. Then there was the inscription, tailor made to give it maximum romantic appeal. And finally there was the undeniable fact that she had been beautiful. The degree of accuracy attainable these days through plasti-flesh facial reconstruction, with only a skull or even part of a skull to go on, was absolutely amazing. Close to one-hundred percent. And when Grebbs first looked upon Mary's three-dimensional face almost a year after he'd discovered her bones, it nearly took his breath away. She was everything both his waking and sleeping mind had dreamt of since the age of fourteen, cloaked in fantasy, but had failed to see clearly till now because a certain part of him even in sleep feared that reality could never measure up to the dream. He'd been wrong.

But long before he gazed upon the countenance of Mary resurrected, her face was familiar in every home via the InterNews; and even in two dimensions her beauty had captured a nation's imagination for a short while. "Mary Out O' the Earth." Grebbs was never sure just who it was who first had called her that, playing off the Irish reference in the inscription and off where she had been found. But it had a certain lyrical ring to it that seemed to fit – both her beauty and her mystery – and it had stuck.

Mary Out O' the Earth.

When the crime lab in Detroit was done with her face and head they gave her to the University of Michigan, where they made a plasti-flesh body to cover her bare bones, and clothing exactly copying that which she had been found in to cover that – and archeology, the "collection and study of evidence remaining from mankind's life and culture in ages past," will probably never seem quite so mundane and without passion to anyone who happens to enter Kelsey Museum by way of the new State Street Annex. Because that is where she stands, just inside the doorway, gazing out upon the spot where she and David, clothed in different flesh, once kissed. The effect is haunting and never fails to produce an awed hush.

The plaque, with her lyrical new name . . .

Her stunning beauty . . .

And her sad, wistful smile, which some say was never shaped that way, with so much longing and just a touch of irony, when first they gave her back her face.

10 October, 2027: 5:30 p.m. - Brockton, Massachusetts

The place was electric, so charged with adrenaline and emotion that Mark Rigert could almost imagine his – and everybody else's – hair standing on end. But even if it had, most people wouldn't have noticed. The sport of arm wrestling has more than its fair share of eccentrics, and these were the World Arm Wrestling League Nationals. Shaved heads, six-inch handlebar mustaches, even such oddities as a man with a bone through his nose and another with the words "Over the Top!" tattooed across his forehead, were all part of the scene. Most of the really good ones, however, were all business, as professional in their demeanor and approach as a Russian gymnast at the Olympics.

Mark was all business.

They had just called his name for the finals. If he could beat this next man, Poole, winner for the last two years, he would be the League's right-handed Heavyweight Champion – and $20,000 richer. His pulse was pounding. His whole body was singing to him again, the way it might have if one of the really bad-news eccentrics had gotten in his face and said something dirty about his family. But in this place there was a whole chorus of adrenaline-laced songs, and it might not be enough.

His arm hurt. The middle of his back hurt too, because he didn't have a left hand to grasp the upright post provided as an anchor against all that pull and it torqued on his spine in the same way carrying a really heavy suitcase a great distance in one hand is worse than having a second one on the opposite side to offset things. And he'd already fought through five hard matches to get this far, including one quarter-finals match where he'd come within a hairs-breadth of losing before finally reversing the other man's arm for the pin. No, the song alone was not enough, and for just one moment he panicked, because winning this title had come to mean so much more than just money and the prestige. He'd allowed it to become a symbol of wholeness. Of life with no holding back and with no-excuses-please.

Then he knew what *would* be enough, where he could go to find the ultimate best in himself. The seats inside the John Brzenk Sports Palace and Recreational Hall were arranged in ever-ascending circular tiers, like theater in the round, with the padded table where the contestants locked arms the low spot and the circle's center. Mark quit his pacing back and forth in front of that table, and despite the fact that his name had been called over the public address for a second time, strode purposefully away. Up the stepped aisle between the north and west quadrant of seats. Up past the aisle seat where Brzenk himself, legend in the sport of arm-wrestling and the man for whom this hall had been named, sat, where he paused for just a moment and gave the man – still strong, still, at sixty-three, looking as if he could change a tire without benefit of a lug wrench or a jack – a knowing smile, as if they shared some secret.

Up three more tiers where he stopped again. Seats one, two, and three on his left and everything dear in his life. "Mom. . . . Dad . . . This is it," he said gravely.

David Rigert took his son's hand, took it in the traditional arm wrestler's grip, and squeezed, then gave a short pull. "You'll win," he said, and his eyes were shining.

The woman to David's right didn't say anything right away. She couldn't get any sound past the fact that this was the first time her stepson, whom she couldn't have loved more if she had given birth to him, had called her "Mom" instead of "Carol." Then she found her voice, just barely, and said ". . . proud of you!"

Then Mark looked at Jenny, whom he'd been married to in spirit since they were both fourteen but legally for only the past year. Jenny. She of the perpetually shining eyes and the gee-its-great-to-be-alive disposition that had been a constant all her life, except for a single dark period which had been his fault, seven years ago. So much joy, so much love in those eyes . . . "Jen," he said. "I've gotta want this about ten percent more than 'with all my heart.'" He leaned in then, leaned across David and Carol, and she leaned toward him until their foreheads touched and his hand was cupping the back of her head. "I need some magic, something to put me over the top." He closed his eyes a moment. "You know the words . . ."

And because she knew him as well as she knew her own heart, she did know. "For you . . . my life," she murmured, and kissed his cheek. "You *are* my life!" They remained that way for several seconds, heads pressed together, eyes closed, shutting everything out but each other. Then he straightened, looked right at her, and repeated the words: "For you my life." And it was so much more than merely an echo . . .

Just by the way he carried himself on the down-trip to the table, by the light in his eyes, there was no question in anybody's mind who the next National Champion was going to be.

17 July, 2020; 12:30 p.m.

They had just completed a walk in the woods, the same woods Mark had run to five long weeks ago on the day Mary had arrived and he'd met her coming out of his father's bedroom, and there had been plenty of time for talk. Now they were in the open field, and the low wind and midday sun did things to Carol's hair that made David want to catch hold of it in both hands and pull her to him. God, he loved her .All the more for what she'd just said to him, less than a minute ago.

"Tell me . . ." she'd asked, looking off to the south, where the distant house and barn looked as idyllic and full of the sun's promise as would be their lives there together for the next twenty-three years. "If someone slipped some kind of mind-altering drug into Mark's food, and because of it, while he was 'under the influence,' so to speak, he hurt you, badly . . . would you forgive him? Would you still love him?"

He'd nodded his head as answer to both questions, not trusting his voice. And then, just to make sure her point was clear, she'd said, "Drugs are kind of like magic. Black magic. Black magic *spells* . . . And I guess I know about spells . . ."

And there it had been. The forgiveness he hadn't been able to grant himself, because how could he have done what he'd done to her? He didn't understand it himself, and though he was sure in the deepest levels of his mind that his passion for Mary had come mostly from some exterior source rather than from his heart, how could he tell her that? It seemed so unworthy a reason to serve as the cornerstone for the rebuilding of their relationship . . .

But now, coming from her lips . . .

He'd felt like falling to his knees, making solemn promises, solemn vows, all the while smothering her with kisses. Instead he'd slipped an arm around her waist quietly; and she had laid her head against him just beneath his chin. It had felt right. It had felt like forever, in a way that all the suggestive power in the world could not have reproduced, and he knew that he had loved her all along – beneath, through and during everything else – with a love built slowly, over a lifetime, once act of kindness, one revelation of goodness and light at a time, the way nature builds its greatest monuments one grain of sand, one shifting, eroding, transporting molecule of water/gust of wind at a time. And because he was just as shy for words in the face of all that emotion as he had been with Mary, just as awkward and even more overwhelmed, he actually had – finally – gotten down on one knee. And what she had said, what she had said, less than a minute ago . . .

"Yes."

Printed in the United States
By Bookmasters